RISE
OF THE
ELITES

TRIALS OF THE BLACK THRONE

E. M. LACEY

Light of Oracaii,
shield between two worlds.
Take heart, own your calling.
Haven to the unclanned,
voice of truth, speak.
Bridge of Oracaii

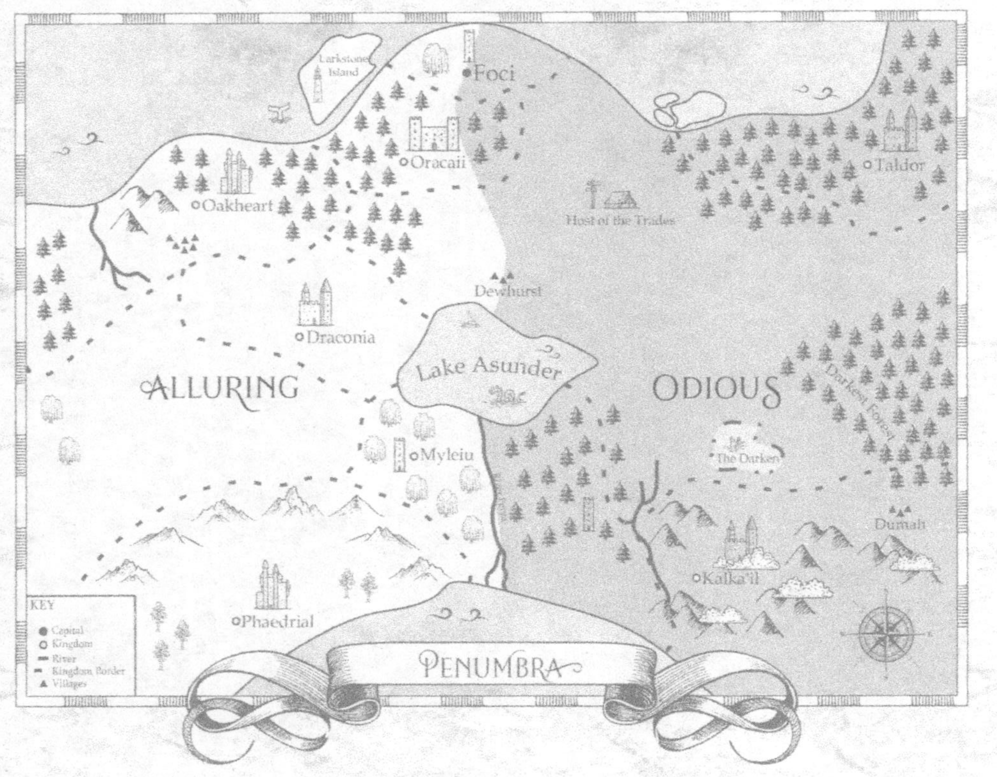
ALLURING
ODIOUS
PENUMBRA
Larkstone Island
Foci
Oracaii
Oakheart
Taldor
Host of the Trades
Draconia
Dewhurst
Lake Asunder
The Darken
Darkest Forest
Myleiu
Dumah
Kalka'il
Phaedrial
KEY
Capital
Kingdom
River
Kingdom Border
Villages

PROLOGUE

THE SUN SET ON THE HORIZON AS THE SYLO BIRDS BEGAN their song. Everyone in Penumbra, a magical world parallel to the human realm, knew what that sad, melodic tune meant. It was time for the leaders of Penumbra, known as the Elites, to gather at the temple Foci, to mark the beginning of a new season and the long-anticipated shift in power. For in Penumbra, only two seasons existed. The Rising, when the dark powers were quieted and the light blossomed. And the Falling, when the light powers settled and gave way to dark energy. Now was the time of the Rising.

Chosen by the High Spirit, the Elites were charged with keeping watch over the supernatural world and maintaining the balance between Light and Dark magic, both in their magical homeland and in the human realm. Each side is given its time to rule with the constraint that neither would shift the balance too far in their favor while at power. It's a delicate balance that often found itself teetering, and if not for the meeting at Foci and the changing of seasons to keep matters in check, the opposing powers of Penumbra would have long ago gone to war and annihilated one another.

Inside the Colosseum, structured from the earth itself, the Elites took their place. Those who were led by dark took to one side while the light took to the other. The Elites along with their council and guards settled in as the ceremony began. Typically, they would elect a member of each side to recount the season, noting anything of key importance before proceeding with the shift of power. This time was different. The Dark had tilted the hands of balance further than they should have during their rule and the air was tense.

Just as the time came for the council to call their representatives, they heard a sound that stopped the hearts of nearly every being in the room. For the first time in over 200 years, the twelve deathly chimes began ringing. One chime for each of the original elites. And as the first one rang out, the air turned cold, and all sound stopped. It was a sound every Elite dreaded to hear. The sound that signaled the end of an Elite's rule. Anxiously they waited for the twelfth and final chime, and as the eerie sound fell to silence, an altar appeared in the center of the room.

A hooded being emerged from the altar, cloaked in shadows. The prophet. She was the High Spirit's messenger and her arrival confirmed that one of the Elites was doomed.

"Six. Six to fall, Six to rise, to right the wrong. Balance must be restored."

Whispers of shock spread through Foci. Six elites would fall. Every pair of eyes widened and darted around wondering which of them it would be. Some fell to prayer, while others stood tall, accepting the fate that was to come.

Six chimes rang out and again they waited. The prophet held her hand out and a scroll appeared. She began to read the names of those who would fall.

The first to be called came from the side of the dark, the shifter Elite, Cyrus Ostara. The six-foot-two blond-haired wolf shifter stood from his seat as his council members stared in disbelief. He turned to his guard, Thomas, and nodded. As he climbed down from his seat, Mei Ching, the female Jaguar shifter and council member, stood to watch him. Cyrus approached the prophet and as he did, he shifted to his wolf. He let out one final howl as his form vanished. The sound of his howl echoed throughout Foci for a moment longer.

The second to be called brought some relief to the dark as it was a name from the light, the Orc Elite, Ryza the Black. This was not a punishment for their transgression, it was an equal playing field. Ryza was one of the largest Elites outside of the giants. He stood over seven feet tall and was built for battle. Like those before him, he made no protest. He turned to his clan members, bowed, and headed for the Prophet. On the side of the light, those he passed bowed their heads, a show of respect and gratitude for his service and his sacrifice. As he made it to the prophet, the Orc stood tall as his spirit was claimed and his form vanished.

The third to be called was a name that brought pause.

The dark Elite was the Irin, Anael. Anael was one of the longest standing Elites and the only one who hadn't appeared worried until his name was called. With a tightened jaw the Irin stood. His crimson wings spread from within him and he took to the sky as if he would try to escape his fate, but a moment later he landed with a force so hard it cracked the floor of Foci. He turned looking only at his people, as the crimson color faded from his wings and he too disappeared.

The fourth to be called was the vampire Elite, from the dark side, Alexander stood. His pale skin stood in sharp contrast to the red glow of his eyes as he hissed, unhappy to have his name called. Unlike the others, the members of his clan seemed almost pleased with his demise. They forced somber expressions as their leader departed, heading for the Prophet. With each step towards the center of Foci, Alexander lost the shield the Elite title gave to him. Though it was night, the sky opened with a beam of sunshine that met him at the base of the altar. Within moments the vampire, once impervious to the effects of the sunlight, began to disintegrate. His burning left a charred mark on the stone floor.

The fifth to be called was the dragon Elite, Horace, who was once known as the devourer. He stood from his position on the side of the Light, turned to the other members of the House of the Blue Flame, and allowed his honey brown skin to partially shift to reveal the sea blue scales of his dragon. He plucked one scale from his arm and handed it to the council members. This was his gift to she who would replace him. In a vibrant show, he turned to descend the steps of the Colosseum while allowing his blue flame to dance across his skin. When he reached the altar, he shifted into the massive beauty that was his dragon, shot one blue streak of fire into the sky, and by the time the light had faded, the dragon was gone.

The sixth to be called was the phoenix Elite, Paereon. The bird of fire sat perched on the highest level of Foci looking down on his fellow Lights. When his name was called his full lips lifted in a sad smile and his mint green eyes glistened before shifting to a golden hue. Hanging around his neck was the Obsidian stone. Worn by each of the phoenix Elites, it was a symbol of their strength. Accepting his fate, Paereon removed the stone and handed it to Olise, his trusted guard. She would ensure its safe handling until the new Elite was chosen. Allowing his flamed wings to blaze once more he glided from his perch to the prophet's altar. Before his feet could touch the ground, the phoenix turned to ash, never to rise again.

With no more names to call, the Prophet's scroll disappeared from her hands and the hollow voice spoke once more. "Six. Six have fallen, six will rise, to right the wrong. Balance must be restored."

CHAPTER 1

West Loop, Chicago

LIGHT OF ORACAII, YOUR TIME IS NOW.

Onyx Jones rolled over in her small bed, running her hand across her face. Thinking she was still in that space between wakefulness and slumber, she ignored the words.

She groaned at the swell of intrusive headlights from the street below. Peeling open an eye, as light spread across bland, puke green walls and traced the scratches in the wood flooring. It flared bright in the corner of her bedroom as a long strip of red material shifted into the available darkness. Once the headlights passed, again coating her room in gloom, the floor groaned under the weight of the *thing* in the corner.

Onyx jerked upright, sliding back in her bed until her back connected with the wall, clutching her sheets to her chest. Her eyes locked on the spot the sound came from.

7

Peace, Chosen, a deep, masculine voice said.

The words bounced around in her head. Her scalp tingled. Her fingers longed to scratch it, but the presence in her room kept them locked on the sheet. Sheets were a poor shield, but they were something, as she struggled to identify the *thing* in the corner.

You have nothing to fear from me.

It took a few tries, but Onyx found her voice. "Who are you?"

A friend of your mother.

The tingling along Onyx's scalp ceased with the shadow's words. "My mom?" she whispered. Her heart struggled to regain its normal tempo as her gaze dropped to the sheets. "I barely remember my mom." She took a deep breath, returning her gaze to the shadowed corner and with a firm voice said, "Besides, friends don't hide in shadows."

I am confined to them. A stretch of silence bridged his next words. *It is part of my agreement with the Prophet.*

Onyx frowned. "Prophet?"

Her gaze darted to the door and back to the corner concealing the speaker. Her door was closed. It was old, like everything else in the building. She had to put some muscle into opening it, so a quick getaway was out of the question. She drew the sheet up to her chin.

You must leave this place.

"I'd love to, but this is all I can afford at the moment."

It's not safe here.

"My aunt's a little crazy, but she ain't gone kill me."

My warning holds. Leave this place and do not return.

"Where do you suggest I go?" Onyx worked to keep

her voice at a whisper. "I don't exactly have any friends I can stay with."

There is a place where you feel safe. Go to it. Cassius will find you.

"Who the hell is Cassius? Why should I listen to you?"

Your life depends on it.

Onyx could have sworn the room rumbled from the thunder in his tone. She drew the sheet higher, stopping at her nose.

Get up, daughter!

Onyx startled at the growl. It was bestial.

Run!

Onyx scampered from the bed, ducking into a corner near her only window. It was far enough away from the talking shadow and parallel to the door.

The loud pop of her room door opening pushed Onyx deeper into her corner, as her Aunt Helen walked in and flipped on the light, illuminating an empty room. Onyx's gaze darted to the corner where the shadow spoke. An old, faded aqua-blue bag with *Bahamas* printed along the sides stared back. Five boxes of shoes were stacked beside it.

Her room was barely bigger than a closet, which forced her to live lean. Her clothes were folded neatly in a six-cube shelf system. It was a bookcase, but it made for a more practical storage place. She had a few books stacked on top of it. No family pictures.

"Where you been hidin' that?" Gaudy nails laced with fake jewels, sharp as little daggers, crooked toward Onyx's neck. Helen Jones filled the doorway, which should not have been possible. She was barely an inch over five feet in height. She had the kind of lean, muscular frame that required no workouts.

Onyx slid trembling fingers over her chest to her throat. Her questing digits stopped at the edge of cool metal. *Jewelry?* A finger pushed up, bumping against an odd protrusion. Its smooth surface was warm to the touch, unlike the metal housing it. Curiosity beckoned her eyes to identify the strange object around her neck, but years of living with Aunt Helen killed the urge. Onyx knew that whatever it was, it looked expensive, and it being around her neck meant it was Helen's by default. No one out shined Helen, especially Onyx.

Helen crossed the threshold, entering the room, her gait predatory. Her eyes burned with accusation as they fixated on the thing around Onyx's neck.

"Who gave you that!" Helen rushed her. Onyx dodged, spinning out of her reach, then dashed into the living room.

Onyx moved behind the sofa. It placed her in front of Helen's beloved smart TV. She was too cheap to have it mounted, but she had a nice stand. Helen was being Helen; anything that belonged to her was sacred. She wouldn't make a move that would hurt her television.

Helen's eyes narrowed. The wheels of her twisted mind turned as she again aimed gaudy stiletto nails at Onyx's neck.

"You got a boyfriend?" She paced along the large windows facing the street, or rather the shop across from them. "Drug dealer?"

A retort settled on the tip of her tongue, but Onyx knew better than to take the bait. Helen wanted a fight.

One their upstairs neighbor would hear. They would call the cops. It happened once before when Helen found out an out-of-state college had accepted Onyx and gave her a full ride scholarship. Onyx should have known something was up when her aunt got all helpful. The day before she was supposed to leave, Helen started breaking stuff, getting loud and hit herself a few times. The neighbors called the cops. When the cops arrived, Helen flung open the door, screaming victim and the cops believed her. Who wouldn't? Her aunt was short and she was a giant, standing at six-foot-three. Her piercings and blood red mohawk with the intricate tattoo work along the sides of her head didn't help. Onyx was guilty before Helen described her fictional crime. Her aunt contacted the college and informed them of her brush with the law. Once Helen was done, all Onyx could hope for was a job that paid a little more than minimum wage.

"Answer me. Who gave you that?" Helen's head tilted. Her expensive burgundy weave washed over her shoulder. It was early and her aunt was already outfitted for shopping. Dressed in black tights, a leopard skin top and pleather jacket. She wore Uggs. It was still technically winter in Chicago; it was the middle of April.

Onyx's dark eyes flitted around the living room for objects her aunt might launch at her the moment she moved away from the television. The only projectile-worthy objects were the remote control band her aunt's cellphone. Both were essential to Helen, so she was safe.

Onyx pressed her hand against her throat. "I... I... don't know what this is, or where it came from."

"What do you mean, you don't know what you're

wearing? It's a goddamned sterling-silver collar with enough stones in it to put me in a nice condo with money left over."

Onyx shifted toward the door. There was a full-length mirror in the living room, a foot away from the door. Helen always liked to give herself a once-over before she graced the public.

Onyx used her peripheral vision to get a look at the jewelry her aunt wanted. A glint of silver drew her eyes to the mirror. A gorgeous sterling collar adorned her throat. The large stone she'd felt earlier resembled a ruby, but there was something about its color that made her doubt. Something inside moved with her every breath; it flickered, shifting around within the stone as if it were alive. The stone didn't sparkle like the other jewels. An evenly spaced row of diamonds spanned the collar, each set within a spiral of unique swirls and twists. It looked good on her, contrasting nicely with her dark chocolate skin. The ruby complemented her crimson hair.

"Don't you forget." Helen's eyes widened as she calculated the value of the thing around Onyx's neck. "It's your job to take care of me, the way I had to put up my life to take care of you." She sauntered carefully toward Onyx, weaving through end tables and an easy chair, hand out. "Give it here."

Like hell! Onyx thought. She would never raise her voice at her aunt, though Helen deserved more than high-pitched screaming.

"Why do you want it?" Helen folded her arms across her flat chest, chin tilted up, back ramrod straight. She was too short to look down her nose at her niece, but fifteen years of scathing looks and her sharp tongue stripped Onyx's confidence, bending her low.

"Because it's mine." Onyx searched the space her aunt occupied, looking for a route that would place her as close to the door as possible.

"Nice things aren't for you!" Helen held out her hand, expecting Onyx to obey, which she normally did.

There was something about the collar that made Onyx stand her ground. She didn't recall someone giving it to her. She didn't pick it up on the way to, or from, the community center where she worked.

Where did it come from?

Onyx did something she never thought she would do. Her lips parted, her gaze hardened, then she said it. "No."

Helen jerked back as if slapped. "What did you say?"

Onyx swallowed. "I said, no." Her hand rose to her throat, she placed it over the collar. "This is not yours! Someone wanted me to have it, so I'm keeping it."

Helen's artfully painted lips parted in a snarl. "How dare you!" she hissed. "I raised you!"

Onyx managed not to roll her eyes. Her aunt always resorted to the sad story of the fictional life she surrendered.

"When my baby sister Olivia died, I took you in." Helen's voice trembled as her eyes watered. "You were just eight years old. I sacrificed my job with the City to take you in. You're twenty-three now. I've paid my dues." Her trembling voice hardened, just like her face, as she said, "You owe me."

Onyx knew very well that her aunt hated working. She had been glad to take in her niece. She fostered her own flesh and blood for a check. That check allowed her aunt to live rent-free for years in a ratty apartment over a restaurant.

According to her aunt, they lived on the Gold Coast, at least, that's what she told her friends. In truth, they lived in a questionable part of the Loop, next to a drug rehab center and the Brown Line elevated rail station. The apartment itself was a citation away from being condemned. The bathroom was a joke. Duct tape held together the toilet. The shower was *meh and* the kitchen was a crowded box of barely functioning appliances. Her aunt had it painted, ordered fancy-looking furniture from Ikea and labeled it a high-end condo.

"I deserve that piece of jewelry," Helen snapped, then something shifted. She grinned knowingly. "You can consider it payment for rent." She shoved her hand forward, wiggling her fingers expectantly.

Anger wrapped its fingers around Onyx's throat and squeezed. Helen did nothing. Onyx worked, paid the bills, bought the groceries and got things fixed. The landlord had stopped caring about the place long ago. If anyone was owed anything, it was Onyx. Her breath hissed from her nose. Her lip curled slightly.

"No." Onyx anchored herself in her spot. She was bigger than Helen. Helen knew she couldn't move her if she didn't want to be moved.

Helen placed herself between Onyx and the door. "You owe me everything you have!"

Onyx ran her hands along the pockets of her jeans. She had a few dollars, her AirPods, cellphone and the pouch which held her Ventra card, debit card and ID; all the things she needed to survive away from her aunt for a few days.

Onyx surged forward, shoving her aunt out of the way. She grabbed the doorknob. Her aunt screamed at her as she descended the steep stairs toward the main entrance. Onyx paused briefly to unlock the door.

"If you leave, don't come back!" her aunt spat.

"Don't worry," Onyx grumbled as she tore open the door. April's chill wrapped its arms around her. She scowled. She forgot her jacket. It didn't matter. She felt better as she stepped onto the sidewalk. A tinkle of bells sent her into an awkward spin. She jerked her leg up, nearly stumbling as a huge black cat ran behind the garbage can at the bus stop, which was five feet away from their front door. She growled at the stupid animal, then scanned the streets. They were empty, which meant her commute to Hubbard Community Center would be swift. If she had any luck, the local crazies would be roaming the streets and not on the train.

She paused briefly to load up her music and put in her AirPods. She braced herself for the cold and began her trek to the Center, unaware of her four-legged shadow.

CHAPTER 2

Penumbra
Orc Capital of Oracaii

HAD THE HIGH SPIRIT FORSAKEN ORCS?

Twenty-seven days and still no Chosen. There were no reports of dreams or visions from either the High Spirit or the Prophet. Orcs were not creatures of magic, but all who existed in Penumbra, magical or non-magical, could have visions or dreams when it came to the will of the High Spirit.

The High Spirit was Penumbra.

The High Spirit was its magic.

Jahll, son of Jahrayne, stared into the vibrant blue sky with its rose-tinted clouds from the balcony of the King's room. Though no king had been chosen since Ryza's fall, Jahll's role as his second in command gave him access to his King's quarters. He leaned his weight on the railing, wondering if a Chosen would be called among them. Elites were called from every being in Penumbra. Orcs sat at the table of immortals, but a significant shift happened after Ryza took his place among them.

Before Ryza the Black's rule, Jahll would never have seen a sky with color. Orcs were part of the Odious. Creatures of the dark. The Orc capital of Oracaii once sat under a slate-gray sky. Their lands were barren. The caves were the only part of their territory which bore fruit. Caves gave them metals: iron ore, silver and gold. Smithies profited from their skill and those with a temperament for trade did well in the markets, while the rest of Orcdom sold their talent for slaughter, tracking and war to the highest bidder. Those without such talents suffered.

Jahll had not been born during the Darkest Times, when Shades culled Orc territories. A time when Orcs would raid Fae and Shifter lands, leaving a trail of corpses and bastards. Orcs were not so bloodthirsty that common sense left them. They stayed out of Dragon and Phoenix lands, while some Orcs ventured down the darkest path: cannibalism. Consuming flesh altered the devourer. It darkened the mind and mutated the consumer. Orcs had become monsters to be put down. What was left of them after the culling barely filled the streets of Oracaii. Many wandered, creating small villages within the darkest parts of the forests. Some made their homes in caves. Orcs became the ghosts of Penumbra until the calling of Ryza the Black.

Orcs were the color of mud, brown or deep green

with eyes that were black, mud gray or brown. Their ears were long and pointed like Fae. All Orcs, male and female, were similar in their appearance: wide, flat noses, tusks, large thick lips, claws and canines. They were a few feet shy of being giants, capping off at the height of nine feet. Ryza stood at eight and a half feet, but he was not as thick as the average Orc. Even the females of their species were stout, their skin tough. It took a lot to pierce the hide of an Orc. Place armor on an Orc and they were nearly unstoppable. When Ryza discovered the Knowledge Stone, or rather, the Knowledge Stone found him, the ways of the Orcs changed along with their place in Penumbran society. Orcs became one with the light.

Jahll dragged the rough pads of his fingers along his collar bones. A silver brace with a red jewel should have been there. Pulling his fingers away, he wrapped his hands around the balcony railing. Laughter floated from the streets below. He watched a game between two youngling Orcs. They took turns chasing each other, giggling when one was caught, signaling for the other to give chase. The game continued until they receded from sight.

"Sir."

Jahll straightened, the speed of his turn causing the bottom of his hooded cloak to snap. Two Orcs, part of the palace guard, knelt in respect, several feet away in the middle of the room as he descended the balcony steps. Jahll noticed the door remained open.

Jahll bowed his head slightly as he approached the pair. His cloak was cinched, concealing his skin, which, thanks to his mother, was abhorrent. White blotches draped his shoulders, across his right side, spanned his ribs, stopped over his heart and formed a patch in his hair at his left temple. A thick white patch ran along his outer right thigh. In close quarters, he kept his cloak on with the hood up, unless meeting with the advisors. In battle, Jahll's disfigurement could be hidden with mud, which matched the color of his unblemished skin. Nothing could be done about his left eye, which was the same pink as his mother's. She was an albino.

Strange coloring on a female was appealing, mainly to the diplomats who collected the exotic. On a male, it encouraged the sharpening of combat proficiencies. His looks married to battle skills generated fear in both the enemy and within the company of Orcs who joined him in war. He collected the tongues of those bold enough to classify his appearance to weakness. He wore those tongues on a necklace before passing them on to his mother. She stored them in jars which Jahll set in prominent spots in his quarters for guests to consider.

He stopped at the top step leading into the main room. Looking down at the pair of kneeling soldiers, he said, "Speak."

"The Chosen has been found," the Orc spoke to the floor, not daring to raise his head or gaze to Jahll.

Jahll balked at the word being used for someone other than himself. He wanted to crush the head of the Orc who uttered the word. Instead, he remained motionless, his face indifferent to the news, though inside he raged.

"Continue," Jahll said.

"The Prophet appeared to several of the royal advisors. She…"

"She!" Jahll lunged toward the kneeling pair, who quickly rolled out of harm's way and onto their feet, weapons drawn.

Jahll's teeth gnashed together as his canines cut into his gums. His top lip curled back. The well of fresh blood took the edge off his anger, as he lowered his head instinctively, aiming his tusks at the soldiers. Tension in the room was palpable as the soldiers carefully lowered their weapons, while back-stepping cautiously toward the main door.

"Continue," Jahll ground out the word, which tasted as bitter as it sounded to his ears. He didn't want to hear any more, but he had to hear all of it to plan.

Both Orcs stopped their retreat, shared a look, then half bowed, eyes wary as they watched Jahll.

Jahll moved away from the pair and took the King's chair, which widened the space between him and the messengers. Once seated, the Orcs took a knee. The original speaker resumed.

"It is said that our king had a child he kept from our world."

Jahll leaned back to appear relaxed as he clutched the chair's armrests. "Why would our king do such a thing?"

"It is unknown, sir. Perhaps he wished to keep her from the sights of males who saw her as means to the throne."

Jahll chuckled, a gruff sound, as he considered the error of his former king. By keeping his daughter away from Orc lands and society, she was ignorant by default. She would know nothing of the Rising.

"Continue," Jahll said.

"The Prophet appeared to an advisor in a dream. She revealed the name and location of the Chosen. Also, the route to the Junction through which she can cross into Penumbra was revealed. A company of our finest soldiers has been deployed to escort the Chosen back to Oracaii."

Jahll leaned forward, resting his elbows on the armrests and his chin on his knuckles. "Who is in this company?"

"Iyska, Taqual and Gryn of your squad, sir."

Jahll grunted acknowledgement before motioning for the speaker to continue.

"The company departed four days ago. They will contact the Chosen in the human world and escort her back."

"So, they held the knowledge?" Jahll scratched his chin as he again leaned back in the King's chair, his weight causing the wood to complain. "Is there more?"

Both Orcs shook their heads.

"Leave." Jahll watched the pair leave the King's quarters as fast as they could, without breaking into a full run. He waited until they closed the door before he rose and went over to the King's bed. Beside it, he kept a necklace his mother gifted him when he joined the guard. A charm etched with the symbol of his father's insignia: a serpent coiled loosely around a riolin's neck, carved in black wood. The chain it hung from was riolin-hide. Riolins were scaly black steeds with black leathery wings. Spikes ran from the crest of their heads down their necks, ending just above the withers. Their tails were serpentine. The necklace was spelled so that only he could see it. His mother, Ivy, said it was for protection. He later discovered she used it to spy on him.

He picked up the necklace, wrapping his hand around the charm, he closed his eyes and pictured his mother.

"Mother, I have need of you."

My son, how may I serve you?

Jahll's left brow arched at the phrasing of her question. Ivy was no one's servant. "What is your game?"

None, my son. It's rare that you call for me, so I assume you need my help with something.

"They've found the Chosen."

His mother's laughter danced around in his skull, irritating his scalp. Jahll wanted to scratch but stayed his hand.

I know and have planned appropriately.

"What are you up to, Mother?"

Making sure my son takes the throne.

Jahll's mouth opened with another question. It would never reach his mother. She cut her link to the necklace. His mind emptied of her presence, leaving questions in its place. How did she know of the Chosen before the advisors?

Ivy was no witch, though many called her one. Her blood wouldn't allow it, but she found ways around the rules. Jahll knew she gained most of her knowledge through Penumbra's dark market, the Host of the Trades. It only appeared at sundown in the darkest forest and vanished the moment the sun touched the horizon. Many in Oracaii had ideas about his mother's practices but those ideas never became facts. If his mother's little cottage in the Darkest Forest remained a secret, she was safe. For now, his mother would do what she felt necessary to secure him the throne. Jahll returned the necklace to the stand. He only wore it when he was in battle or moving around the grounds.

Jahll did a slow turn in the King's room, examining the space fated to be his. He considered Ryza's knowledge of his offspring. Was she a secret kept *from* him, or a secret kept *by* him?

Jahll trudged to the balcony. There he stared across the capital's expanse. Oracaii's palace was enormous and sat in the heart of their territories. The high wall and gates obstructed his view of the forest, but not the lush caps of the purple, blue and green treetops. At the farthest edge where the trees brushed against the mountains, a dark line marked the beginning of the Odious. He leaned against the balcony railing, his mouth twisting in a smile as an idea formed. His mother taught him that women were the ties that expanded bloodlines. A son is one thing, but a daughter is *a* bridge.

Jahll's blood was dirty. His father, Jahrayne, fell in battle, at least that was his mother's story. Once he began training as a warrior, he discovered the truth. Jahrayne was a coward. Fled in the height of a battle against Ogres that had crossed into their territory. His father fell, but by the blades of his own company. His father was a disgrace and his mother an abomination. A king's blood would wash away that shame. The Chosen would purify him. If he bred with her, his younglings would set him in Ryza's bloodline.

The Rising Challenge demanded death. Jahll would use his mother to defy it. He needed the female alive long enough for him to sire a youngling. He would be king in both blood and power. Ryza's daughter would make that happen.

CHAPTER 3

THE PAT-PAT-PAT OF THE PUNCHING BAG CALMED ONYX as she danced around, bobbing, weaving, then striking. She'd been at it for two hours. The center's gym was her haven. Its occupants were her clan. They were a collection of broken things. Trash in the eyes of society but treasures to Nancy Mays, who ran the place.

Nancy Mays, whom the kids called Mama and the adults referred to as Mama Mays, ran the community center, which was two separate buildings connected by a covered walkway. The main building was two stories. The first floor had four offices, a conference room, a cafeteria, a small gym, complete with locker rooms and showers, and a reception area. One of the four offices was converted into a computer/game room. The second floor had six classroom spaces. One was a nursery. The others were used for workshops and afterschool programs. The second building was a two-story apartment connected to the center. The dorms were on the second floor. Key cards were required to gain access.

Each dorm could hold four teens. Furnishings included a pair of bunk beds, two shared closets, a study area and reading nook. The dorms could house a total of twenty-four residents. Gym style showers and bathrooms were on both ends of the second floor. Boys on the south end, girls on the north end. They were coded for key cards which were assigned to the residents. The first floor housed a security desk, a clinic, five counselor offices and a recreation room with vending machines that were also coded to the key cards.

Hubbard Community Center spanned across a block. It was in an ideal location, near the local redline train station. They were off 35th, which was close to the Illinois Institute of Technology, or IIT. Mama Mays had a sweet deal with IIT which allowed the residents to attend summer programs in exchange for part-time labor. She spearheaded a literacy program off grounds through a partnership with the many advocates in the community. Small businesses were strong but advocates for communities of color made things happen. Between the afterschool programs and tutoring at IIT, Onyx earned a decent income. Mama Mays hooked her up with a few service grants, too.

On the outside, Mama Mays looked like anyone's grandmother. She was short and round. A prosthetic limb completed her left leg below the knee. It was the price she paid for testifying against a brutal attack on two girls in her program. Mama Mays let her hair go white two years ago, deciding to put the money she spent on hair dyes and rinses back into the community center. Honestly, her hair color was the only thing that clued people in on her age. She was sixty-five, but spry, mentally sharp and a fighter.

She worked hard to keep the Center running but a month ago, something changed. Onyx didn't know what, but whatever was wrong killed the fire in her eyes. She smiled less. Frowned more. The Center wasn't a pigsty but with kids running around, there were always toys, books and gadgets lying around. The place was spotless, which was a sure sign that something was wrong. Mama Mays was constantly wiping things down, sweeping and chewing her nails. She snapped at anyone who brought her bad habit to her attention.

The kids scattered when she walked down the halls. Normally they flocked to her, showered her with questions, or displayed their latest pictures or grades. One kid, Israel, who was seven years old and barely spoke, graced Mama Mays with a freestyle rap. Hubbard Community Center had gone quiet. So quiet that Onyx noticed three massive men, all well-dressed, barge in and push pass Ginger, the self-appointed screener of visitors.

One shoved Ginger so hard she fell.

Onyx abandoned the punching bag, running over to check on her. She offered Ginger a hand up, which she took gratefully. Ginger was a thirty-year-old in an eleven-year-old body. Ginger was light skinned with dark purple bantu knots and piercings lining both brows. She had a small nose ring, like Onyx, and both ears were riddled with hoop earrings. Ginger was lean muscle over long bones. She was tall for her age. She got teased for it, but the teaser would regret it. She lived to fight and it didn't take much to provoke one.

Though Onyx was the adult, she trusted Ginger's instincts. Poverty and trauma had a way of aging a kid. It made them wary. They were more adept at reading people and they trusted few. The preyed upon recognized predators. The three men who stormed into the center were predators.

"Who are they?" Onyx jerked her head in the direction of the trio.

Ginger grumbled, glaring after them as they filed into Mama Mays's office. Their girth filled the hallway. All of them had dreadlocks which flapped like capes in their wake. Onyx shifted to follow them, but Ginger grabbed her shoulder. Onyx stared at the girl; eyebrows raised.

Ginger shook her head sharply. "They're with the state. I don't know what department, but they've been giving Mama the business for about two weeks."

Ginger pulled Onyx off to the side. Both girls were far enough out of sight that anyone in the hall couldn't see them, but they had a vantage point from their position that allowed them to detect movement, should one of the men head their way.

"What kind of trouble is Mama in?"

Ginger shrugged. "I asked the other kids. Israel said he saw them walking around the building." Ginger leaned toward the hall, checking around before speaking again. "They might be inspectors or something."

"So? Mama keeps this place tight. I doubt there's anything here that's not up to code."

Ginger wrapped her hands around herself. "You know how rich folks been buying up property round here. Maybe someone's got their sights on this place."

Onyx chewed on the idea. It was a reasonable argument, but the buyouts had been happening for years. So, why now? Why the big push to get Mama's block?

Ginger snapped her fingers in Onyx's face. "Hey, you still with me?"

Onyx blinked. "Yeah, I was just thinking about what you said."

"What we gone do if Mama loses this place?" Ginger was already entertaining the worst-case scenario.

Onyx caught Ginger's flailing arms and held them to the girl's sides. "None of that." She put her face in front of Ginger's, not allowing her to look away from her. "We don't know what's up, but I am going to find out." She looked over her shoulder. Her back was to the hall, blocking their vantage point. She lowered her voice. "Nothing's wrong, 'til it's wrong. When we find problems, what do we do?"

Ginger brightened. "We solve them." Ginger cleared her throat. Onyx detected the tapping soles of shoes echoing off the halls, punctuated by the painful thump of Mama May's cane. Ginger and Onyx played the role of frightened girls as they watched the men. Mama Mays trailed them, clutching papers that looked legal with their stamps and staples.

Ginger leaned in. "That don't look good."

Onyx scowled at the men, jaw locked, as she noted their dismissal of the woman they should be bowing to. Mama looked her age at that moment, which curled

Onyx's fists. She growled, a habit of hers when she was pissed and those men had definitely pissed her off.

Both Onyx and Ginger trailed Mama Mays as she followed the rude men. Onyx did her best to read over Mama's shoulder as they moved closer to the main door. Ginger and Onyx nearly crashed into Mama Mays as the last of the trio spun on her. He raised his finger at Mama Mays and both girls were ready to throw hands. His gaze slid over to the pair briefly then back to Mama Mays.

"Look, Miss! You got three days to get things straight." His gaze slid up and across to Onyx. "We'll be back. At that time, be ready to vacate."

Ginger squeaked. Onyx's growl grew in volume. She strode forward, only to have Ginger block her progress with a simple shift in position. "Ginger."

Ginger laid her hand on Onyx's stomach and whispered as discreetly as she could. "Don't embarrass Mama Mays. Not in front of them."

"But..."

"You know how she feels about fighting."

Onyx pointed at the man insulting Mama Mays. "Look at him!" she hissed, as the man gave Mama Mays his back, opened the front door then slammed it behind him.

Mama Mays stood trembling.

"Mama?" Ginger moved closer, placing a timid hand on Mama Mays's left shoulder. "You okay?"

Mama Mays patted Ginger's hand with her free one. She clutched the papers tighter, raised them to her face and screamed at them. She pushed past the girls and headed to her office. Onyx was on her heels.

"Mama." Onyx kept a careful pace, not wanting to cause the older woman to stumble. She caught the office door before it closed.

"Mama, talk to me." Onyx followed her in, stopping at the visitor's chair. She dropped into it.

Mama Mays took her seat, tossing the papers. A fluttering, curling cloud floated onto her desk when she lay her head.

Onyx gathered the papers, stacking them into a pile, unsure of the order. She turned the stack toward her and began to read: Order of Eviction.

"What's this?" She pulled the papers closer and began flipping through.

Mama Mays pushed herself up and gave her a look. "What does it say?"

Onyx picked up the stack of papers and waved them at her. "They can't do this!"

"Well, they have," Mama Mays groused.

"No, they won't." Onyx clutched the Notice of Eviction to her chest, jumped up from the chair and rushed from the office. She was sure Mama Mays called her name, but she ignored it. Her goal was to get out of the building and to the men who delivered those documents.

A big white Cadillac Escalade was parked along the curb. Two of the three men had already entered it. The last one, the rude one, was about to get in when Onyx called out.

"Stop!" Onyx screamed as she picked up speed. Her hand surged forward, reaching for the rude man. He scowled, shifting into a fighter's stance. She slowed, stopping into her own combat position. She wanted a pound of flesh. If he were willing to give it, she would take it.

"Stay your hand, Taqual!" A woman's voice drew the man into a casual stance, though his eyes were ready for war.

"Who are you?" Onyx's limbs relaxed a little, as she moved toward the SUV, eyes darting between Taqual and the half-lowered dark tinted window.

A pale white hand slid from the open space. The owner was thick. Fat fingers waved toward Taqual. "Move. Let her pass."

Taqual grumbled but side-stepped, leaving enough space for Onyx to pass but keeping her within reach, should he need to subdue her.

"Stop," the woman ordered when Onyx was within two feet of the window.

"Look." Onyx waved the papers at the window. "You can't do this. This place..."

The hand waved dismissively. "Get off your soap box. As you can see from the papers you hold in your hand, what you say we can't do, has been done. In the time it takes your matriarch to get a lawyer and a court date, her properties will be ours."

Onyx ground her teeth.

"I have a proposition for you," the woman said.

Onyx took a step back, hands fisting at her sides.

A rich, throaty laugh floated from the dark interior. "Look, child. The window of opportunity will remain open only for so long. So, hear me out, or watch as everything your matriarch values crumbles."

Onyx preferred choices that could be settled with either her fists or an argument. "Fine."

The woman called Taqual to the truck. She passed him something through the window. He remained by the door as the woman inside resumed speaking.

"I hold the contracts to your matriarch's property." She gestured toward the building behind Onyx. "It has promise. It is, as you say, prime real estate."

"But you'll be putting kids out that need this place! Why…"

"Would I do that?" the woman finished the sentence. "Little girl, haven't you picked up on the fact that money makes the world go round? It's not a saying. It's not an ideal. It's a hard and fast fact. The sooner you learn it, the easier things will get."

Onyx fixed her gaze on the shiny black tires. It helped her keep her expression neutral, though inside she could feel scalding heat build in her chest. If she opened her mouth, it would pour out. She had to listen, which was hard when she was mad. She swallowed as she worked at focusing on the woman's words.

A business card appeared under her nose. She looked up to see Taqual's ugly face. She snatched it and flipped it so she could read what was on it.

"The address on that card is where you will meet Taqual and his company. You will be at that location by sunset. If not, the agreement is null and void."

What was she agreeing to? Onyx shook her head. She didn't hear an agreement. Her gaze darted to the window. She wanted to ask the woman to repeat what she said, but

Taqual standing in front of her and the woman's belief that Onyx was naive kept her mouth shut.

Taqual pivoted, opened the door and got in. Once the door closed, the woman spoke again. "Remember, sunset or no deal." The window slid up, leaving Onyx to stare at her own reflection before the SUV pulled off.

Onyx watched the truck disappear around the corner. She looked down at the card in her hand. The meeting place wasn't far from the Community Center. She slid the card in her back-right pocket. She would meet them to help Mama Mays keep the community center, though she wasn't sure about Taqual and his goons. No matter what, she had to try.

———

Taqual stared at the white avatar across from him. It was a soft bodied human as pale as the Orc witch, Ivy, who manipulated it. He hated Ivy but was wise enough to do her bidding. Her predictions never failed.

Females! They had no place in Orc society except as breeders and entertainment. He pressed the back of his head into the seat as he slid down. The glamour Ivy cast irritated his skin. His Orc hide was tough, but magic didn't mix well with it. Orcs were not made for magic. Ivy should have been put to death the moment her curiosity for it surfaced. She breathed because her son, Jahll, was the only acceptable successor. He was Ryza's second, plus his views leaned toward the ways of blood and war.

Taqual turned his head toward the window and watched the scenery pass. The human world with all its stone buildings, noise and lights had no appeal to him, but it did to others. He watched a shriveled, dirty beggar approach the SUV. His lip curled into a snarl. In Oracaii, Orcs were taught to provide for themselves from the womb. They learned to live with nothing if need be. The way of war demanded it.

The avatar across from him laid its hands on its knees, letting him know that Ivy had released her control. Human eyes stared at him, bright green and full of terror. It would remember nothing of its enslavement. Once they reached their destination, the juncture through which they would cross over into Penumbra, the magic would dissolve the moment their feet touched Penumbran soil. The spell on the human female would break and she would return to whatever she was doing before it took hold.

Females! The half-Orc female Ivy bartered with was too stupid to be queen. If she were, she would have killed them all, including the human across from him. The female, Onyx, was weak, ignorant to their ways and not savvy enough to handle basic Orc negotiations.

CHAPTER 4

A FAMILIAR TINKLING OF BELLS GREETED ONYX WHEN SHE pushed open the door to Mama Mays's office. An obscenely large Maine Coon cat was sprawled across her desk. Mama Mays was lost in scratching its ears, sliding her worshipful fingers under its chin. The tinkling bells were wild as the cat writhed with pleasure while its favorite human loved up on it. Onyx cut off the love fest when Mama Mays began baby-talking and cooing at the cat everyone called Black.

"Mama, have some pride," Onyx scolded as she entered the office fresh from her shower. The cat stared at her with gorgeous olive-green eyes. The low light expanded its pupils, giving the weight of its stare a near human quality. Mama Mays continued stroking its thick black fur. The cat was beautiful. It wore a black collar with silver bells. Onyx absently reached for her own collar. It was hidden under the black turtleneck she kept in her locker. She added a black puffer vest over it, zipping it up to the neck. It helped conceal the collar.

"Black's a good kitty." The cat tilted its head toward Mama Mays, who scratched it by default. "He keeps an eye on this place." Mama Mays began the slow process of sitting down, sliding her cane forward, leaning it against the edge of her desk. She kept her chair positioned in a way that all she had to do was twist her body toward it, then drop onto the soft cushion. Once seated, she gave Onyx her full attention.

"He's not a dog," Onyx said.

"He's better than a dog. Dogs are loud, messy and need too much attention."

Onyx stood on the visitor's side of the desk. She lay the Notice of Eviction down. Her gaze passed over an assortment of letters. Several had nasty red Past Due stamps on them. She scanned the postmarks, noticing they were several months old. Onyx took the visitor's seat, she reached for the nearest envelope. She gathered several, scanning the sender's information. One name tightened her grip on the envelope as she pulled it closer. She opened it and removed the contents. A single sheet of paper. She read it.

"Alderman Jay 'Jessie' Jessup." Onyx looked up from the piece of mail.

Mama Mays sighed, nodding slowly, as she fixated on Black, who crept toward her. He stopped at her chest and pressed his head against her collarbone.

"Didn't he spend a lot of time here when he was a kid?"

Mama Mays swallowed as she stroked Black's head. "He helped me get funding for this place." She looked around the room, her gaze troubled. "Introduced me to the people who partnered with me to get programs going, which help the kids here succeed."

Onyx raised the sheet of paper. "This says he's cutting his ties and withdrawing from the contracts you two set up."

Mama Mays wrapped her arms around Black. The cat meowed and rubbed its head along the side of her face.

"He can't do that!"

"What is it with your generation and denial?" Mama Mays's eyes were flat when they finally met Onyx's gaze. "Justice is fiction." She huffed as her hands slipped from Black's fur. "At least round these parts, it is." Mama Mays drew a pile of assorted letters toward her chest. Black leapt out of her way but stayed close.

"Money makes the bad good and the good bad. Folks are labeled one of two ways: those with money and those without." She pointed at herself. "I don't have any and this place..." she waved her hands around the room again, "it runs on grants and the kindness of others." She made a noise that Onyx figured to be laughter but turned out to be more of a moan choked by a cough.

"I learned years ago kindness is plentiful under the eye of a spotlight." Her gaze drifted to several framed articles. "It's a well that dries up once the hype dies down."

Onyx stared at her lap, eyes settling on her left wrist. She ran her fingers across her old friendship bracelet.

Chipped acrylic paint spelled out the name Willow. Her first and last real friend. The slap of an envelope hitting the surface of the desk in front of her pulled Onyx from her thoughts.

"It's the first of many who withdrew their help with the programs I have in place."

Onyx caught the envelope, repositioning it for a better look. She scanned the envelope, noting it was from IIT.

"Why would they stop helping you? Don't they get grant money or something for participating in community service programs?"

"They do." Mama Mays leaned back. "If participants in the program put the college's reputation at risk, they back off."

"How does the Community Center put the college at risk?"

"Cops. They've been rolling through lately."

"That's not strange around here." Onyx shrugged. "We're the northernmost part of the South Side. You know, once you exit Chicago's South Loop, everything's considered questionable."

"Yes, but they've been bothering the boys."

Onyx turned in her chair, staring at the door, as if she could see through it to the small basketball court to the right of the building. The court was off the alley. It would be the route she took when she left to meet the White lady's goons.

"The only thing bad on the boys that come to the center is their mouth and that's only when I'm not watching," Onyx said then chuckled to lighten the mood.

"Don't matter. The boys stopped using the basketball

court because I asked them to. I thought it would help, but the cops started popping up near their homes. Derrick told me yesterday that a cop trailed him as he walked home."

Onyx leaned forward, pressing clasped hands against the edge of the desk. "Is he okay?"

"He's scared but not hurt."

"Why's this happening now?"

"Who knows why rich people do what they do? What I do know is, someone with deep pockets promised Jessie something. Jessie, being Jessie, is always going to go the way of the dollar."

Onyx leaned back in her chair, taking an envelope with her. She tapped it against her thigh. "Good ole Jessie imagines himself the future Al Sharpton."

Mama Mays chuckled. "That boy always enjoyed seeing his picture in the paper."

"What are we going to do?" Onyx held the envelope aloft.

Mama Mays gestured between them. "We will do nothing." She laid a finger on her collarbone. "I am going to call in a few favors." She looked off to her right as she contemplated her options. "Besides, this is grown folks work."

"I have some money tucked away. It's not a lot, but it might help." Onyx lay the envelope down.

"You ain't got to do nothing. I'll take care of my own mess."

"But this isn't just your problem." Onyx's gaze darted to one of the framed articles lining the wall behind the desk. The largest frame carried her story. Three small frames underneath held the only existing pictures of Onyx's mother, Olivia. Helen didn't have any pictures of her sister in their small apartment. The Community Center was the only place she could come to see her.

Mama Mays turned, following Onyx's gaze. She snatched up her cane and brought it down hard. Rising from her chair, she stepped in front of the assortment of articles and photographs.

She tapped her cane against the prosthetic, using her free hand to grab her chair for balance. She'd locked the wheels so the chair wouldn't get away from her. A habit she'd taken up when she lost the lower half of her leg.

"Don't you dare." Mama Mays's words were full of tender warning.

"But they're going to take everything," Onyx mumbled as she began twisting her friendship bracelet, not meeting the older woman's gaze.

"Onyx Janae Jones!"

Onyx jerked upright; friendship bracelet forgotten.

"You listen to me." Mama Mays slapped her hands on the desk with each word uttered. "Don't worry about what you think folks gone take from me."

Onyx's gaze darted to the stack of envelopes.

Mama Mays leaned her elbow on the hard top as she aimed her finger at Onyx. "No matter what happens, I'll always be a safe place for you."

"Why didn't you just adopt me?" Onyx jumped up from her seat and began pacing behind her chair. She paused, aiming her finger at Mama Mays. "You knew my mama better than her own sister. You care more about me than my aunt. You..."

Mama Mays gestured for Onyx to stop. "Don't drown yourself in all the coulda' beens. Law is law. Social services and the courts recognized your aunt as guardian."

"Because she's blood," Onyx spat as she scooted to the edge of her chair. "Blood don't make family."

Mama Mays gave a resolute nod. "We know that, but law is black and white. Ain't no space for the gray."

Onyx growled.

"Stop that."

Onyx cleared her throat and slid back in her chair.

"Haven't I always opened my doors to you?"

"Yes." Onyx folded her hands over her chest.

"Have your back?"

Onyx nodded then swallowed, turning her face away from Mama Mays.

"You know I will fight for your best interest."

Onyx glanced at the top of the cane leaning against the desk, gaze shifting back to Mama Mays.

"You've sacrificed more than you should."

Mama Mays looked down at her prosthetic. "This ain't nothing."

"If you hadn't jumped in to save me and Willow…"

Mama Mays's eyes rolled slowly up from her leg then settled on Onyx. She grabbed her cane, setting it between her legs and pressing her weight on it as she leaned forward.

"Was I supposed to let those bastards get away with what they did?"

Onyx cleared her throat but said nothing.

Nancy Mays tapped her cane on the floor. "Answer

me." She leaned back in her chair. "Was I supposed to remain silent so they could try again?"

Onyx's head jerked up, eyes blazing. "No. You could have asked them to keep your name out of the police reports." Onyx shrugged as she stretched her arms out. "You didn't have to talk to reporters."

"Sure. I could have stayed quiet, but I'm not gone stand around and watch a pack of wild dogs slaughter mine." Mama Mays's cane groaned as she leaned her weight on it. "I ain't never been a coward and won't ever be. There's too much of that going on around here now. Nowadays cowardice has catch phrases like *snitches get stitches*. What the hell is that?" She threw up her hand, gestured around the room then rounded the desk. "Got babies getting killed in they own front yard while a bunch of cowards hiding behind guns walk around like they the shit."

Mama Mays stopped in front of Onyx, who stared at a pair of worn, black, orthopedic shoes. "Places like mine wouldn't exist if I rolled over and looked the other way. It takes real balls to speak up and do something about the problems everyone else complains about."

"But they nearly killed you!"

"Am I dead?"

Onyx shook her head.

"Well, then."

"But…"

"But nothing. You was a baby and so was Willow. Every one of those bastards got what they deserved."

"Torn apart," Onyx whispered the words. A rusty, metallic odor filled her nostrils, making her mouth water.

She flexed her fingers on her knees as she inhaled deep, nearly choking on the memory of fresh death. The sensation of a wet scalp dangling on the end of the dreadlocks wrapped around her fist. Her vision blurred from the blood in her eyes. Every sound was distant, like she was underwater.

"No." Mama Mays used her free hand to tilt Onyx's head up, dragging her out of her memory. "Not torn apart but sent to Hell where they belong."

Black meowed his agreement as he padded to Onyx's side of the desk.

"You ain't got time to mourn devils." Mama Mays released Onyx's chin. "You ain't got time to worry about me."

"But I do."

"But you shouldn't." Mama Mays ground her cane in the floor.

"You sayin' so won't stop it."

Onyx stared at a wall of black fur as she began twisting her friendship bracelet. The soft swish of the cat's tail across the desktop was a welcome distraction. Mama Mays always knew what was best. She never let anyone see her suffer. She had to be strong for her kids. Onyx ran the tip of her finger across the chipped letters, pausing at the "O". Mama Mays worked hard to keep her secrets, but all the kids knew. A couple of them were selling whatever they could to earn money that barely filled the mysterious envelopes left on her desk.

"Onyx." Mama Mays beat the edge of the desk with her knuckles. "Onyx Janae Jones."

Onyx pulled her gaze away from soft black fur to a face laced with fresh wrinkles. "Yes, ma'am?"

"You too young to have the weight of my world on your shoulders."

Onyx's cell phone buzzed. She reached into the pocket of her puffer jacket and checked the caller ID. She tossed it. Black barely missed getting hit by the phone as it landed on the desk, sending envelopes over the edge.

Mama Mays hmphed at the word on the screen: Hell. It was how Onyx referred to her aunt when describing her to others. "She why you here?"

"When is she not?"

"Well, you can stay in one of the dorm rooms."

"I know." The fatigue of the day found its way to Onyx's voice.

"Why don't you go get yourself some rest? You don't look like you've had much, if any."

Onyx agreed as she dragged herself out of her chair. Mama Mays escorted her to the door. She heard the soft thump of the cat as he joined them. Onyx allowed herself to be pushed from the room. Mama Mays didn't follow her but returned to her office.

Onyx headed down the hallway, turning the corner which led to the back of the building. A big, dark, gray door with a reinforced lock was where she was headed. It opened to the courtyard. She stepped out onto the walkway and checked the windows and the general area for an audience. Finding none, she trotted off toward the basketball court then dashed off down the alley.

Several minutes after Onyx disappeared down the

alley, the center's back door swung open again. Black the cat trotted out. He stopped several yards away and sat, wrapping his tail around his body as the heavy door clicked shut behind him. He blinked, then surveyed his surroundings. He lifted his head, sniffed the air then let loose a loud yowl. Four cats and a large black dog rounded the corners of the building from several directions. They all stopped in front of Black and sat at attention. The animals stared at the cat who, after a few minutes, got up and trotted over to the door that had closed behind him. He rubbed his large, furry body against it. Bright white glyphs crawled along the surface. They spread across the walls and along the pavement. Black turned, sat and observed his handiwork. He did not move until the last glyph covered the roof. Once the spell sealed, he rose and trotted past the four cats and dog into the alley. There his trot became a run as he followed Onyx's trail.

One by one, the four cats spread out around the building, shifting into their human forms as they moved. A pair of teenaged boys and girls, each dressed in clothes typical of the neighborhood, found shadows in which to linger. The last animal, a black Cane Corso with blue eyes, trotted over to the dorms. There he scratched and barked at the door. Elias, as always, let him in. Elias was seven years old and only spoke to Mama Mays and his puppy in whispers.

The door clicked to a close behind the boy and the dog. Black's glyphs flared as the spell activated.

CHAPTER 5

Penumbra
Oracaii Throne Room

IT FELT GOOD TO SIT ON THE BLACK THRONE. JAHLL LEANED into the high-back, bare arms sliding down the crystal arms. He flicked his thumb along the edge, snatching it up at the sharp bite of its teeth. He examined the thick dark red droplets then rubbed his fingers together. Did the throne ever cut the old kings? He grunted, exhaling steam from his wide nostrils.

He twisted in the throne, eyes traveling along the Wall of Kings. Reliefs, painstakingly carved by the best artisans of Oracaii, of the old kings astride their capals in various battle poses. Capals were the only mounts big enough to carry an Orc. As large as Earth's African elephants, they looked like a cross between a buffalo and a mountain goat. A capal's horns were thick, curved and served as reins. There was a spot primed for Ryza. It would be added to the wall once the new king took the throne.

Jahll's snort morphed into a growl as he turned away from the Wall of Kings. His fists were clasped as blood from his cut trickled across his knuckles onto black stone. His head snapped toward the large russet slabs of metal, sealing him away from the world. A familiar voice pulled him from the throne.

"You can't enter!" Altos, one of his personal guards, groused.

"He's my son!"

Jahll groaned as he began to descend the steps.

"Mother," he sighed, readying himself for her dramatic entry. Choosing to meet her, Jahll began what felt like a pilgrimage toward the throne room entrance. He'd only taken four steps when the doors swung open. Ivy stormed in, a cloud of gossamer and a symphony of swearing. A tangle of braids floated in a puff of hair as thin as a spider's web. The braids were long, ending at her waist, each with rings of silver which were like chimes when they beat together. The ends held together with bands bearing symbols that did not belong. Most Orcs were wary of his mother's eccentricities. Eyes flitted from her like butterflies keeping her dalliances secret.

Jahll didn't know the origins of the symbols nor what they did for her. What he did know, was that they smelled bad. The magic she carried pushed him back a step the moment she crossed the threshold. Layers of gossamer folded like wings at her back. A collar of pink and white stones anchored her top, shielding her breasts from sight. A series of necklaces layered her neck, the most prominent one, a medallion bearing his father's mark. It was her proudest piece. Jahll wore an identical medallion. He kept his hidden beneath his tunic.

Ivy wore sweet perfumes to cover up her mischief. It didn't work with him. Growing up in the midst of her magic sharpened his nose to it. A pungent cloud of bitter spices and decay enveloped her. Her every step sent noxious tendrils up his nose, which he wrinkled as she got closer. He braced himself for her grand embrace, parting his lips just enough to breathe and not choke.

Ivy threw her arms out, her face a beacon of pride as she rose on her tiptoes. He bent low for her to reach. She pulled him into a hug and he nearly choked.

"My son!" She released him, taking a few steps back. She examined him the way mothers do. Hands on hips, face full of pride and a smile brighter than the sun.

Jahll scanned the room as his mother looked her fill. He chose a table where they would speak, six paces to the left of them. It was out of plain sight and was far enough where a passerby would not hear their conversation. Jahll motioned for Altos to close the doors before he led his mother to the table.

"What's so important that you had to make a scene?"

Ivy reached across the table, taking her son's hands into her own. "The Chosen will not make it to Oracaii for the challenge."

Jahll snatched his hands from his mother's grasp. "You had her killed?" He snorted as he slowly got to his feet.

"Jahll!" Ivy rose with him. She reached for him again; he shunned her touch then beat his chest.

"It is I who decides whether she lives or dies." His

voice was guttural, low, as he switched to human tongue, which few Orcs spoke. "I have plans for the female that have nothing to do with death," he snorted again as he circled the small space he occupied, "yet."

"But son, with no Chosen the throne is yours." Ivy gestured at the black throne.

"Will it truly be mine?" Jahll hissed. "Will the High Spirit recognize me as an Elite if I have not fought *her* Chosen?"

"The High Spirit will honor who the Orcs select." Ivy took a step toward her son, who took an equal step back.

"If by some miracle, the High Spirit allows me to be the next in succession due to some unforeseen accident, I will be in battle for days. Rest will be no option. I. Will. Fall," Jahll snapped.

Ivy's haughty expression vanished. "Son…"

Jahll slashed his hand across the space in front of him as if batting away her words. "I am the King's second, a warrior of warriors, but I have yet to meet one who can endure endless combat."

"I will kill…"

Jahll thrust his finger at his mother. "You would make me a lesser Orc because of your mother's fears?"

"No, son."

"I am not an Elite. I am mortal." He turned away from her, adding more space between them. "I cannot endure three days and two nights of straight combat." Jahll rested his hands on his head, his shoulders slumped, as he sat on the edge of the table nearest him. The face he turned on his mother was weary. "I cannot let you help me in *your* way. The fight must be fought as I see fit."

Ivy approached her son with caution. "I cannot call off a kill contract once it's struck."

"You need to find a way to cancel it, or hope she is able to fend off your assassins." Jahll's tired eyes bore into his mother's. "If she doesn't survive your threat, I will be forced to cull my own kingdom of its best warriors. If I do that, I earn the survivors' respect for my ruthlessness, but I pull Oracaii's teeth." Jahll leaned back and stared at the ceiling, which was a map of Oracaii and its hidden villages. "I hope to return the dread of Orcs throughout Penumbra. I can't do that dead and without an army at my back."

Jahll sat upright before pushing away from the table. He headed for the entrance where he stopped. "You need to fix what you've started," he said without bothering to look at her. He left her alone in the throne room as he contemplated his next step. Spies would have to be sent out to collect the names of those with ambitions. He would know by sunrise if he would have to kill them.

Of all the ungrateful beasts to walk the lands! Ivy stalked through the castle halls in a cacophony of beads, chiming jewelry and gossamer. Her son was the only soul she cared about. She spent years manipulating his way into Ryza's court after his father's death. Jahll had no idea how long she'd worked to prepare the throne for him. She'd killed. She established ties to the disgusting human world to keep her hands in the life of the Chosen. In the end, Ivy's work would bear fruit. As the saying went, "A warrior without confidence is a coward, doomed to fall before the sword." An ugly smile spread across her face.

She jogged down the palace steps, hissing at those who scurried from her path. Their whispers of *lugat,* the orcish term for ghost, didn't go unnoticed. Rage drew out the parts of her meant to stay hidden. Ivy did her best to numb her face and add dignity to her steps. Squaring her shoulders, tipping her chin higher than those around her, she slowed her pace. Her gait was still quick, but her motions were regal, at least to her knowledge. If she were to be queen to her son's king, she had to adopt the persona. Benevolent Queen to the Commons of her people and Blood Queen to her enemies.

To solve her son's problem, she needed to think. She couldn't think when in a fury, which meant she needed to work it off. Ivy smiled; it was genuine, as she reached the side alley leading to the old tunnel that opened into the dark forest. She made sure no one was watching when she touched one of her magicked necklaces to the old lock. It popped open. Entering the tunnel, Ivy recited the words which resealed the lock without missing a step.

Her means to bleed out her anger waited in her cottage.

CHAPTER
6

THIS WAS THE PLACE. ONYX RETURNED THE BUSINESS CARD to the breast pocket of her puffer vest. The stench of urine and garbage had her reconsidering her decision. She stood at the mouth of the alley. Pinching her nose muted the smell. She breathed from her mouth as she entered. Old bottles and cans lined the rear wall of the buildings. There was a mattress propped against an abandoned dresser. All the drawers had been removed and were stacked neatly next to it. A chair with three legs lay on its side next to the discarded furniture. Sparkling shards of broken glass lined the walls like someone swept it there. Her gaze shifted to the pockmarked asphalt. The City would ignore them until next fall or election season. Until then, Old Hershel took care of it. He owned *Who Kut You*, the neighborhood barbershop. It bordered the alley and the main street. He hired the local kids to clean up and fill the potholes when he had a little extra money.

Her gaze traveled along the graffitied walls. The artist's perspective was a view from the field to the storefronts. It captured Old Hershel standing in the doorway of his store, smiling. Several of the regulars, Jo-Jo the Wino holding up his sign and Dawg, the local mutt, watched. Faceless customers of the liquor store and the barbershop leaned against the walls or their backs were to the artist. It was a nice piece. She searched for the artist's tag. She found it on the lower part of the wall: Josiah. Onyx smiled. She'd heard of him, but this was the first piece she'd ever seen in person.

A can skittered behind her. She spun, fists raised, as she searched for the source. A loud meow announced her shadow. She gaped as Black trotted down the alley toward her.

Onyx watched him, wondering why the tiny bells along his collar were mute. She should have heard his tinkling approach. Black stopped directly in front of her and sat on his haunches. His tail flicked slowly left then right, head tilting up, he stared at her.

Onyx stomped her foot, then shooed the cat. He flicked his tail and yawned.

"Go away, cat." Onyx spoke through gritted teeth. Black lay on his belly, still looking up at her. He tilted his head to the right, eyes locked on hers.

Onyx stomped her foot again. "Get!" She waved her hands to shoo him away, closing the slight space between them, hoping to spook him. Instead, he looked down his nose at her boot as if he were offended by it.

"Stupid cat." She bent to pick him up, but he darted out of reach. She grabbed patches of her mohawk, the desire to pull was strong. She let go of her hair and turned away from the cat.

Cats were weird. Black ignored her most of the time. Why was he following her now? He wasn't a dog. They were needy. She pivoted, fixing the cat with a glare as he sat regally.

"Why are you being all clingy now!" she whisper-yelled. "You ignore me all the time." She untangled her hands, placing one on her chest. "I'm not Mama Mays. She's your girl." She shooed the cat again. "Go to her."

Black yawned, then blinked.

Was that judgment in his eyes?

Black tilted his head again, this time to the left, as if the new angle would bring clarity to what it was he was observing.

"Don't you judge me," Onyx accused just as her cellphone buzzed. It was loud in the alley's quiet. She checked the screen and frowned. Her aunt. She immediately ignored the call. There were fourteen missed text messages. She made a face, quickly deleting them. She aimed her phone at the cat.

"Go away." Onyx headed for the dumpster, unsure of which side of the alley she should wait on. It probably didn't matter. She could hop into the SUV on either side. Besides, if Black saw she didn't care, maybe he would leave her alone.

Once she reached the dumpster, she noticed the thick chain and padlock wrapped around it. It stank, but it wasn't overflowing with trash. Leaning against the wall,

Onyx slid down it until her butt connected with the asphalt. She sat on the side, which hid her from the eyes of passersby. She got as comfortable as she could when Black trotted around the dumpster and plopped down in front of her.

"What do you want?" she snarled at the cat. Black just stared at her. Onyx considered how she could get rid of him. She glanced at the padlock and chain. She couldn't toss him in the dumpster, which would be ideal.

Black meowed. His tail swung forward, curling over his forepaws. He fixed her with that stare again, like she should know what he was thinking or something. She leaned forward, putting her face in front of the cat's. Brows drawn, she bared her teeth and hissed. Black blinked but didn't move away.

Onyx straightened, leaned back and rested her head against the plaster wall. Her phone buzzed again. She fumbled with it, pulling it close to check the caller ID. It was her aunt again. What did she want? She let the phone slide from her hand as it began another round of buzzing.

She drew her legs up, wrapped her arms around them and rested her chin on her knees. Black meowed. Maybe if she didn't react to him, he would go away.

Onyx faced the grungy side of the dumpster. Graffiti coated the lower half. Someone had spray-painted Black Lives Matter with a brown fist raised in salute. She looked over her shoulder when something tapped on the bottom of her jacket.

Black backed up and sat on his haunches.

"Why are you following me?" she ground out. "What do you want?" She shook her fist at the animal.

You're not safe, a strange, accented voice filled her head.

"What the..." Onyx scrambled to her feet, drawing as close to the wall as she could.

They plan to kill you. Black raised a paw and aimed it at Onyx.

Onyx shook her head vigorously, beating the heels of her hands against the sides of it. "This can't be." She stared at Black. "Animals don't talk."

Black stretched as a disc of pale green light spread beneath him. His eyes flashed red, as thin spindles of white and yellow light rose in an awkward dance. It surrounded Black, then washed over him, creating a stat-icky cocoon. Onyx saw it as an opportunity to run. She had taken a step when the light splintered into a cloud of shimmering embers. A man now stood in place of the cat, an impossibly tall one. He had a runner's body, with long lean muscles. His skin was as black as the cat's fur and so was his hair; both glistened in the light. His hair fell in waves across his shoulders and down his back. His eyes were currently red, conjuring the word "devil." Her gaze shot to the top of his head. There were no horns. Maybe he was half demon or an imp of sorts.

A light tinkling of bells drew her gaze to his neck. Around it was the same black collar with little silver bells. The sight should have been funny, but the man wearing it made it look sexy. He was shirtless. His pecs were spec-tacular, each with an intricate tattoo just above the nipple. She was tempted to lean in for a closer look, but she resisted. There was more of him to inspect and her eyes had a mind of their own. They raked his long, languid torso, lingering on a perfect eight pack. Her gaze dipped lower, locking on hip bones peeking from the low rise of black leather pants. She pressed a hand on the spot just under his ribs, ran it across the top of his abs, then pulled it away. She turned it over to check for ink. Her palm was bare.

"Nice, aren't they?" His warm breath bathed her scalp and kissed the tip of her spine. Her head jerked up, catching a self-satisfied grin. Her scowl made him laugh, exposing the tips of fangs.

"You're a Shifter!" Onyx found herself back in the corner between the dumpster and the wall. She'd read about them in urban fantasy novels. They weren't real, at least, they weren't supposed to be.

"Your father sent me to look after you."

Her eyes narrowed. "I don't have a father."

The Shifter shook his head. "You do."

"It's news to me."

"Which is how he wanted it."

"Why would he want that? I mean, did he hate me? Hate my mom?"

"No." The Shifter shook his head. "To know him would have been the end of you."

"I don't understand."

Onyx sized up the Shifter in front of her, eyes dropping to his hands. The tips of his fingers sported long nails. No. Those were freaking claws! Her gaze darted to his.

"Who is the *they* you're talking about?" Again, her eyes dropped to his claws then back up to his face. "You look like a killer to me."

The Shifter rolled his eyes. "If I were going to kill you, we wouldn't be having this conversation."

Onyx's pride pulled her out of her corner and dangerously close to the Shifter.

"Look, little female. It was your father's wish for me to look out for you."

"First," she looked him up and down, making it a point to appear unimpressed, "who are you calling little?" She folded her arms across her chest. "Second, protect me from what!" Her voice raised; its echo surprised her. She backed up a little and lowered her voice. "Look, man, I've had one hell of a day."

"I know. I was there," the Shifter said.

"Who are you?" She narrowed her eyes at him.

"Your matron calls me Black, but my name is Cassius, friend of Ryza the Black and left hand of the King."

Onyx stared blankly.

A long, soft chime broke the momentary silence. Cassius shook his head. "Look, there is no time for histories and all the minute details that go with it. If you didn't catch it before, the men you plan to meet aren't men. They're coming to kill you."

Onyx flicked her hands at his words. "Those guys were a bunch of mindless goons and very human."

"Things aren't always what they seem."

"Tell me about it." Onyx swung away, giving him her back. She pressed her forehead against the wall, then smacked it. It stung, so she wasn't hallucinating. The heat radiating from Cassius's body was real, too. It drew beads of sweat, which slid down the small of her back. He laid his hand between her shoulder blades.

"I must ask you for an impossible thing." He stepped closer; his breath warmed her scalp. Her eyes closed as she tilted her head toward him.

Cassius placed a second hand on her right shoulder, his claws pressing into the fabric of her shirt. A little more pressure and they would pierce both her shirt and flesh. "I need you to trust me."

Her lips parted, a retort on the tip of her tongue, when the growl of an engine pulled both their eyes to the mouth of the alley. Onyx expected a White Escalade, instead, a black Chevy Tahoe came into view.

Chimes sounded again, this time in two short bursts as the front of the Chevy Tahoe pulled into the alley. Cassius's grip tightened on her shoulder as he spun her around. He crouched behind the dumpster, pulling Onyx with him. His eyes searched hers, pleading. "We have no more time."

Onyx watched the headlights creep along the ground and along the walls as it advanced into the alley.

Cassius snapped his fingers. "Look at me."

Her head jerked in his direction.

"Don't tell them about me for your safety. I will learn what I can about their plans and, if I'm lucky, get the name of the Orc who sent them."

"Orc." Onyx blinked slowly. "Wait. Orc?"

Cassius nodded his head. "As I said before, I don't have time for details, but I will tell you all you need to know as soon as I can."

The growl of the SUV's engine ricocheted in the hollowness. Rocks popped under the weight of its tires, startling Onyx, though it shouldn't have.

"Onyx." Her attention snapped back to Cassius. "Will you trust me?"

Onyx nodded.

"Don't let them know I'm different." The fine spindles of green light danced around his body. "They'll have their ideas regarding what I am because of your collar." Cassius aimed a claw at the sterling collar she hid under a turtleneck. She'd forgotten about it.

Cassius shifted back into his cat form. The black collar with its silver bells chimed like mad. He scurried over to her as the Chevy Tahoe stopped beside the dumpster. Cassius pressed his feline body to Onyx's legs as they both watched the front and rear passenger doors to the SUV swing open. Onyx spared a glance at the driver's window. The same pale white woman sat behind the wheel, her eyes facing forward. Her head didn't move as the same three hulking men rounded the truck to stand in front of Onyx. They'd exchanged their business clothes for street clothes, choosing to don hoodies, jeans and combat boots like hers. Only theirs were more expensive.

The one called Taqual wore a dark green hoodie with a Green Lantern Core symbol on the front. He seemed pleased to find her huddled with the cat in a corner. The idea that anything she did made him happy pushed her to her feet. She scooped up Cassius and clutched him to her.

Even at her full height, Onyx was shorter than the trio in front of her. Taqual shared a look with the other two. They began speaking a weird language. It was guttural, like their teeth were too large for their mouth. After a few seconds of conversation, the man closest to the SUV tapped on the driver's door. The woman pulled off, not once looking over at them.

Once the SUV was out of sight, green hoodie reached for her. Both Cassius and Onyx hissed as she ducked out of his way. The other two moved in. Onyx got in a few well-placed kicks to the knees. She took a few cautious steps back into the middle of the alley.

"One scream and the cops come running." She stopped, cradling Cassius to her chest. "I thought you were here to make a deal, not to manhandle me."

The three men remained where they stood. All of them promising her a slow death with a look. She rolled her eyes as if her heart weren't beating uncontrollably. Onyx never backed down from a fight, but she wasn't sure how well she would fare against three enormous men.

Taqual pushed to the front. The other two advanced toward her when Taqual threw up his fist for them to stop. Their obedience was instantaneous, pegging him as the leader. He muttered something to his companions. They stepped back.

"I will not apologize, as I do not like you. But my orders are to get you to our meeting point. There you will fulfill the debt of your matriarch."

Onyx looked up and down the alley, then at the men. She jerked her chin in the direction the Chevy Tahoe took. "Didn't our ride leave?"

Taqual snorted. It was an ugly sound. "No, female."

Onyx balked at the word "female."

Taqual looked up at the darkening sky, then scanned the alley. "Look, female, we have no time for questions."

His companions pivoted right, facing the wall behind the dumpster. Taqual moved to stand in front of the wall. He looked over his shoulder at Onyx.

"You must come with us now." He again faced the wall and lay his hand on it.

"Into the shadows, out of the light, hide no more from human sight."

As soon as the words were spoken, a fissure formed in the spot where his hand rested. He stepped back as tremors overtook the alleyway. The neatly stacked furniture jostled, then toppled over. The dumpster shuddered and banged against the wall. Everything, including Onyx's teeth, rattled, drawing her gaze back to the expanding fissure.

The fissure bled into a perfect oval. It spread, gaining girth and height. It stretched higher than the building on which it formed. Shafts of lightning pierced the ground in front of the opening, leaving no scorch marks.

Water. Why did she smell fresh water? Lightning preceded rain. She should smell ozone. She looked up at a dark yet clear sky. Staring into the gaping hole. She rose on her tiptoes as Taqual stepped into the opening, squinting as she strained to see where it led. Inside were pulsing colors, a mix of grays and vibrant cotton-candy pinks, oranges and reds. Taqual's companions entered. Mists rose within the pulsating tunnel, hiding them from sight.

"Will you honor our deal?" Taqual taunted.

Onyx looked at Cassius, then down the throat of the tunnel. The edges of the opening shimmered like embers and the fissure began to narrow. It was closing.

Onyx tightened her grip on Cassius, who yowled in protest as she dashed in. The fissure sealed as soon as she was inside.

The alley was quiet again except for the buzzing cell-phone that lay under the dumpster.

CHAPTER 7

South Side Chicago
Hubbard Community Center

IT WAS GETTING LATE; THE SUN WAS SETTING AND ONYX hadn't responded to her calls. Helen didn't see what her niece liked so much about the community center. She scanned the exterior, old bricks in need of tuck pointing and bits of trash flapping around in the wind. Onyx's little episode had forced her to change plans. Instead of shopping and communing with her friends, she was forced to go all James Bond. She pulled her peacoat tighter as she stood outside the front door.

She adjusted her sunglasses, sliding them down her nose, as she watched dirty little children run around inside. One of the little creatures came screaming toward the front door and stopped. When it, a little girl, noticed her, she stood on her tiptoes and sized Helen up.

"Who you?" The girl clutched an old, ragged pink

bear. The toy sported blue overalls and was missing its left eye. The girl wore matching overalls. She had both of her bright brown eyes.

"I'm here to see the woman who runs this place." Helen waved her hand at the interior. Her face was a billboard of revulsion as she aimed it at a poster.

A smile bloomed on the girl's face as she hoisted her bear over her head and did a dance. Her braids bounced as the beads in them clacked together, reminding Helen of beaded curtains from the '70s.

"Oh, Mama Mays!" She twirled, dashed away, halting before she was completely out of sight. She spun in Helen's direction, held up her index finger, letting her precious bear drop to her side. "I'll be right back."

The child dashed around a corner. The sound of her tapping feet faded with the growing distance.

Helen, not surprised by the child's rudeness, tried the door. It was unlocked. So, she pushed it open and stood in the doorway surveying the interior. It was clean but worn. The lobby was a decent size, a perfect square, with sparse furniture. Two chocolate-brown loveseats sat on the left and right walls with faded spots thinned from wear. Dimpled cushions and dents in the backs of each piece from years of use. Game stations lined the wall near the hall.

Helen was certain that hall led to the infamous Nancy Mays. There was a buzz about her long before Onyx came to live with her. Nancy Mays became a permanent fixture in their lives when Onyx made the news. Helen scowled, eyes traveling across the many pictures and photos of the woman with local children. There were even a few with her posing with local politicians. She even had one with Oprah in front of Harpo Studios, a few years before Oprah's move to Hollywood.

Helen frowned. Nancy had a way of getting into her business when it came to Onyx. She'd check in whenever Onyx showed up at the Center with a bruise, or Onyx would come home with bags of hand-me-down clothes and toys, which Helen would promptly take to the dumpster.

Onyx would sneak out and bring some back in. She thought Helen didn't know, but she did. The toys and clothes were a great talking point to her friends when she expounded on her generosity. None of her friends associated with people like Nancy. They were rich. They had big jobs that made them lots of money. Helen knew how to talk like them, act like them and she spent every penny Onyx gave her to look like them.

From a child's perspective, Helen thought as she moved deeper into the lobby, the center was like Neverland. It was a place where no grownups trod. Nancy Mays was Peter Pan. Nancy didn't pretend to be a child, she let them be. Here they were free from the burden of family, society and predators.

Helen looked around for a place to sit, nose wrinkling at the selection. She pulled a handkerchief from her Coach purse and dropped it on a decorative chair. It too was as old as the other furniture. She was glad she didn't plop in it because her butt touched wood as soon as she settled. The cushion looked soft, but it was just as busted as everything else.

The pitter-patter of the girl's racing feet broke her

momentary silence. A lethargic tap of a cane joined the song of soles. Helen looked up in time to see the child burst from the hall, dancing and spinning with her raggedy old bear. Facing the mouth of the hallway as the girl bounced in place. She pointed at Nancy, then twirled to point at Helen.

"Here she is, Mama! It's the lady whose lookin' for ya!"

Helen cringed at the gleeful shriek of the child's voice; grateful she had no kids. They were dirty, loud and expensive.

Nancy emerged, stopping in the mouth of the hallway, leaning heavily on her cane.

"Dasha!" Nancy's affection for the child prompted a momentary pause. Helen could tell the child bathed in Nancy's praise. "Can you be still for me?"

Dasha began her bouncing, twirling dance. The child probably had ADHD. Helen watched the girl run in a small circle. Nancy stepped into the lobby, bent slightly, resting her hands on top of her cane.

"Dasha." Nancy didn't raise her voice. She uttered the child's name, soft and sweet.

Dasha looked over at her matriarch and slowed. Nancy offered her a smile which seemed to be a glorious reward for the overactive girl because she stilled. Stopped right in front of Nancy, bear clutched to her chest.

Nancy cradled Dasha's face then touched her forehead to the child's. "Dasha. Dasha. Dasha. My pretty little hummingbird."

Helen could tell the child was ready to burst from her spot, but she didn't. She stayed in place and giggled.

"Baby, I know being still isn't your thing, but thank

you." Nancy planted a kiss on her forehead then lay a hand on the child's shoulder. Her expression sobered.

"Now, Hummingbird, I need you to do something for me."

Dasha bounced. "Yes, Mama?"

"It's almost time for the afternoon snack." Nancy shared a conspiratorial look with the girl. "Can you get everyone together?"

Dasha nodded vigorously.

"That's a good girl," Nancy said, as Dasha sped off down a different hall. It probably bled into some gym or classroom. Nancy watched until the girl vanished around the corner. She straightened then turned a dubious gaze on Helen.

Helen popped up from the chair and stomped toward the other woman, stopping inches from her.

Nancy looked her up and down. "I hope you understand, your proximity comes with consequences."

Helen scowled and took a few steps back.

"I thought so." Nancy seemed satisfied with the distance. "I'm not a child and stomping up on somebody will get you stomped."

"Look, old woman..."

Nancy held up a halting finger. "First, let's get a few things straight. As I said before, I'm not a child. Second, you're on my property. Third, if you don't check how you address me, you will leave my property."

Helen opened her mouth.

"Think about your next words." Nancy pressed her cane into the floor.

Helen closed her mouth and softened her face, doing

her best to push the contempt from her eyes. She offered Nancy a smile, hoping her face didn't shatter. She swallowed, moistening her lips, though she didn't need to, before she spoke. "I'm looking for my niece."

"Who might that be?"

"Onyx Jones."

Malice hardened Helen's gaze. Nancy blinked and it was gone.

"She's not here," Nancy said after a few seconds.

Helen scanned the area, searching for signs of Onyx. Onyx carried little, so figuring out if Nancy was lying to her was going to be a challenge.

"Look! We had an argument this morning and I wanted to make things right." Helen hoped her plea appeared concerned. She needed Nancy to help her find Onyx. There was plenty for them to work out, like where she got that sterling silver collar with the big red ruby in it and where the rest of the valuables were.

Nancy narrowed her eyes, examining Helen as she folded her arms across her chest. "You still haven't told me who you are and why I should tell you anything, not that I know anything."

Helen took a deep breath. "I'm Helen Jones, Onyx's aunt."

Nancy scowled. "Oh, you're *that* Aunt Helen."

Helen glared right back at Nancy. "Yes, I'm Onyx's aunt."

"Like I said before, your niece ain't here."

Helen threw out her arms, waving them at the lobby. "Well, where the hell did she go?"

Nancy said nothing.

"At least tell me when she left."

Nancy closed the space between them, stopping inches away. "Look," she aimed her finger at Helen. "Onyx is an adult. She can go where she wants and do what she wants. It's not for me to keep track of her."

Helen stomped her foot and growled. "I'm her guardian." She pointed at herself, pressing her index finger into her chest. "It's my job to make sure she's safe."

Nancy arched a brow. "Um-hmm."

"What does that mean?"

Nancy shook her head, raising a hand for Helen to cut the theatrics. "Look, I know plenty about you without her telling me. All my kids tell their story in how they move, their trust or lack of it, their anger, or their fear. You don't care about Onyx."

Helen stiffened her back and squared her shoulders. "How dare you!"

"Girl, you been hanging round them boujie folks, ain't 'cha?" Nancy chuckled.

"What!"

Nancy made a face. "Girl, cut the crap. You ain't rich and you ain't important. You just a leech and you bleedin' that girl dry."

"I don't." Helen snatched up her purse and threw it on her shoulder.

"I bet you stopped working once Onyx was old enough to. You guilt that girl to provide for you."

"No, I don't," Helen insisted as she dropped her gaze. She stared off at the love seat to the left of them.

"Yes, you do. I bet you remind her every day how you

saved her. How, if it weren't for you, she'd be on the streets."

Helen lifted her head, setting her anger on the other woman. "She does owe me," she hissed, taking a step forward. "I gave up everything to raise her!"

Nancy rolled her eyes. "You didn't have a damn thing before that child came to you."

"She owes me," Helen growled.

"She don't owe you a damn thing, you leech."

Helen curled her fist. Nancy's gaze dropped to it then raised to meet Helen's eyes.

"You better think about that." She jerked her chin toward the curled fist.

Helen uncurled her hand, flexing her fingers as if she were working out a cramp.

"Now I know why she stays away from you."

"You don't know nothin'!" Helen hissed.

Neither woman noticed the slowly growing crowd of children pooling into the lobby. They lingered in the hall, clogging it with their bodies.

Helen glared at them, then spun away. She stomped to the door, grabbed the handle and yanked. She paused in the open doorway then looked over her shoulder.

"You hold on to these kids like they're yours, but they ain't. You're a sad woman, Nancy Mays." Helen shook her head.

Dasha crept forward, wrapped an arm around Nancy's waist and held her bear tight in the other.

"I love every child here like I birthed them myself. There's no shame in that." Nancy hugged Dasha close to her. "If you see it like that, then shame on you."

Helen growled and stormed out of the Center. The door slid to a close behind her. It had a pressurized spring denying Helen of the satisfying slam. Some kids jumped.

Dasha looked up at Nancy. "Who was that?"

Nancy looked down at Dasha. She squeezed her a little tighter as they both stared at the door. "Nobody."

CHAPTER 8

The Juncture Between Realms

SHE USED THE TIP OF HER BOOT TO TEST THE STURDINESS of the ground, cloud, or whatever it was. It was pretty solid, so, Onyx took a tentative step forward. Mists tore apart like a spider's web. Bits of it stuck to her skin as she moved. Onyx wanted to shake it off. No. She wanted to scrub it off. It was nasty and she hated spiders, but if she did, it would severely ruin her tough façade. Onyx didn't know the weirdoes she'd entered the portal with, but she was smart enough to know that they liked to flex. Taqual didn't particularly like her, nor she him. He was a dick. He waved his misogyny like a banner. All he was missing were the dragging knuckles.

Onyx kept him in her peripheral vision. She dropped Cassius the moment they entered the portal. Did she trust Cassius? Not really. Knowing his name and knowing he was coming along put him in a better light than the cavemen leading her to God knows where. The shadow said she could trust him. There was something about the shadow, his sense of urgency, that killed ill-will.

Her head swam, provoking a mild case of vertigo. She paused, allowing it to pass. Taqual grunted for her to keep moving. She flipped him off before she did.

The spiraling mists kept to the floor, sides and ceiling of the tunnel. It cleared up at her knees, ending several inches above her head in a perfect circle. She appraised the distance between where she stood and the bright, pulsating exit. It didn't seem like a long haul.

A chime set her to search for the source. She spied a poufy black tail swishing a few inches above the mists ahead of her and followed. Taqual trailed her. She kept her head facing forward, acting as if she were both fascinated and frightened by her surroundings, which wasn't far from the truth.

She was about to cross into another realm. Maybe another planet? Was the air breathable? Did the animals talk? Was it full of Shifters like Cassius? Her pace quickened, curiosity overriding uncertainty. A soft resonance followed by two rapid, high-pitched rings drew her to search for the poufy black tail. Cassius meowed as his tail sank beneath the mists like a shark fin in the ocean.

Don't let your mind wander. Stay alert.

Onyx's gait faltered but went unnoticed by Taqual. She fixed her eyes on the exit. The other two men were far ahead of them. Distance didn't diminish their size; mists billowed in wide arching funnels, warping their features. Every step closer to the exit, the mists jumped in time with their steps. The moving mountains of frothy mist shifted. The process wasn't smooth like Cassius, but more spastic.

A pair of hulking beasts with mottled dark green skin stepped from the writhing froth. Onyx was a fan of comics; she had gone to several comic cons, even volunteered with an organization that supported writers and artists in the industry. She loved the art, though the character's bodies were exaggerated in musculature, but what she observed at the end of the tunnel made the Hulk look like a ninety-pound weakling. The beasts had long torsos, wide chests and shoulders and the muscles! They wore no shirts, just muscle and skin covered in what look like brands rather than tattoos. Jagged marks like a sickle crisscrossed across the expanse of their backs. The one on the left wore a shoulder pad with spikes and an armband on the bare arm. Both beasts wore dark fur-lined kilts sans the Scottish tartan. It looked more like leather, with bits of metal in spots. A curved blade slapped against their hips. The beast on the right had what looked like a spiked flail. The weapons matched the size of their bearers.

Onyx was close enough to the exit now to admire the shafts of sunlight crisscrossing between thick brown and orange tree trunks. There was something in the air that caught the light. They fell like snowflakes and shimmered in the sunlight. Tiny starbursts formed a dazzling curtain at the mouth of the tunnel. As she neared the exit, more of the little snow-like particles shimmered frantically, creating a blinding starburst. Onyx used her arms to shield her eyes from the glare. The heat from it pushed her back a few steps. Something pricked the space between the heel of her palm and wrist. The sting of it lasted for a few seconds and, like the glare, it dulled and was soon forgotten.

Onyx lowered her arms, rubbing her wrist absently. There were no mottled green beasts at the tunnel's end. Gone were the chiming bells of Cassius's collar. She heard only the thump of Taqual's footsteps behind her. She scanned the swirling mists below her knees, catching no sign of movement. Had Cassius abandoned her?

Her pace slowed as the scent of fresh grass permeated the tunnel. Emerald-green blades fluttered in the wind outside, beckoning her to lie on them. She stopped. Why did she want to lie down in the grass? She shook her head.

Duck!

Onyx dropped to the ground. A hollow whoosh filled the space where she once stood. She rolled on her stomach and looked up. Her scream ricocheted through the tunnel as she stared into moss-green eyes. Taqual had changed, just like his counterparts. Thick meaty lips peeled back, exposing feral teeth, yellowed tusks, which were chipped in spots tilted in her direction. Silver and red rings lined the base of each tusk. She could see the intricate carvings as his smile spread. Taqual had piercings in his nose, lip and along his brows. There was even a chain in his left nostril connected to a hoop in a skull ring that connected to his left tusk. Long dreads morphed into black hair the consistency of a horse's tail.

He roared, showering her with spit and burning her with his breath. He drew back. The glint of his blade set her on autopilot. She kicked him in the chest, sending him flying back into the mists. She rolled onto all fours, pushed up and sprinted for the exit.

A roar echoed through the tunnel as she reached the shimmering curtain of starbursts. She braced herself for a flash of light, throwing her arms again over her face again. Heat washed over her, marking the crossing. She'd made it past the threshold.

Something loud approached. She dove, falling to the ground, avoiding the clash of bodies and steel. She lay face down in the grass. Dirt pelted her prone body as guttural grunts faded in and out around her.

Move!

"Where?"

Left! Now!

She rolled.

A wail overtook the noise of battle as she rolled. She covered her ears once her body came to a stop. Large leaves pressed against her forehead. Onyx pulled her body closer to the bush when something lodged into the ground inches away from her back.

The roar of a large feline punctuated by a thud sent Onyx into an awkward rise. She regained her footing, twisting to see what fell behind her. Cassius sank his claws into Taqual's back.

Cassius caught sight of her. His eyes glowed red before his words hammered inside her head.

Run! Find somewhere to hide. I'll find you.

Onyx looked around. Clusters of bushes and trees lined the edge of the clearing she stood in. She dropped back down, hoping the shadows along the trees would provide enough cover. Using her forearms to pull her body along, she crawled, peering through the baseline of shrubs in search of a hiding place, as the world around her was upended by giants.

Cassius's yowls and the monster's grunts were all she heard as she continued her search. A hand clamped around her ankle and yanked. Her fingers dug into the pliant earth, creating grooves as she used her free leg to kick at her captor. She flipped onto her back for better aim and nearly pissed herself. Moss-green eyes burned into her. He sneered, raising what looked like a battle-axe. He swung down. Onyx spun away, landing a kick to Taqual's ankle. He stumbled away but did not fall.

Onyx crawled backwards; eyes trained on the beast pursuing her. It moved with deliberate slowness; battle-axe raised. He twirled it a few times for dramatics as she continued to back away. His body, four or five times her size in muscles and height, progressed in her direction. He did an elaborate spin and leapt, swinging his weapon up as his body took to the air. He brought it down as he descended.

The trill of steel coupled with a few sparks kept him from killing her. A long thickly muscled arm darted out between them, swinging an even larger axe shielding her from the mottle green beast's blow. Onyx's gaze traveled the length of the arm to its fearsome owner. A beast, much like the others, now stood between them. It was the same in every way except for pale orange skin, blond hair and big blue eyes. It had a thick braid held together by silver bands with several loose braids bound with colorful ribbons.

The pale orange beast was better at fighting because it

blocked every blow the mottled green one threw with a pair of axes. It even giggled a few times as it danced away from deadly swings, as if playing a child's game.

Dressed in a simple shirt fashioned from sackcloth. Strapped to his left shoulder was a black pad like the others. It had no spikes, but a steel crest with the same sickle-like markings the other beasts had stamped on their flesh. He had on black leggings and boots similar to Native American moccasins, only they stopped under his knees. Around his waist was a thick leather belt with metal skulls and sickles. A few hooks clanked together. A string of bells trilled as he leapt with lethal grace, planting his knee in the other beast's chest, baring his teeth at the fallen one. His tusks were unblemished white.

The pale orange beast bellowed, the muscles in his neck taut as he tightened his grip on the twin axes. Several others like him joined him as the fallen monster rolled on his feet and tore into the bushes. He angled his tusks toward the defeated monster, swinging his axes in a wide arc away from his body. They crossed behind him before he dropped them in their sheaths.

Onyx collapsed on the grass and stared into the canopy of trees overhead. They were beautiful shades of red, oranges, pinks and deep green. Sunlight streamed through open spaces, creating speckles of light on the ground. She smiled lazily, grateful to be alive, as she felt the rumble of footsteps around her.

Someone called her name in the distance. The colorful canopy melded together in a kaleidoscope of messy colors.

She heard her name again, garbled, as if underwater,

which was silly. She lay sprawled on the grass, surrounded by monsters. The pale orange one leaned over her, offered her a hand and a gentle smile. She reached for the offered hand. At least she meant to. Her body didn't respond. She closed her eyes, intent on gathering her strength. She heard the word *"bitten,"* as darkness swallowed her whole.

CHAPTER 9

Penumbra

TAQUAL GRIT HIS TEETH AS THE HOOFBEATS OF HIS CAPAL echoed through the tight tree lined path of the Red Corridor in the Darkest Forest. It was called that due to the blade sharp needles protruding from the bark. Rumors were whispered about the trail. Its trees and the ground beneath him drank the blood of wounded travelers or those unfortunate enough to be cut by its needles. The path was carved from magic. Sigils shimmered along the trail. He was near the end of it. The Host of the Trades lay on the other side. Blood from his wounds splashed across the rocks, leaves and grass as he rode his capal hard. Sigils flared, taking on the color of his blood, which vaporized in their fading magic.

His mission failed but a sliver of promise remained. Taqual wanted the female's head but was denied that pleasure. Help had come for her. But he left behind

"

another means to fulfill his purpose. He set loose a graul before he attacked her in the Juncture. The tiny insects were akin to Earth's mosquito. Similar in body structure, the graul's translucent bodies made them hard to see. Their wings made no sound and they had a preference for human and fae blood. Their venom induced sleep. If not treated with antivenom, their prey would sleep for seven days. On the eighth day, the victim would die.

Taqual grinned at the girl's destiny. It was his will to kill her. Slit her throat or take her head, but the graul's venom would finish what he could not. She would sleep through the deadline for the challenge, at which point it guaranteed her death, freeing the throne for its rightful heir, Jahll.

Though mounted, his lungs burned as if he were on foot. His injuries flamed with every jostle of his mount. Taqual clutched the reins tight, enduring the pain as he leaned into his saddle. His body was molded to his capal as his mind raced.

He gnashed his teeth when his capal slowed. Capals were bred for the jagged slopes of mountains and caves. They could also bear the weight of an Orc in full armor, but they were skittish around magic of any kind. The Red Corridor and the path into the Host of the Trades were heavily warded against carnivores.

The most fearsome were the Night Hares. They were not native to the forest near the Trades, but everything was old in the dark markets. If you had the coin, you could buy your heart's desire. Night Hares were appealing to females. They were black fuzzy creatures with big purple eyes. Their babies fit in the palm of a human female's hand, but a mature night hare was a quarter size of a capal and flesh eaters. It was said that a shopkeeper had bred and sold them as pets. The same breeder became his pet's meal. It took the Nameless Assassins to kill them. Weak-hearted women and their cuckold husbands released their pets into the forest, where they thrived.

He reached for a thin blade he kept tucked between his belt and chain mail vest he slipped on before he entered the Red Corridor. He held it against his side. The blade was pliable. A flick of the wrist and the blade became a whip. His grip tightened as the opening came upon him. The hooves of his capal drowned out the scurrying night hares. They were swift and could easily keep pace with his capal. He measured his breaths, numbing himself to his injuries. Taqual knew the Red Trail well. He'd done many runs for palace advisors and a few for Jahll. He trusted his capal. It knew the way. His job was to keep them both alive to the trail's end.

The tree lined path opened up. Dead leaves were replaced by blood-soaked sand. The last leg of the Corridor had its own name: Fool's Trail. The sand laden ground changed the timbre of his capal's hoofbeats. Death smells, screeching and scurrying feet overwhelmed his senses. Insects buzzed. As soon as they stopped, Taqual readied his blade. Two strides into the silence, Taqual sensed the first of the hares barrel toward him. The warding sizzled as their furry bodies connected. The warding did its job, but some creatures of the Darkest Forest made it through, which was why he had his blade.

He felt the weight of it against the air. He waited for it

to draw close, then he swung his blade, slicing it in half. Its fallen body drew the others to feast on it. Taqual knew there would be more.

He flicked his blade, clearing it of blood, pulling it close to his side as he continued on. Their chittering gave them away. The flare of magic on both sides of the trail alerted him of the night hares' location. They screeched as they sacrificed themselves for the opportunity of a meal. Only two out of the cluster of hares made it onto the trail, their bodies jerking from the magic they defied. The dark hares charged and like the others, Taqual unleashed his blade, whipping it around him. The wet thud of their corpses rained upon the ground, giving him and his mount more time as they neared the Trades.

The tempo of his capal's hoofbeats changed. The pliant forest floor hardened, hollowing out the beat of his capal's trot. Hooves clopped atop the cobblestone path. Taqual sat upright in his saddle, discreetly returning his blade to its hiding place. He had several weapons tucked away on his person. Their discovery would come when he sank them in the bodies of his opponents.

Taqual squeezed his thighs against the sides of his mount, slowing its gallop to a trot. He needed to find an orange tent. The witch would meet with him there, not physically, but by other means. The tent, like the rest of the Trades, was warded against discovery.

Taqual's gaze caught the shimmer of glyphs. He wasn't sure what kind. Dark elves, Shifters and other creatures visited the Trades. Some of the most powerful magic-wielders forged the spells which hid it. It was only visible at night, guaranteeing its anonymity.

He heard there was a Spell of Transition cast on it. If the location was ever under dire threat, the Host of the Trades would transfer to another location along with all its occupants. Being entangled in such a transfer was to break ties with your kind. One would be a rogue, a creature of no land. To become such was to swear fealty to the unnamed ruler of the Trades or walk among the dead.

Taqual pushed his capal through onlookers foolish enough to stop and stare at him. The Trades was a grim place. It wasn't like the markets in Oracaii, which were full of color, pleasant scents, laughter, and culture. It was full of shadows and the scent of decay and dark magic lingered under the smells of food.

Orcs may not be magic wielders, but they could smell it and die by it. His gazed flicked between his armor and the streets. He hated Jahll's mother, but he hid it well. She had her uses. She had the armor of her agents warded against magic and other things.

Taqual pulled a warded charm Ivy left with him from the confines of his chest plate. It was never good to leave blood or any parts of oneself unattended while in the Host of the Trades. The moment the charm touched the armor, it flared as magic did its work. His wounds stopped bleeding. All signs of his injuries vanished though the wounds themselves were far from healed. It was some kind of suspension spell. He'd used it a charm like it before on a different mission for Jahll. His wounds would bleed again the moment he neared Oracaii. The charm would turn to dust once the spell died.

Taqual scanned the banners over the entrances, bringing his capal to a stop when he found what he was looking for. He dismounted, entered the tent, which was empty and waited.

The snap of the thick black curtain startled him, but Taqual schooled his visage, appearing unphased. An emaciated human female, covered in dirt and dressed in rags, entered. She held herself like a queen, measuring his worth with her gaze, curling her lip in decision. Her stench pushed deeper into the tent, seizing his throat, tempting him to cough. Instead, he swallowed, blinked slowly and showed no signs of offense.

The female was as small as an Orc youngling without the weight. Her dark, matted hair hung like frayed ropes down her back. Her skin was the color of a pig. Pigs were not from Penumbra, but Orcs liked their meat. So they stole some from the human world and bred them in Oracaii. They were part of their normal livestock.

The female's eyes were the only part of her that had life to them. They were as blue as a spring sky. There was a faint glow to them. Her lips were thick, cracked, with a cut across the top lip. Her features were sharp from starvation, prompting Taqual to wonder what she looked like well-fed and rounded.

"Taqual."

The power in her voice surprised him. He nodded acknowledgment.

She walked across the padded floor to a blood-red bench. Taqual turned away from the door as she passed. Her overlarge, smoke-gray, rag of a dress hung loose, baring her shoulders and part of her back, revealing a maze of welts. Bruises were the only color on her pale skin. She moved fluidly. The only stiffness in her was from pride.

There was minimal light inside the tent, as was the way of the Trades. Only two torches lit the space. There was one in the sconce to the right of the entrance. The other was lodged in the ground beside a narrow stand, an altar, on which a velvet-red box was perched. A black silk cloth concealed the contents. An orb of enchanted glass covered the flame of the freestanding torch. The glass granted the tent's occupants the power to dim or brighten its light.

The tiny female took her place on the crimson bench, back straight, legs folded, hands braced on each knee, chin up, eyes resigned. She took a deep breath, then bid him to approach. His lips drew back, flashing his canines.

The tiny female's eyes lost their light as veins of black took over the white until onyx marbles stared back at him. Taqual's hand went instantly for his blade, but the tiny female raised her hand for him to stop.

She chuckled. It held a familiar disdain.

"Witch!" Taqual hissed.

The tiny female's face soured. "Now, now, Taqual, that's not nice."

Taqual growled.

The tiny female's fingers dug into the flesh of her knees as Taqual began pacing. He could not see her eyes, but he could feel her watching him.

"I take it you failed." The tiny female's voice gained the timbre of Ivy's.

"The Chosen had unexpected help."

The tiny female snorted. "Help?"

"Yes. There were others at the Juncture."

"Did you know them?"

Taqual stopped pacing and gave her a look. "Of course not! Had I known she had skilled warriors as shields, I would have planned accordingly."

"No matter. It's good that you did not kill her yet."

"How is that good? The Chosen still breathes, which is an obstacle for Jahll's ascension to the throne."

There was a lightness to the tiny female's voice that worried him when she spoke again. "She will survive despite her exposure to Graul venom."

Taqual glared at the tiny female.

"I was aware of your *back-up* plan long before your company departed on your retrieval mission." The tiny female chuckled. "Remember, I am very familiar with the Host of the Trades and know all those who deal in poison."

"Her existence is not good for Jahll."

The tiny female growled. "Oh, I know it. You know it, but Jahll has plans and he is my son."

"What?" Taqual bent to peer into the face of the tiny female. "The Chosen has to die! The High Spirit demands a soul as trade for the throne and immortality."

"She *will* die, but how she dies, I will arrange."

"Jahll must kill her in the ring to gain the throne unchallenged."

Taqual straightened, running calloused hands across his chin as he wondered what the witch was up to.

"I need you to return to Oracaii."

"I can track the Chosen and..."

"You will return to Oracaii and help my son." Ivy's tone brokered no argument.

"Jahll has a full company of Orcs that stand with him."

"But can he trust those Orcs without risk of betrayal?" Ivy stated through the tiny female.

Taqual remained silent.

"My son needs you. Oracaii needs you."

Taqual's right hand fisted, coming down hard over his heart. Oracaii would return to its glory when Orcs were nightmares and filled the hearts of the weak with dread. With Jahll on the throne, they would return to that time. Taqual would be the hand of the king. He would make sure the heart of Oracaii beat in accordance with the king's wishes. For the sake of Oracaii, he would be the death of those that stood against the capital and its king. For the sake of Oracaii he would do what he must, to guarantee Jahll the throne.

"Oracaii and my son require your presence. I have a secondary plan in play. If it succeeds, he will need you to aid him in cutting down those harboring aspirations for the throne."

"But what of the Chosen?"

"She will enter the gates of Oracaii unchallenged." The tiny female's black orbs rested on Taqual. "Do you understand, Taqual?"

He grunted, then bowed to the tiny female.

"I will do as you wish," Taqual said.

The tiny female bowed her head as a sign of acknowledgment to the large Orc.

"Return to Oracaii as soon as possible. There is much to be done before the Chosen arrives."

Taqual grunted, back stepped, then swung toward the entrance. He walked over to it, raised the hood of his cloak, then pushed aside the tent flap. Scanning the immediate area, Taqual had one more stop to make before heading to Oracaii. He had a kill contract to finalize for Jahll's sake and Oracaii's future. The fact that his friend was entertaining the idea of allowing the Chosen to survive stripped him of the doubts he carried when he initiated it. There was a deal to be made for Jahll's own good. He would set in motion his backup plan incase his contract failed.

The tiny female remained perched on the altar. Her head jerked up, mouth wide and her jaws locked. A spiral of black smoke rose from her mouth as the black covering over her eyes receded. Her muscles spasmed as pain sliced through her skull as Ivy extracted her consciousness from hers.

The tiny female collapsed on the bench, not wanting to breathe because it hurt. Instead, she watched smoke from the torch float toward a basket resting on the altar. It formed a small cloud over it. The thin blanket covering it quivered. The black cloud thinned, forming a coil. Like a whip, it struck. It pierced the blanket, tearing into the still beating heart beneath it.

The tiny female forced herself upright; unfolding her legs, she set her feet on the floor. It took a few tries before she stood without swaying. She took a deep breath, bracing herself for the part she hated: breaking the heart which ended the link and the spell between herself and the albino monster manipulating it.

The tiny female pulled the crispy blanket, which cracked in her grasp. Some of it fell away, revealing a charred heart. It belonged to the witch Ivy purchased. Orcs couldn't wield magic, but that albino Orcess knew a lot about it. Ivy knew something no one else did. She'd learned how to use natural witches as conduits. Human magic was potent and hard to detect in Penumbra. Ivy used a fae to help her create a spell that bound humans to her. Ivy killed the fae after she perfected the spell. She used a necromancer to dispose of the body. No one in all of Penumbra was aware of Ivy's little secret.

The tiny female put her fist through the still-beating shell of a heart. It collapsed into a blend of ash and chipped bits of scorched flesh. The ache in her head receded, but not before Ivy called her back.

The tiny female worked magic she wouldn't remember, much like her own name. It was part of the binding spell cast on her. Ivy didn't want her pets to remember their names, or their families.

Ivy kept her talented witches close, disposing of those who were weak. It was the way of the Orcs. Only the strong had the right to live. Though it shamed her, the tiny human female thanked the gods for her strength. She might not remember much of her life before Penumbra, but she was certain of her desire to live.

CHAPTER 10

Penumbra
The Wandering

ONYX LAY PETRIFIED ON A BED OF GRASS AS MONSTERS raged around her. Steel sang and blood rained down. A single drop landed on her wrist, rolling lazily along the inside, over the bones, before sinking into the ground beneath her.

A clump of dirt struck her head. Her fingers spasmed, filling her with hope, which quickly died. Seismic tremors of monsters locked in battle jostled her prone form.

Another tear of blood rolled down the inside of her wrist. Had she been cut again? She willed her eyes to move, but they refused. Locked in a death stare, she watched as a soot-colored beast danced in and out of her line of sight, swinging medieval weapons with sharp blades. Green grass lost its color under the deluge of oil-black blood.

A third tear of blood rolled down the same spot inside her wrist. It was dry. The texture rough, but not abrasive. Something sharp nicked her skin, shocking Onyx awake.

"Where am I?" Onyx hissed and cradled her bandaged wrist to her chest. She scooted away from a strange child wrapped from head to toe in gauze. It shimmered in the scant light, creating a vague rainbow, the kind she'd seen in oily water. It rolled like a wave down the slight body three feet away from her, then vanished.

Her gaze darted to the dingy gray gauze wrapped around her wrist. Onyx wanted to give it a quick sniff, but that would take her eyes off the frail mummy next to her bedding.

"Who are you?"

The frail mummy turned its head. Its face was hidden under a mask of gauze. Bumps where the eyes, nose and mouth should have been told her a face was underneath the strange gauze.

Onyx's wrist throbbed.

"Sor...sor...sorry for touching you without permission," the mummy was a girl. Her voice was like an orchid, delicate yet pretty.

"What did you do to me?" Onyx held out her wrist, turned it over to check the gauze for blood.

The mummy girl pressed her chin to her chest, which garbled her words. "I treated the graul sting."

"Graul?" Onyx pulled her injured wrist back to her chest, securing it with her uninjured hand. "What the hell is a graul?"

Both Onyx and the mummy girl's attention jerked to the tent flap, which snapped when thrown back by the giant from Onyx's dream.

It looked like it had escaped the ruins of a fire but could not get rid of the soot. Deep grooves trailed its arms. Raised scars from claw marks covered its right pectoral. There were more claw marks along the ribs and back. Its pointed ears stretched past its head. They were torn in spots and pierced in others. A scorch mark in the shape of a starburst stretched from its chest, ending at the left clavicle. A silver spike pierced its wide nose. Medium-sized tusks jutted from the bones near its nose, just above its lips. Three bronze bands with black lettering and silver swirls were at the base of its tusks. Onyx shuddered as her mind wondered what its teeth were like.

It wore its hair in a long black braid, held together by a bronze band. The braid looped like a noose, ending between its broad shoulders. A spiked pauldron capped its right shoulder like a murderous shoulder pad from the eighties. A leather strap connected the spiked pauldron to a waist belt. A long leather loincloth embossed with silver skulls stopped at its knees. A collection of tiny skulls, hanging from hooks on its waist belt, rattled as it walked. Onyx's brows furrowed at a small purple flower carved from wood which jostled amid the skulls.

A second giant entered. She remembered it from the fight in the forest. It wore no weapons, but a plain shirt the same gray as the bandage around her wrist. It wore dark green leggings tucked into tan leather moccasin-style boots, which ended at the knee. Its pale orange skin seemed delicate compared to the thick hide of the darker one. The marks of battle decorating its flesh were as dull as its blunt tusks, making it less menacing. A bronze band like the other tamed its flaxen hair, only its braid had colorful ribbons woven in. Its braid hung loose, bouncing against the back of its knees as it skipped inside. Its features were as soft as its color. It paused when it noticed she was staring. Onyx gasped at the human blue eyes staring back.

"What does the ant say to the mountain?" Cassius said from the outside of the tent.

A goofy grin spread across the pale orange giant's moon face. "Move, said the ant."

Cassius poked his head into the tent. "Okay then, mountain, this ant says move."

The pale orange giant chuckled as it joined the large soot-skinned one seated at the foot of her sleeping pad. Onyx pulled her legs up, pressing them to her chest.

Cassius ducked into the tent. He paused beside the girl in shimmering gauze. Onyx noticed the mummy girl was as still as a deer yards away from predators. She stared at the girl's chest, not sure if she breathed.

Cassius crouched beside her and cleared his throat to gain her attention. The girl turned to him. Cassius pressed both his hands together, forming a prayerful fist. He raised his clasped hands toward his head, which he bowed.

"*Ke*," he said and repeated the bowing.

"*Ke*," the girl said, inclining her head in kind, but did nothing with her hands which remained on top of her legs. "She is well."

Cassius offered his hand. The girl took it. He pulled her up, then bowed dashingly. The girl curtsied.

Cassius slid from his bow into a soldierly stance. "Honor be to you."

"Blessings and health to you and yours." The girl did an about-face and dashed from the tent.

"Who was that?" Onyx stared at the tent flap.

"A healer," the pale orange giant offered. He toyed with his braid, stroking the colorful ribbons.

"What was she wearing?" She waved her hands up and down her body.

"Faceless Robes," Cassius said.

Onyx made a face, brows furrowed, lips twisted in confusion.

Cassius settled next to Onyx's sleeping pad. "They're warded garments worn by the most sacred among the Wandering."

Onyx gestured for him to pause. "Hold up. The Wandering?" She looked over at the pair of giants at the foot of her sleeping pad, then back at Cassius. She gestured toward the pair of giants. "They're the Wandering?"

"It's who we are," the soot-skinned giant said. He gestured toward Cassius and the pale orange giant next to him, ending with a hand on his chest. His voice was a low rumble of thunder, which resonated in the quiet parts of the tent.

"It's a poor name for marauders."

The pale orange giant giggled. "We're not marauders. We are clan."

"Family," Cassius punctuated the pale orange giant's words.

"But you killed those other..."

"To save you." The soot-skinned giant stretched his arms toward her. "You are the Chosen. Dark words traveled through the forest about your discovery. Plans to assassinate you were not far behind." The soot-skinned giant slammed a fist into the ground. Chunks of dirt exploded around it. He raised that fist, uncurled a finger from the mass and aimed it at her. "You are the High Spirit's choice to succeed the last Elite. You are to attend the Rising. Win it. Then take the throne as your father did."

"Hold up." Onyx scooted back on the sleeping pad, thankful for the cluster of large pillows at her back. She leaned against them as she worked to digest the soot-skinned giant's words. Her head ached. She ignored it, choosing to focus on the words: rising, father and throne. "What are you talking about?"

She pulled her legs under her before addressing the gray giant. "I don't have a father and the only thrones I know of are toilets, so you're going to have to hit me with some details."

The soot-skinned giant jerked back as if she hit him. "Details? What details do you require? You are the Chosen, the future Queen of Oracaii. What more do you need?"

Onyx fisted her hands, pressing the knuckles into the sides of her head. "God!" She huffed, then stared at the intricate embroidery on the bedding beneath her. It was beautiful and the fabric was her favorite color: purple.

She withdrew her fists, resting her hands on the plush bedding.

"I don't know what you're talking about." She slowly raised her head, meeting the gray giant's eyes. "I don't know you. I don't know what you are." She gestured at the room. "I don't know this place."

The soot-skinned giant lay a hand over his heart. "I am Gryk the Hammer, right hand of the King." Gryk nodded. "I am Orc." He motioned toward the pale orange giant beside him. "Joseph is Orc, too."

"Orc?" Onyx gave Cassius the side-eye. "Are you an Orc?"

Joseph giggled. "Cassius is not Orc. He's a Shifter."

"I am a Shifter, yes," Cassius began. "I'm also Orc by adoption."

Onyx cocked her head, eyes narrowing as she studied the handsome Shifter.

"He was blooded by the King. He is Orc by our law." Gryk offered.

Cassius leaned in, pointing at a puckered scar on his pec, an inch above the nipple. It looked like the one she'd seen on the other orcs who tried to kill her. There were different markings on the opposite pec. "It's the mark of the King." He tapped his hand against the mark. "Ryza," Cassius aimed a clawed finger at Onyx. "is your father, blooded the entire clan."

"The old King is dead," Joseph said.

"So are we," Gryk stated plainly.

"You look alive to me." Onyx glanced at the tent flap and back at Gryk.

Gryk opened his mouth but Cassius stopped him. He

lay his hand over the King's Mark on is right pec and with the other, he waved toward the tent's opening. "Our situation is dire, which has made us all anxious. So, let's start with the Wandering." Cassius set his hands on his knees. "The Wandering as a people shouldn't exist. We are a collection of Penumbra's sins."

"So you're outlaws?"

Cassius shook his head. "If you would let me finish, you'll understand."

Onyx drew an imaginary zipper across her lips then motioned for him to continue.

"The law here is strict with regard to trespassing upon another's territory. Different beings are allowed to enter another's land only by invitation." Cassius spread his arms to encompass the confines of the tent, gesturing toward the flap. "We are a colony of bastards. We take in outcasts from all of Penumbra, usually the offspring of a forbidden coupling."

"Why is that a problem." Onyx caught herself, throwing her hands over her mouth.

Cassius arched a brow before continuing. "A forbidden coupling would be a child of a Shifter and a Fae. Such a child would be killed at birth or left in the darkest forest by a midwife or a member of the family."

Onyx's mouth parted with the weight of her questions, but a look from Cassius stopped them. "Sorry," she whispered.

"We are considered unclanned among the races of Penumbra."

"But you were adopted by the king."

"Yes, we were." Cassius folded his hands in his lap.

"Unfortunately, upon the death of a king, all oaths and ceremonies are meaningless. If the new ruler wishes to destroy all that belonged to the old king, it is the duty of the guard to make it so." Gryk leaned so his body touched Joseph, who began to rock. It was a subtle motion, accompanied by a low keening.

Gryk countered Joseph's lament with a soft baritone hum. It was a touch louder than Joseph's whine.

"Even now?"

Cassius nodded, face grim. "We are like ghosts. No land to call our own. We can't stay in one place for long for fear of discovery. For us to be discovered means death."

"You're stuck?" Onyx couldn't imagine applying the word helpless to the three strong males before her. The homeless in her world were harassed by the authorities, but they were never killed.

"Yes." Cassius scooted closer to Onyx. "But you will save us."

Onyx stood so she could get away from Cassius. She backed up, careful of the pillows. Eyeing the distance between herself, the three males and the tent flap, she was trapped. Cassius was fast. Her gaze darted to the thick black claws and back to his face, which showed no signs of humor.

"I can't save you." Onyx held up her bandaged wrist and waved it in front of her. "As a reminder, I was the first one down in the last fight. What makes you think I can help you?" She lowered her arm and used her unin-jured hand to grip her elbow.

"You're the Chosen."

"And that means what?" She looked down her body. Still wearing the same jeans, combat boots and turtleneck, the puffer vest was missing. There was nothing extraordinary about her. Not even her height in the presence of the trio sharing tent space with her. She lifted an arm and made a show of making a muscle. "There's no superpower here."

Gryk, Joseph and Cassius stood up but did not approach her. It was Gryk who spoke first, half bowing, raising his head enough so that their eyes connected. "You are not alone. *Afar Angathfark*. By the forge of my soul, I offer my life in service to the Chosen Queen, as her right hand."

Cassius mimicked Gryk. "Life and death are by your word. As I am the left hand of the Old King, I shall serve the Chosen Queen, with my life as both sword and shield."

"I'm not your Queen."

"You will be." Gryk straightened. He looked at her as if she were a goddess. Normally such a look would fill any girl with pride; instead, Onyx's stomach churned.

She shook her fists at the Orc. "I'm not your Queen! I'm not some super-soldier who can defeat hordes of monsters and make everything right and good again." She began pacing the small square of space next to her bedding. "Hell, I can barely manage my own life, there's no way I can help you with yours." Onyx stopped abruptly, gesturing up and down her body, ending with a dismissive wave. "I'm not your girl."

Cassius aimed a claw at Onyx's neck. "You wear the knowledge stone."

Onyx wrapped her hands protectively around her throat.

"Ryza was the only one to ever wear it." Cassius folded his arms around his chest.

"In truth, he was the first," Gryk said.

"So?"

"The collar appeared to you today." Cassius narrowed his eyes, his posture unchanged. "Am I wrong?"

Onyx grunted, lips pressed tight, as she glared daggers at the Shifter.

"Do you think it a coincidence that the pressure on your matriarch was made public today of all days?"

Onyx looked away from the annoying Shifter, hating that he was right. No one knew Mama Mays was in trouble, but anyone who knew Onyx, knew she would do anything to help. She didn't have much by way of money, but her credit was good. If she'd known about the problem, she would have co-signed a loan or something to keep the doors of the Center open.

"As I said before the crossing, time is not on our side. The Rising is only a few days away."

Onyx growled, cutting him off, as she stalked up to the Shifter, stopping inches away from him. She raised her gaze to meet his. "Look! You say this like I know what it means." Slashing her hand toward the ground, she curled it into a fist, drawing it back around in a mock punch, stopping just short of Cassius's ribs. "I don't." She unfolded her fist, letting her hand drop to her side. "I don't know if I want to know what it is."

"Sadly, it's not your choice."

"Like hell!' Onyx's voice crackled with power. She was

unaware her eyes glowed red, but she noticed Cassius take several cautious steps back, slowly raising his hands as he moved. She sized him up like a meal, muscles taut.

"It is the will of the High Spirit." Cassius paced his words. "It is the way of things."

"Well, I'm not from here."

"Half of you is a child of this place which ties you to its laws." Cassius leveled a finger at the collar beneath her turtleneck. "The knowledge stone marks you as the Chosen; as the Chosen, you must make the Rising and complete it."

"What the hell is this Rising?"

"You must fight for your place as the Elite." Cassius lowered his gaze and arms as he stopped moving.

"I'm not fighting anybody." Onyx swatted away Cassius's words, then stalked off to the opposite side of the tent, aware that the two Orcs blocked the exit.

"Then you'll die," Gryk said matter-of-factly.

The air fled her lungs. A sedate pivot brought her face to face with him. "What do you mean I'll die? I haven't done anything to anyone here. I don't know anybody." She jerked her chin at Cassius. "Except for him and that's barely."

"You are the Chosen. You must answer the Rising," Gryk offered.

"Still, I don't know what this Rising is. It sounds like a death sentence."

"It is for the loser," Gryk said.

"So why would I want to participate?" Onyx waved her hand toward Gryk, then to Joseph. "I don't stand a chance if I'm fighting anything like you two."

"You will be ready by the time we reach the borders of Oracaii." The two Orcs and Cassius laid their right fists over their hearts and did a half bow.

"I will teach you what I can as we travel," Gryk said.

"I'll help, too!" Joseph clutched his braid and stroked it obsessively.

It was hard to find an angry word for Joseph. He was large, scary and could probably kill her without breaking a sweat, but there was something tender about him. Sweet. He reminded her of Israel from the center. Her next words were rough on her tongue, but necessary. "Thanks, but I can't." Onyx stared at her boots. "This is not my fight."

"My clan will die if you do nothing!" Cassius snapped. A feline snarl sharpened his words.

"I'm not responsible for your people." She pressed her hand on her chest. "I'm responsible for those I left on the other side of that portal."

"You are nothing like your father," Gryk growled.

"Why would I be? I don't know him."

Silence thickened as the Orcs, the Shifter and the young woman glared at each other.

Onyx squeezed the fists planted at her sides, finding comfort in the scratch of her leather workout gloves. Soon that dull scratch gained an edge morphing into a burn. The nerves in her left hand were on fire as it shook. Her eyes sealed against the pain, teeth snapping together, barely missed her tongue as she sank to her knees. Despite the agony, a light drew her. She peeled her lids back in time to see a red light in the symbol's shape she'd seen on the other orcs drift like a leaf toward her hand. It floated above it, rippling like water. In a flash, the red symbol flared, then sank into her left hand.

Tears fell down Onyx's face as she clutched her burning appendage. She saw no fire, but it burned hotter. Her body curled over the now throbbing appendage.

Gryk and Cassius were at her side. Gryk rolled her onto her back as Cassius pried her hand away from her chest.

Onyx hissed at his touch, head pressing into the sleeping pad as she again sealed her eyes against the pain.

"I'm sorry, but I need to see." Cassius carefully stripped the workout glove from her hand and held it up.

"By all that is dead!" Gryk roared and Joseph began to cry.

The gentle press of the pad of Cassius's thumb drew Onyx to look. The back of her hand bore a red mark. It had the consistency and sheen of a ruby. There were intricate spirals and jagged lines. Some lines crooked at the tip like a scythe. The mark started at her knuckles and ended at the tip of her wrist.

She drew the marked hand closer. It gleamed in the scant light. "What is this?" her words trembled.

"A Rising Challenge has been issued." Gryk frowned at the mark.

The queasiness in her stomach intensified as she looked to Gryk and Cassius for an answer.

Cassius moved her hand, so the mark was easier for her to see. "This means someone knows you've been found and are here."

"But I don't want to fight anyone."

Cassius gave a weak shrug as he shook his head. "It

doesn't matter, a challenge has been issued. This mark," he turned her hand for emphasis, "it will spread. Because of the timing, I'm not sure how it will act. Twenty-eight days have passed since the six Elites fell. There are thirty days before the Chosen officially become Elites. At that time, the Chosen are granted immortality from the High Spirit. During the thirty-days of being selected, a potential Elite can be challenged, which is why you have the mark. Normally the Rising Challenge must be responded to by way of the arena in three days. Because of the Graul attack, you've lost a day."

"What happens on the last day of this mark?" Onyx stared at the Challenge Mark as if it were a poisonous snake.

"It will cover your heart." Cassius turned grim eyes on her, "When that happens, you die."

"But..." Onyx began, her gaze darted around the room finally returning to the mark. "I should get an extra day."

Cassius shook his head then covered her hand with his. "The High Spirit's laws are non-negotiable. We have to get you to Oracaii."

"Oracaii?"

"Yes." Cassius squeezed her hand gently, then let it go.

"We leave at sunrise," Cassius said to Gryk, who nodded and began the arduous task of getting Joseph up and out of the tent.

"I'm not ready," Onyx whispered to herself as she fixated on the shimmering mark. "I can't," she muttered to herself, "I can't. I'm not ready."

Cassius wrapped his hands around her right boot. "Onyx." He moved so he was in her line of sight. "Onyx."

She jerked but looked at him.

"Don't fret. Your father has given you all you need to succeed." He pointed at the collar. "We're going to help you."

"You're only doing it to save your skin," Onyx said as she dropped her gaze to her lap.

"True." Cassius cupped her chin, lifting it until he had her attention. "I promised your father I would protect you. As your left hand and as his friend, I will forfeit my life to honor that promise. Do you understand?"

Onyx blinked. She jumped at the crunch of leaves underfoot followed by running.

Gryk darted to the tent flap, pushed it aside and inspected the area. "No tracks."

"We're all a little jumpy," Cassius joked. He took up her hand again, raising it to his forehead, which he pressed to her palm. "By all the dead, I offer my life for yours on this journey. My beast and my magic are yours."

Onyx swallowed, despising the palpable beat of her frantic heart. She acknowledged his promise with a nod, wondering if she would escape death a second time.

CHAPTER 11

HELEN JONES WAS ALWAYS ONE TO HAVE THE LAST WORD. She feigned closing the door only to duck in, insult her Uber driver, slam the door and sashay away. She'd give him two stars and make up something to validate her rating just for fun. It was practice for her career as a writer. She would write a book one day, an autobiography, from the comfort of the penthouse she would buy with her niece's money.

Onyx was holding out on her. That piece of jewelry around her neck would have Helen in a penthouse, a vacation home and real brand-name wardrobe. Right now, she needed to find her useless niece, who had returned none of her phone calls. Helen paused, tossing a curse at or mean-mugging anyone who dared ask her to move as she held up her cell phone. There was a tracking app downloaded on Onyx's phone. Should her niece decide to liberate herself, Helen would find her.

She stared at the pulsing dot on the phone's map. Measuring her location against where she stood, Onyx was very close. Helen watched the flow of people, noting a few folks glancing off into an alley several feet away. It seemed she was right about Onyx hooking up with a drug dealer. Criminals hung out in places with shadows and stench.

She stomped over to the mouth of the alley, bracing herself for the smells. Keeping close to the wall without actually touching it, Helen took a few steps in, scanning its length. It was as long as the block, opening into the next street. There were no people loitering about, nor any animals that she could see. Her nerves were wound tight at the prospect of seeing a rat. She'd probably soil herself should a roach scurry out into the open. The thought of owning a sterling silver collar with a ruby big enough to choke a horse pulled her deeper into the alley. The sparkle from the diamonds wound into the network of chains still made her palms itch.

It was getting late. A fact that forced her out of the apartment, compelling her to visit Nancy and her brats then linger in a neighborhood she despised.

Helen knew she pushed Onyx too far sometimes, driving her to leave, but she always came back. It might be at sunset or in the wee hours of the morning, but she always came back. There was something different about the way she'd left this morning. A vibe. Something just felt off.

Helen moved cautiously through the alley, following

the blip on her cellphone screen. Cellphone in her left hand, her right hand jammed in her pocket and wrapped around a can of mace. The blip led her to a dumpster. It reeked but wasn't overflowing. She spied the large locks and chains sealing it shut from both the homeless and rats. Giving it a wide berth, she examined the ground, noting the usual fast-food wrappers, crushed cans and bottles. Helen tapped the screen and pulled up her call history and dialed Onyx's phone.

Helen squeaked when the phone buzzed, though she knew it was coming. She followed both the sound and flashing lights to a sidewall. Her face twisted in disgust. She carefully lowered herself, so she was on all fours. Tilting her head, she searched the ground beneath the dumpster, spotting Onyx's cellphone propped against the wall and a dirty shoe. She gathered her nerves, wrapped them in courage and reached for the phone. She pulled it from beneath the dumpster, flipped it over and scowled at the screen. The ungrateful heifer ignored all her calls!

Helen's grip tightened around the phone as she rose to her feet. She wiped her hands on her leggings. She needed to find Onyx. Get information about her hidden fortune, then gain access to it. Helen looked up from the phone and around the general area. There were no open back doors into shops or clubs. There was nothing to point her to her niece. Onyx had no real friends outside of that damned community center. Where the hell was she?

Helen dropped the cellphone when it vibrated in her hands. A new text! She immediately scooped it up, unlocked the screen and read the message, brows rising as she did so. It was addressed to her.

If you want to know about your niece's newfound wealth, get in the truck. You will be dropped off at the Law Firm of Gorman and Stein. We're on the fourth floor, Suite 419.

Helen frowned at the message. How would anyone know she was the one with the cellphone?

As if to prove a point, the growl of an engine bounced off the alley walls and a Chevy Tahoe turned into the alley from where she entered. It crept toward the dumpster. The windows had a dark tint, so she couldn't make out who was driving.

Once the truck pulled passed the dumpster, she heard the locks pop. She looked down at the message again, then at the SUV in front of her. The phone vibrated with a fresh message.

Do you want the information or not?

The driver revved the engine. Helen darted to the door, opened it and climbed in.

CHAPTER 12

TAQUAL JOGGED THROUGH THE STREETS OF ORACAII. THE scent of pork, spices and the underlying aroma of ale flooded his senses, draining away the dejection of his failed mission. The bruised sky matched his pride, but he straightened his back when he entered the masses. Younglings scurried from his path and males averted their eyes as he passed. He was a capital soldier assigned to the throne. The best of the best.

Warmth filled his chest as his eyes settled on the castle's tower. Gleaming black stone edged with red loomed over the marketplace and small dorms of Commons. The outer walls told their history from the first orc to its current ruler.

Commons bore witness to the fading, though they were not in the capital. Ryza's knowledge stone faded. It had recently reappeared with a faint impression, a glimpse of their new royal, a faint sketch of a figure with soft edges. Taqual bore witness to the Chosen. True believers would say the bearer of the knowledge stone would rule, but fate is a tricky thing. Like ash, it shifts with the wind.

His jog slowed to a brisk walk as he took the steps leading to the main door of the castle. Large black metal doors loomed, guarded by a company of seven Orcs. Three visible. Four would make themselves known should someone attempt to pass without permission. The doors were engraved with the jagged crest of Oracaii. At its center, a red glass replica of the knowledge stone. The guards parted once Taqual reached the top step. He pushed open the doors, heading straight for the throne room. Jahll was waiting. His brisk step stuttered as he considered Ivy might be with them, though it was not her place. She had a way of working her way into areas where she did not belong.

The guards he passed thrust their chests out and beat their battle staffs on the ground. It was the custom for Orcs of lesser rank to do so before an officer. Taqual ignored them, steady in his pace, even as he rounded the corner to the throne room. The doors were closed, but nearby soldiers pulled it open as he came within a few feet of it.

Jahll sat on the top step, next to the black throne. The advisers were all seated at the long table before the throne, each of them harping. They were loud enough for him to catch the conversation. The advisers worried the Chosen would not make it to the capital in time to accept the throne, as if no one would challenge her. None of them seemed to catch the stormy look on Jahll's face, or they didn't care.

Taqual slowed his walk to a somber march as he neared the frantic scene. The advisors were currently issuing a grim warning, of which Jahll could ignore. The heir was not the end of them, Taqual thought. It would be Jahll who would restore the Orcs to their former glory. A time of blood and murder.

Jahll stood as Taqual approached and the advisors turned and faced him.

"What news do you bring of the Chosen?" Akyr the historian bowed his head in greeting. Akyr, like most Orcs, had done his time on the front lines and his body bore witness to it. Scars from a Dragon's claws spread across his chest. He lost an ear and bits of his nose had deep gouges. There was a gash under his left eye that few were aware of because of the patch covering it. Nerve damage made it hard for him to use the eye. Instead of straining, he patched it.

Akyr loved their history. He was a fan of the future Ryza was building. He mourned the loss of their king. Like the rest of the kingdom, he was in stasis, awaiting the occupation of the throne. That moment would thaw time and reanimate their future. Akyr was eager for its arrival. Taqual could understand that.

He stopped several feet from them, took a knee and bowed his head before speaking. "News is grim, Akyr."

Akyr clasped his hands and began wringing them. "Tell us," his words whooshed from him.

"There was an attempt on the Chosen."

"Why aren't you with her?"

"They do not need my presence. She has a new escort." His head lifted as he scanned the advisors, ending his survey with a discreet glance at Jahll.

Anxious whispers erupted as the advisors voiced their theories.

"It seems Jahll," Taqual extended his hand to Jahll, "had the foresight to send a second company for the Chosen's protection. That company intercepted the assassins." Taqual cast his eyes to the ground, as it was hard to be deceptive among his elders. Theirs were the stories that led to his lust for battle and devotion to the throne." They will escort the girl here."

"Did they send word of the assassins' identities?" Heran stepped forward to address Taqual. His deep blue robes swished as he moved. His robes, like the Orc, were plain. Heran, because of his scholarly lineage, was spared from battle, but he trained. Should he need to guard the castle, he could.

Taqual pushed into an honor stance, back straight, arms folded across his chest, fists resting in the crook of his arm and at the base of his elbow. He raised his head, peering above the head of his elder. It was disrespectful to meet their eyes unless it was initiated. The rule worked well for Taqual because his deception would pass.

"No, Elder Heran. They sent no word except they would be in time for the Rising."

Heran leaned forward and patted Taqual on the chest. "Good lad." His voice was light with joy. "This is glorious news for us. The stone will return home."

The pair thanked Taqual for his news before turning

their attention to Jahll.

"You will be an excellent hand to the new queen." Heran did a bearing of teeth, which was a smile by Orc custom. No fangs or lowering of tusks, both were acts of aggression. Akyr and Heran left the throne room in a cloud of excited chatter.

Once they were alone, Jahll closed the space between them, grabbing the neck of the Orc's chest plate and dragging the other Orc within inches of him. "What do you mean another company saved her?" Jahll hissed.

Taqual removed himself from Jahll's grasp. "It is as I said, a company of Orcs showed up." Taqual put distance between them before he said another word. "They were at the other end of the Juncture. They engaged as soon as my company stepped out."

Jahll appeared both relieved and angry about the girl's survival. He looked over his shoulder at the throne, then at Taqual. He wanted no competition for it, which the female was. "Did any of the company know who you were?"

"No." Taqual gave his head a firm shake. "There was a Shifter with the female."

"A Shifter!" Jahll closed the space between them again. He scowled down at the other orc.

"I give you the news!" Taqual took three deliberate steps back. "I did not plan the mishap."

"Mishap," Jahll griped. "What type of Shifter was it?"

"I don't know."

Jahll growled.

"It struck from behind and did not relent. I only saw claws and red eyes. It was in its half-shifted beast form. It walked on two legs but moved with its speed and hit with the strength of a Shifter."

Jahll pivoted and stalked toward the throne. "Maybe it was a herald of the High Spirit sent to guard the female."

"Maybe." Taqual shrugged.

Jahll's eyes narrowed as he stared at the black throne. He would ask his mother about the High Spirit. If there was a way to keep it from interfering.

"What is your will?" Taqual did a half bow. "Shall I kill her?"

Jahll walked over to the steps leading to the royal dais and sat on the top rung, just shy of the black throne. "No. You will be my herald. You will protect her."

Taqual frowned, but a stoic expression quickly numbed it. "But she..."

Jahll motioned for him to stop speaking. "That female is my way into the royal bloodline."

"She must die for you to gain the throne and become our new Elite."

"I am aware and it will come to pass," Jahll promised. "I must leave the grounds to secure my plans for her."

Taqual studied his friend and superior. He had great respect for Jahll. In battle there was no Orc more ruthless. Had his mother's influence blurred his vision? Ivy was poison. Like poison, it only takes a little to kill.

Taqual bowed, aware that he'd remained upright too long. "As you command, so shall it be done."

Jahll bobbed his head, then dismissed him.

Taqual exited the throne room, hoping his transaction in the Host of the Trades would finish the work he started.

CHAPTER 13

Penumbra
Darkest Forest

THE GIRL IN THE CAMOUFLAGE CLOAK MOVED AS FAST AND as quietly as she could until she reached the mouth of the Red Corridor, where she paused. She traded her Nameless Robes for more practical travel clothes: leggings, a form-fitting shirt, gloves, soft-soled leather boots and her cloak. Nameless Robes were useless anyway. The moment the wearer stepped beyond the declared boundary of the Wandering, they turned to ash. A safeguard against theft and potential unwinding of the spell which powered them.

The girl peered around the edge of the slick wall at the surrounding area. It was clear: grass, trees, moon lilies and long shadows stretched along the warded path. The way home was off the warded path. She was aware of the night hares but there were rumors of nurls moving into the territory. Nurls stepped out of nightmares to prey upon all creatures in Penumbra. Five rows of razor-sharp teeth and the ability to blend into their surroundings validated the terror they invoked. Everything deadly in Penumbra had developed a taste for human flesh. Humans were slow and soft. Easy prey.

The robust chittering of insects meant the area was predator-free. She shook off the dread crawling up her spine. Everything would be fine. She had all she needed. By sacrificing her stolen capal, she gained both blood and vital organs. Blood was required for the last leg of her journey. If she hoped to make it to her mistress's cottage before sunset, she would need a lot of blood. She ran her hands along the outside of a red pouch she had looped over her left arm. Using her fingers, she pressed the material, feeling for the capal's heart, liver and kidneys. The act alone fortified her waning resolve.

She stared at the mark on the back of her hand. It swirled prettily around a crisp line resembling a herder's staff. It was a stealth sigil. It concealed her scent and sound, but it did not make her invisible. The sigil was her mistress's brand. All her slaves bore marks which aided them in bloodletting and stealth. The wards worked on strangers, but not on her mistress.

The girl pulled a pair of gloves from the waistband of her leggings. They were also warded, preventing the material from holding scent or leaving handprints.

She examined the sky, urgency building at the setting sun. If she did not reach her mistress's cottage before dark, her mistress might kill her if the beasts of the forest didn't.

The girl's chest felt like a rubber band close to tearing. Every breath was torture, but the girl ignored it. She couldn't let her fears stop her as she dropped close to the ground, crawling through the thick blend of grass and vines.

A patch of tall grass rattled to her left, freezing her in place. She crouched lower. Her belly scraped the ground. She cocked her head, noting the distance. Chittering insects slowed but did not stop.

The girl slid her hand to a black beaded bracelet on her right wrist. She twisted it, running the tips along the beads. Offering a prayer to a God who had forgotten her, she scanned the area. Releasing the bracelet, she slid her hand into a small pouch. She let her hand be her eyes as she ran them across the contents, stopping when she found the kidneys. They were as small but mouthwatering to both nurls and night hares.

She pushed up into a crouch, hand still in the pouch, careful to not disturb the surrounding vegetation. She kept low, no bigger than the tallest patch of the wild grass and listened. The chittering died, but her trained ear caught the soft shuffling of paws. From the cadence, the girl determined that a night hare was a few feet behind her. Thick vines and overgrown trees formed a wall to her right. Anything could hide on the other side, so she opted for the left side, which was clear. The grass had patches. A few holes were in the place of those patches, possibly night hare burrows.

The girl aimed for the farthest hole and threw a kidney. It sailed through the air, descending smoothly into a burrow. An explosion of dirt followed by thumping and growls collapsed the burrow she tossed the kidney into. The ground around the nearby burrows rose and fell like a breath. The girl tossed the other three kidneys as far as she could. Each one dropped into a burrow. Clumps of dirt exploded as squabbles broke out in the burrows containing the tasty organs. It was then the girl made her move.

She sprinted down the trail, light on her feet, using the shadows to keep her presence a secret. Her magicked boots left no trail. Her breathing keened like a boiling tea kettle from her lungs, but she kept going, though her vision blurred with tears. Survive. She had to survive. Eleven years in Penumbra. She could make it.

A sand-brown cottage came into sight just as a rash of chittering and thumping rose behind her. Tears streaked her face as she willed what strength she had into her run. The big white door was only a few yards away. She just needed to cross the mistress's witch circle and she would be safe.

The chittering shifted into a strange shrieking. Nurl!

A surge of adrenaline forced the girl into an awkward stumbling run which drove her across the glittering symbols of her mistress's circle. She came to a stop, her back to the forest, mere inches into the safety of the witch circle. Laying her hands on her knees, she struggled for her breath. She tried different ways to ease the burning in her chest, settling on breathing through her mouth instead of her nose. A chill cooled the sweat on her skin, forcing her to stand upright. She remained motionless as she stared at the big white door of the cottage. It wasn't fearsome, but what was behind it was.

She looked over her shoulder. A bunch of night hares on their hind legs stared back, teeth bared and their eyes locked on her. She hurried to the door, twisted the knob, hoping the mistress was still at the capital with her son. Pushing the door open, she slid in and closed it quietly. All was silent. There were no screams or curses lobbed at her upon entry. Her shoulders slumped as she leaned her forehead on the door. Maybe, if she were lucky, she could get a nap before the mistress returned.

She pushed away from the door, turned, only to get knocked off her feet by a single blow. Her head rang, her vision went from black to vivid. She was on the ground, in a corner, curled, which was her default when the mistress was in a rage. Her mouth tasted like copper and salt. She raised a trembling hand to it, coming away with a smear of blood.

A roar shook the cottage, setting the floor to rumble.

"Mouse!" the mistress shrieked at the girl. Her name wasn't Mouse, but it had been so long since anyone had called her by her actual name, she forgot what it was. She was a mouse, quiet and afraid. Like a mouse, she learned to hide in any hole she could find. It's how she existed for the last eleven years. There was no one to save her. She was a human, a nothing. And she couldn't go home. All she could do was survive because she was afraid to die. So, she lived in hell.

Mouse sat up and flipped over, hoping to anticipate her mistress's next move. Hopefully, she could scurry away.

Her mistress enjoyed inflicting pain. Her pink eyes were like jagged stones as they cut into Mouse. Nailing her to the spot by the weight of accusation. She raged in orcish, a language Mouse had become fluent in, but she feigned ignorance. Every word her mistress lobbed at her; a fist followed. Mouse bore the blows. There was nowhere she could go to get away from them. Her mistress liked to corner her. If she ran, her mistress would break her bones. Mouse hoped her beating would end in darkness. A blessing would be a darkness she would not wake from.

Mouse shielded her head with her arms, earning her a kick in the ribs.

Ivy was cruel and cunning. Females avoided her. Males ignored her, giving her free rein. Ivy was like Mouse, in how she moved among the Orcs, but she was a viper in a field. No one paid attention until she struck. By then, it was too late.

Ivy's tusks were long, engraved with spell work her pets could see, but no one else. An Unseelie Fae wove glamour into the etchings. Most of Ivy's body bore spells that protected her from harm. Mouse wasn't sure if Ivy was safe from magic, since magic was used to shield her. The thing Mouse wasn't sure her mistress understood was this: The Hosts bartered and sold their magic without hesitation, but they always left in opening in their work, should their current customer be marked by another.

"Should I seek a new Mouse for the mistress?" a voice came from behind Ivy. The speaker was smaller, thinner and Mouse's only friend, the Seer.

The Seer's voice was like cold water on Ivy's rage. Her face grew slack, then melded into the Orc version of resting bitch face. Ivy lowered her hand, fisting at her side. She backed away from Mouse, the distress at her handiwork rising with each step.

"What have I done?"

"Punished your Mouse for her failure," the Seer's tiny voice cut through the silence. Ivy dropped to her knees; arms crooked like wings as she hovered over Mouse's battered body. She reached for Mouse, who flinched and pushed herself deeper into her corner.

Ivy's face softened as she cooed to her wounded Mouse. She scanned the damage, not liking how Mouse's thin arms looked. The right arm hung at an angle that wasn't natural. The joint at the shoulder was turning a dark red, which would progress to black. It was already swelling, which was a bad sign for humans. Ivy pushed up and turned away. She held out her hands, which trembled like the rest of her. The trembling wasn't from fear, but the anger that still lingered inside. Wrapping her arms around herself, Ivy rubbed them as she paced. Ivy had no reason to be angry with Mouse.

She turned away from Mouse. Her prone form tempted the beast in her to strike. The Seer moved past her and joined Mouse in the corner, settling next to her, leaning close enough to touch her but didn't. She began humming a tune. It was new. Her voice was beautiful, much like she was before Ivy had her augmented for her purposes. Her Seer was a natural human witch. Ivy learned how to harness their power ages ago. Her Seer had several talents: her voice, her sight and her affinity as a conduit. The old fae who traded her to Ivy had already marked her for use.

Agony pierced her heart as she watched the slow descent of the Seer's hands. Her fingers danced above her skin, landing inches away, never making contact. Mouse's rigid body loosened, uncurling to rest in the corner. Her eyes were intent on the Seer who would tend her wounds and bring salves that killed the pain. The Seer moved in a way that kept Ivy from Mouse's line of sight.

Ivy's fists clenched, pink eyes becoming like stones, as she watched Mouse respond to the Seer's ministrations. Why didn't she react that way to Ivy? Why did she shun her? This was her territory. All within its walls belonged to her. She was free to punish and reward as Orc males did. Thanks to Jahll's rank, she was no longer a servant but a queen. Queens are worshipped and feared. So far, Ivy commanded their fear and with a little magic, her slaves loved her, except Mouse and the Seer.

Her brows drew into a deep V, making the piercings clink together like wind chimes. Rage roiled in her stomach, surging into her throat like bile, choking the rising growl. She backed away from the pair until her back pressed against the soft curtain hiding the door to her workshop. She could feel the spell work through the curtain, its presence reminding her she needed to take care. The throne was close. Ivy would be the hand that moved the king. What remained of her plans must be carried out. She needed Mouse, which meant she had to leave.

The Seer's touch on Mouse drew an audible growl, drawing Mouse's startled gaze in her direction. The Seer stiffened but did not turn. Mouse's terror triggered Ivy's need to destroy her prey, to kill.

Ivy spun toward a coat rack beside the front door. She stomped over to it, plucking a muddy brown cloak from it. She slipped it on, not bothering to look back at the pair. Yanking open the door, she said, "I have business to attend to. I will return later tonight."

"I will tend to the mistress's property," the Seer said. Her voice was firm yet offered no threat, but there was something about it that pushed Ivy to leave.

The Seer stared at the door long after Ivy left. She adjusted Mouse in her arms, letting the girl's head rest on her shoulder. Mouse twisted painfully before settling into her magic-induced slumber. She ran a calloused finger across the girl's brow. In her chest, a warmth she believed she'd never feel again, bloomed. Love. Mouse was tiny. Others thought she was weak, but the Seer sensed an underlying strength tucked deep inside. All it needed was a spark, a purpose. She admired the tiny woman who looked more like a child than the adult her age decreed.

The Seer looked off toward the thick white curtain. To the bare eye, it seemed sheer, but the warding woven into the material was powerful. A combination of compulsion spells and old-fashioned hexes for the persistent. The Seer smirked. She'd been in Penumbra for twenty years. Despite Ivy's efforts, she was very aware of the movement of time. She felt the flow of Penumbra's sun and moon, but the tug of her world's stars helped her keep her freedom. She was a child of the moon and its magic.

Mouse moaned as agony etched across her brow. Her face smoothed as she pressed her head into the stark bone of the Seer's shoulder. The Seer's thin arms wrapped around Mouse. A black coven tattoo peeked from beneath the left sleeve of the burlap tunic. It was a murder of crows circling a solstice moon. The final pieces of the binding magic fell away and The Seer remembered. She'd always wanted children back in the human world, with all her human dreams and carefree ways. Her name was Carol Mason. She used to live in Montana. She had a family, a coven and a future before she was kidnapped. Snatched into a Juncture on her way from her coven's Mabon celebration.

Mouse shifted uncomfortably in her arms, reaffirming her need to save her. Mouse had become her family and you look out for family.

CHAPTER 14

Penumbra
The Wandering

ONYX WATCHED CASSIUS LEAVE THE TENT BEHIND THE TWO Orcs. Once she was alone, her gaze drifted to the mark on the back of her left hand. She raised it, holding it so it caught the light. A slow swivel, left then right, cast a jagged red slash against the fabric of the tent. She flexed her hand. The skin around the mark pulled much like a fresh scab, tender, but not uncomfortable. Cassius said the mark was a magical timer: seventy-two hours, but in her case, it was forty-eight. What happened in forty-eight hours?

Onyx lowered her hand, resting it in her lap. The mark was pretty. Its smooth surface reminded her of glass. She had yet to touch it. It was silly, but she feared touching it might somehow set it off like a bomb.

Not wanting to look at it anymore, Onyx searched

around for her workout gloves. They were lying on the ground near the pillows. She plucked them up and pulled them on. With the mark out of sight, the slow burn of anxiety died.

A swish of fabric pulled her mind away from the strange mark to Cassius, who strode in and plopped down at the foot of her sleeping pad. His normally haughty expression was gone. In its place was a look of urgency.

"What?" Onyx straightened, digging the heels of her palms into the top of her thighs.

"Why do you want to leave?"

"Really?" She gestured at the tent, ending with both hands aimed at him like an arrow. "It should be obvious."

Cassius nodded. "Yes, this is a strange land." His tone was dismissive. "It won't be for long."

"What does that mean?"

Cassius batted away her question with the flick of a wrist. "Why do you need to return home?" He leaned forward, studying her as he awaited her reply.

"The Center. I'm needed there."

"Besides the Center, what else is there?"

Onyx drew her legs under her. "What do you mean what else is there?" Her lip curled as she glared. "Mama Mays needs me."

Cassius shook his head. "No, she doesn't."

Onyx jerked back as if he'd slapped her.

"I promised you truth," Cassius declared. "And what I speak is truth."

Onyx's mouth moved, but no words came out.

"Hubbard Community Center is safe. I've seen to it."

Cassius pressed his hand to his chest. The swirls and jagged lines just above his left pec filled with pale green light. "No one who means her, or the children, harm can enter."

"But those jerks..." She pointed toward the outside.

"Two are dead and the third escaped."

"He could have doubled back and..."

Cassius shook his head. "He is on this side of the world, not in Chicago."

"How can you be certain?"

"The lesson in the laws of Penumbra's magic comes a little later, but trust me when I say, the only way back for the escapee would have been through Gryk, Joseph and myself."

"What do you mean by that?" Onyx looked as if she tasted something sour. "And what the hell do you mean by company?"

"Junctures aren't on every corner of this world. For Orcs, who cannot wield magic, they must go to the weak points of Penumbra to cross over. Our opponent's sole point of entry was behind me and the others."

"Fine, but there could be others. Who's watching the Center?"

Cassius arched a brow and lifted his chin. "They're safe."

"Those jerks got into the Center just fine earlier."

"Did they harm anyone?"

Onyx was usually quick on the smart replies, but her mouth had become a tar pit and the word she spoke was a lone bubble, sticky and foul. "No."

"Of course."

The smugness on his face made her want to punch him, but she swallowed her annoyance and motioned for him to continue.

"For a long time, citizens of Penumbra have slipped from our world into yours." Cassius clasped his hands and pointed his index finger at Onyx.

"I figured as much, with the whole portal thing."

Cassius made a face. "Yes. Junctures, or portals, as you call them, allow my kind to cross over into your world."

Onyx shrugged. "What's the problem? Obviously, you know, so what is it?"

"You are the reason for concern, according to the Prophet."

Onyx pointed at herself. "Me?"

"You are half Orc."

Onyx ran her hand along her body, ending with her hands cupping her face. "I'm not an Orc." She jerked a thumb over her shoulder. "If you haven't noticed, I'm not ten feet tall and built like a tank."

"Female Orcs are smaller than males." Cassius mimicked Onyx's original gesturing, opening his hands as if cupping her face. "Your human blood shaped your features, which allow you to pass as full human." He gestured up and down her body. "Your height and thickness of skin is from your father."

Onyx scanned her body. She always wondered about her height. Her mom had barely topped five feet and her Aunt Helen was taller than Onyx's mom by a half inch. Holding up her arms, she examined them. Some girl stabbed her when she was in tenth grade. At least, she dragged a blade across Onyx's arm. Her skin sank from the pressure of the blade but did not give.

"You have a temper too," Cassius said.

Onyx didn't look at him. Mama Mays taught her to accept herself, always saying her flaws were the priceless parts of her. Onyx agreed with most of what Mama Mays said, except for her temper. Her rage was bloodthirsty and blind, forcing her to treat it like a wild dog. She kept it within her sights, cognizant of its movement. To surrender to it was to lose herself and bits of memory. It had happened twice.

"Maybe," Onyx replied.

Cassius huffed. "Orcs by nature are short-tempered and battle ready." He crooked a claw at her. "You have taught yourself to manage yours, but the few times you've succumbed to it, I'm certain those on the receiving end didn't fare well."

Onyx wrung her hands. The last time she was in a rage, it ended with blood on her hands and a scattered array of body parts. Instead of being disgusted by the memory, it conjured the scent of fresh death. It failed to turn her stomach like a normal person; instead, it satisfied something deep inside she preferred to ignore.

Cassius wrapped a hand around Onyx's booted foot. "Do not fret over your rage. Embrace it."

Onyx shook her head vigorously. "I can't."

"You are your father's daughter. Ryza the Black was slow to anger, but when he raged, it was righteous."

Onyx shivered. There was nothing righteous about her rage. She was twelve the last time she gave into it. Willow, her only friend and the only White girl who lived in the Cedarville Projects, was attacked. Rico and his boys had dragged her into the gutted old high-rise behind the principal building. Anyone up to no good hung out there. Even the onsite security team of three stayed clear of it. The security guards only carried Tasers, no guns. With Rico, you had to be ready to shoot back or run really fast, because he would kill you. Murder was Rico's way.

As Onyx replayed the memory, she always believed that Rico was out to get Willow. Most folks in Cedarville harassed her and her mom. They were the ultimate outcasts in a building full of them. No one wanted to speak to them for fear of becoming a target. Onyx didn't care because no one cared for her. Willow was nice. She was kind and Rico was the devil.

Onyx should have known there was something odd about the abduction of Willow. Rico didn't kill her right away. He liked to make a show of his brutality, killing the innocent in front of future victims. Nothing kept a mouth shut better than a display of heartless cruelty. In that, Rico was king.

With Willow, Rico dragged her into the heart of the abandoned building, took her up to the second floor where the only functional apartments were. It was the moment Onyx entered the gate. Mama Mays was behind her when he made Willow scream while he laughed.

Onyx recalled running and someone yelling for her to stop. She ignored them. Instead, she crossed the distance between the main gate and the back building in a little over a minute. She reached the stairs on the ground floor and someone's arms jammed across her neck and lifted her off her feet.

The roar, it didn't sound human, but it was her. She slammed her foot into the knee of her captor. The audible crack made her smile. She spun around, sending a fist into her captor's stomach. He folded like a lawn chair, then fell.

Onyx pivoted, racing up the stairs, taking them two at a time. A shrill scream drowned her labored breathing. She picked up speed, using the momentum to jump, legs aimed at the door, like she'd seen in action movies. Onyx crashed through the apartment door, landing on her feet, heart thudding, as adrenaline flooded her body.

Rico held a patch of Willow's blond hair above his head. He waved it, revealing a bit of her scalp at the end. Willow curled in a ball at Rico's feet. She was crying. Then he kicked her. Onyx felt Rico's boys close in, but she didn't care. They needed to suffer and Rico needed to die.

People say rage is red, but for Onyx it was black. In the thick of it, Onyx recalled the sounds of broken bones, torn flesh and the cries of boys masquerading as men. She was in the middle of stomping Rico in the chest when the softest voice pulled her from her darkness. *Willow.* She called her name, asked her to stop and she did.

Onyx blinked and everything was red. She looked down. Her foot rested in a crater that was Rico's chest. Around her were arms, legs and the broken weeping teens they belonged to. Onyx raised trembling hands, which were covered in blood, soft tissue and hair.

Onyx moved to help her friend when the cops entered the apartment. They kept her from Willow asking her questions she couldn't answer. Her voice vanished, stolen by the horror of what she'd done. Someone escorted her out. She couldn't recall her legs moving or when her feet touched the bottom step. Everything around her shifted into the surreal. Voices grew distant except one, Nancy Mays. She was on her knees, gripping her hands, staring into her blood-spattered face, chanting her name.

"Onyx."

Someone tugged on her booted feet. Looking up, it took her a minute to comprehend that Cassius was the one calling her name this time.

"Yeah." Her voice, a worn soft rasp.

"Where did you go?"

Onyx looked away from the Shifter, focusing on the small pile of colorful pillows. "Nowhere."

Cassius wrapped his hands around Onyx's ankles, forcing her to look at him. "The will of the High Spirit is for Penumbra to remain unpolluted by the worlds beyond it."

"I take it, Penumbrans are purists?"

Cassius shrugged. "The High Spirit has her will which is sent to her people through the Prophet. It's my understanding that the trips between worlds have become messy and encourage further rebellion." Cassius held up his index finger. "Blatant rebellion will not be tolerated."

"So, this place is ruled by dictatorship?"

Cassius chuckled at the comment. "Penumbra's ways are vastly different from your world, but like your world, there are laws. Those laws are in place for a reason." He released her ankles. "For the safety of both worlds, it is best for our people to remain here." He watched as she pulled her legs away, drawing them flush with her chest.

"An Orc wandering down Michigan Avenue would cause quite a stir." Onyx wrapped her arms around her legs, hugging them tight, still refusing to look at Cassius.

"You serve a great purpose as foretold by the Prophet. You need only to trust your instincts," Cassius continued.

"My instincts are telling me to go home."

"Don't be a child. It's not fitting," Cassius scolded. "Penumbra may not be like Chicago, but the sixth sense you carry will save your life."

"What I need, is to go home," Onyx insisted.

"What you *need* is to answer the challenge if you hope to save Nancy and the Center."

Onyx pulled the glove from her hand and displayed the mark. "How does me answering this help her?"

"Every group in Penumbra has an Elite, whether dark or light. Elites are chosen by the High Spirit and gain immortality."

"Elites can't be immortal, or I wouldn't be here!"

"All sins have their price."

"What does that mean?" Onyx challenged.

The look Cassius gave her shut her mouth. "Onyx. I understand you're scared but all you have is three days." He held up three fingers to drive home his point. "You can squander time fighting the truth or you can spend it preparing for what's coming." Cassius waited a few seconds, giving Onyx time to protest. When she didn't, he continued. "Gryk and a few others must prepare for the journey ahead." Cassius rose to his feet and moved to the tent flap. He pushed it aside, then looked over his shoulder at her.

"I'll leave you to decide if you want to own your

destiny or not. If you are content with others who mean you and yours harm driving you to the slaughter, so be it. In three days, you die. If you decide to stand for those who need you, I will kill anything that gets in your way. It's your choice. In an hour someone will come for you."

Cassius left the tent, leaving Onyx with her ghosts.

CHAPTER 15

FOR A LAW OFFICE, ITS DÉCOR WAS BARGAIN BASEMENT. THE bland carpet and Ikea chairs and end tables screamed "new practice." Helen plucked a magazine from the end table next to her. It was an underwhelming intellectual publication about science, not fashion. Helen liked fashion. She mapped out ways to apply high-end looks at the stores where she held credit cards in Onyx's name. Her credit was garbage, but Onyx's was excellent. The assortment of credit cards in her wallet had Onyx's name on them. Since no one checked ID, her liberal use of them wasn't a problem. On the rare occasion a clerk asked, Helen was ready with a fake ID.

She shifted in her seat a third time, careful not to knock over her collection of Gucci and Prada bags. She placed them in a way that anyone entering the office could read the brand. If someone got close enough to peer inside, they would see a Gucci purse and a pair of Prada shoes. Helen would wait until the end of her little meeting to decide whether she would venture into Wolford Boutique. They dealt in one of a kind jewelry, which is probably where that heifer picked up that sterling collar.

Helen flipped through the magazine then laid it across her lap, her mind drifting to her earlier shopping spree. They raised the credit limits on her cards this month. A text message and an email alerted her to that fact. Why? It was a mystery she hoped the lawyer could solve. As far as she knew, Onyx still volunteered at Hubbard Community Center, but earned actual money as a tutor and counselor for IIT.

Her fingers drummed against the magazine's pages as she again examined her surroundings. The firm felt like a pop-up restaurant. New. Temporary. She tossed it back on the table, just as the door beside reception opened. Helen stood but did not move.

A tall, thin man with skin the color of a walnut entered the waiting area. Instead of inviting her back to his office, he let the door close behind him. He wore a dark blue suit with a nickel gray tie. The tie had fine silver stripes in a diagonal pattern. Helen noticed them when they shimmered as he passed under a bright patch of light. The man's hair was in a stylish, close-cropped, gray afro. Its texture and color were like cotton. His olive-green gaze gave her a once over, flitting over to her bags, then settled on her face. From the wrinkling of his wide nose, he was not impressed.

Helen returned the criticism in an in-kind glance. She pulled out Onyx's cellphone and flipped it so he could read the text message. The man plucked it from her hand without touching her. He scanned the message, returned the phone and inspected Helen a second time.

"Which one are you?" She dragged her gaze around the office, then spared him a glance, then focused on Onyx's phone. "Gorman or Stein?" Helen asked without looking up. She scrolled through Onyx's messages. One with an address and time caught her eye. She'd check it later.

"I am Roger Gorman." His voice was commanding without being loud. He didn't offer his hand after the introduction, instead he inclined his head.

"I am Onyx Jones's aunt, Helen. I'm her legal guardian and trustee of her inheritance."

The man's face was awash with understandings as soon as the words "inheritance" and "trustee" came out of her mouth.

"My employer informed me you were in route."

"Why don't we cut to the chase? The text message said you had details about my niece's new trust fund. As her guardian, I should know these things."

"How old is your niece?"

"Twenty-three."

"Since we're shooting from the hip. You know, once your niece turned eighteen, you ceased being her trustee or guardian."

Helen knew that, but she'd done a little homework on the ride over. If she could prove her niece could not care for herself, it would reactivate her guardianship. All that money would be hers. Declaring Onyx unfit would allow her to dump her in an institution to rot while she lived high on the hog.

"So?" Helen watched him.

Gorman chuckled and waggled his finger at her. "My employer was right about you."

"Right about what?"

"Don't worry about it." He turned and headed for the door leading to the back office. He motioned for her to follow. Helen gathered her bags and followed Gorman, who walked into the first office to the left of the door. It was as bare bones as the reception area. No pictures of family or clients on the desk, wall or shelves. The only sign of authenticity was a framed law degree mounted on the wall behind his desk. He waved at the guest chair as he sat in a leather executive chair.

"Now what?"

Gorman stopped her. He pulled out a drawer, removed a black file and slid it over to Helen. She caught it, spun it around so she could read it.

Helen opened the folder. Inside were bank statements. She flipped through them, discovering several additional accounts, all without her name on them. She scanned through other documents detailing properties being held in trust for Onyx. The trustee's name was redacted.

Pain formed a ring around the crown of Helen's head as she closed the file. She ran her hands over the smooth surface a few times before looking up.

"What's in that file is just the beginning." Gorman held out his hand for it. Helen complied.

"How do I make it mine?"

Gorman leaned back in his chair, folding his arms of his chest again, surveying the woman in front of him. After several seconds, he held up two fingers.

"Come back in two days." He returned that hand back into the fold of his arms. "I will have all the necessary documents to make your request a reality."

Helen leaned back in her chair, considering the man in front of her. "Just like that?"

Gorman nodded.

"Nothing's that easy."

"True." Gorman leaned forward, resting his arms on his desk. "My client is motivated to sever your niece's ties to her life here."

Both Gorman and Helen stared at each other. Helen was the first to blink and break the silence. "What's it going to cost me?"

"A percentage of your niece's inheritance."

Helen growled.

Gorman burst into a fit of laughter. "You didn't think I was going to work for free."

"You're supposed to help me."

"Rob your niece," Gorman stated.

Helen scowled.

"Even accomplices get a cut of the spoils at the end of a successful robbery."

"I'm not robbing anyone."

Gorman slammed his fist on the desktop. "Let's cut the bullshit, shall we?" He leaned in. "Look, Ms. Jones, I'm sure you've gotten by with fooling your rich friends into believing you're one of them, but I'm a lawyer. I deal in bullshit, day in, day out. I can smell it a mile away and you're full of it."

Helen's eyes narrowed.

"Do you want the money or not?" Gorman challenged.

"Every penny."

"Well, you're going to get 85 percent of her fortune, because I'm getting 15 percent off the top. If you don't want what my client's offering you," Gorman waved a dismissive hand toward the door, "leave and don't come back. If you're ready to make this happen, come back in two days."

"You'll get your 15 percent," Helen groused.

"Damn straight I will."

Helen snatched up her bags and stood. She made it to the doorway before Gorman asked her a strange question.

"Once you've acquired your niece's wealth, would it bother you if you never saw her again?"

"No. Once I've got the money, I have no use for her." Helen raised the Gucci and Prada bags for emphasis.

"What happens when people ask about her?"

"She's a grown-ass woman. She can come and go as she pleases. It just so happens, she left and I ain't seen or heard from her in however many days or months. Of course, dates and times will be adjusted based on who I'm speaking to."

Gorman flashed perfect white teeth. "Excellent."

Helen smiled too.

"You can go now." Gorman pulled a new file after he returned Onyx's to the drawer. He opened it and began reading its contents. Helen cleared her throat. Gorman paused briefly to check the time. "Return in two days.

Let's say, ten a.m., that way you'll have enough time to do all the necessary paperwork for the banks."

"How soon will I have access to everything?"

"When you come back, everything will be ready for transfer. All it will take is your signature and a notary. If you like, I can have five thousand dollars in cash ready for you upon signing. It should be enough to tide you over for a couple days until everything updates in the system."

"That works just fine." Helen pivoted and trotted out of the office.

Gorman pulled out his cellphone once the main door closed behind Helen. He composed a quick text, alerting Ivy that her rat had taken the bait. He would keep her posted on the progress. After he hit send, he leaned back in his office chair, folded his hands behind his head and started daydreaming about the big payday his client would deliver once Helen severed her niece's last tie to Chicago.

CHAPTER 16

Penumbra
The Wandering

ONYX RAN HER FINGERS ALONG THE CHIPPED BEADS OF HER friendship bracelet. There was a nameplate at its center. The letters were chipped but still legible: Willow. She was the only girl her age brave enough to be her friend. She stuck with her no matter what and when they made the bracelets, they chose colors that reflected how each girl viewed the other. Willow had a big, vibrant heart, so Onyx picked bright, brilliant colors: luminous yellows, oranges and greens. She threaded them next to the nameplate, which she considered the sun. It was a flat wooden plate with two loops on the side. She painted Willow's name in the center, filling the "O" the same yellow as the sun. She even added a few orange flames to frame it. Onyx raised her wrist, holding it to the sliver of sunlight streaming through the creases of the tent. Onyx thought she was going to gift it to Willow, but her friend had a better idea. They would keep the bracelet they made to keep each other close, no matter how far they were. Families move away. Friends lose contact. In Willow's case, she disappeared from the Cedarville Projects. Lost in the chaos of police, reporters, gapers and well-wishers.

"Willow." Saying her name out loud was like a soft wind to a dying ember, it flared. The sudden warmth of it died as Onyx returned her hand to her lap, twisting the bracelet so the scarred surface showed. Her life mimicked the bracelet, worn with fissures along the pressure points. The glint from the mark on her left hand reminded her of Joseph, Gryk and Cassius. Like Willow and Nancy Mays, they had faith in her. Onyx shook her head sharply. No, they had faith in her father. She was a piece of him, but she wasn't him.

Lacing her hands at the back of her neck, she pulled, unlocking them. She slid them down her collar bones. The tips of her fingers grazed the hard silver collar under her turtleneck. It too was an object of faith. Onyx withdrew her probing hands. Leaning forward, she pressed the heels into her legs. She was not a reliable idol.

A moan bordering on a pained wail startled her. It alarmed her that it came from her. Coils of anxiety constricted her chest, stunting her breathing. She rubbed it, hoping to push down her rising panic. She wanted to return to the shadows, a nobody. It's what she knew. It's what she was good at.

I'm nobody's savior.

She needed some air.

Onyx jumped up and ran from the tent, nearly

crashing into someone. Retreating a few steps, muttering a loop of apologies along the way, Onyx finally looked up. A tall woman stood in her path. Her statuesque frame was more cartoonish, in a graphic novel way: long, lean and seemed weightless. Her luminous white skin conjured the word ghost, but ghosts weren't corporeal beings, at least, not in Chicago. The woman held up a small, gilded cage with a trio of disgruntled birds with white feathers and purple and gray crests. The woman's long white braid swung behind her. Several dark green bands lined the end.

Her clothes were straight out of a medieval movie. She wore soft green breeches. A long beige tunic cinched at the waist by a dark brown belt. Her shoes were like Joseph's, moccasin-style boots. Hers were the same color as her belt. The only color to the woman was her crisp yellow brows, which curled at the ends much like the crest of a bird. Her sharp, narrow nose had a tiny silver-bead piercing.

"*Pax tecum.*" The flurry of wings and squawks ceased, then the woman curtsied. "Forgive me, Chosen." Her voice was a melody away from a song.

Onyx waved and watched, noticing how the left sleeve of the woman's tunic moved like a pendulum. It was empty with a knot at the end.

"I am Caladrius." A slight bow of her head followed the introduction. The gilded cage resting at her side. "I am called Cali by everyone. I will accompany you to Oracaii."

Onyx cleared her throat. "I'm Onyx."

Cali's smile was a radiant display of perfect white

teeth. "Word of you has made its rounds among the Wandering. We are all excited that you are with us." Cali's hand flexed on the cage's handle. "If you need anything, ask and it will be done." Cali curtsied again.

Onyx nodded absently as her gaze darted around, searching for a path, a way out of this mess.

Cali frowned. "Is something wrong, Chosen?"

Onyx wrung her hands, eyes refusing to meet Cali's.

"Please, Chosen, follow me." Cali walked pass Onyx to a row of colorful trees. She paused at the edge, noticing Onyx hadn't moved. Cali pivoted, face grim. She joined Onyx, leaving a foot between them. "My Chosen, your mind must be full of the weight of your calling."

Cali shifted her hand forward. Onyx glanced at the cage. There was no door. The birds could fly off if they wished, but they didn't.

"Please, come with me to the clearing. There you can breathe, scream, or cry in private."

Onyx's head jerked up. She blinked a few times before nodding.

Cali did an about-face, looked over her shoulder at Onyx; after two steps, Onyx followed.

Cali led them through the trees onto a path lined with black stones marked with sigils. They flared bright green as they passed. Dry leaves, twigs and rocks composed the path. Onyx noticed she couldn't hear their footsteps as they walked down the trail.

Their walk was short. Cali made a left by a tree with a blue trunk. They moved toward the sound of rushing water. A cluster of large palm branches formed yellow fans. Cali pushed back the leaves, exposing large stones beside a purple stream. The surrounding flowers were beautiful. Cali named each one as they moved carefully through them to the large stones. Onyx favored the moon lilies with their soft yellow petals ringed with deep purple. Its pistils were deep purple, but the tips were soft yellow. Cali said they pulsed like Christmas lights at night.

Cali chose a patch of grass beside the stream where she set the cage down. Onyx hopped on the stone studying the other woman. Cali's ears were normal, which surprised her. She expected them to be pointed like an Elf.

"What are you?" The question was out of her mouth before she could stop it.

"I am a Grand Caladrius Shifter."

"A Cala-what?"

Cali sat; legs crossed. "A Grand Caladrius." She smiled, though it was half-hearted. "My second form is an Orc-sized white bird. My kind exist to serve royalty." She held out her hand, index finger elevated above the rest. One bird hopped from the cage and onto the waiting finger. Cali pulled it into her lap. The bird stepped from her finger to her knee. "Grand Caladrius served in both mortal and Penumbran courts for millennia." She made a grand gesture toward the canopy. "It was my duty to keep the king healthy and safe. I am a healer of the body and mind." Her face fell, "At least, I used to be." She clasped her armless sleeve. "A healer can't heal if they're broken."

"You can still help people." Onyx's habit of lifting the spirits of her fellow broken kicked in. She slid from her perch to scoot toward Cali. She settled two feet away, close enough to see the bird's lovely purple eyes.

Cali shook her head as she deftly removed a small pouch from a loop on her belt. Her thin fingers undid the string, then she shook out the contents: three tiny collars with small brown tubes corked at the top.

"I teach the mothers of the Wandering how to heal. They teach their sons and daughters. I have my function here, but I don't trust myself with the care of another."

"Why?"

"Consider the reasons behind why you reject your calling."

Onyx was startled at the directness of Cali's question and the speed at which their conversation turned.

Cali picked up one of the little collars. The bird stretched its neck as Cali made an adjustable loop, then placed it around its neck. It pressed its head against her fingers. Cali scratched its head absently as she considered Onyx.

"I understand the war inside you." Her scratching fingers halted and the little bird hopped from her knee. Another bird took its place. "I know what it is to have the fate of others on your shoulders. My king was slaughtered and his kingdom destroyed. The Salvagers spared no one. Not even the children or animals. Any creature exhibiting a talent of value, magical or not, were taken."

"Salvagers?"

"Agents of the Host of the Trades. They collect rare creatures, for a price, like my sisters and me. They burned our home, collared us so we couldn't shift." Cali lifted her head, exposing her neck revealing a deep red collar. Tiny black pebbles gave it a studded look, but upon closer inspection they formed an array of symbols, lines and stylized figures. It reminded her of hieroglyphics. "We were then delivered to the Host of the Trades, where we were sold. My sisters, Myna, Aria and I would bring a hefty sum, considering we were the last of our kind." Cali stroked the bird's crest, letting the tip of her nails linger between the feathers. The bird tilted its head, its beak slightly ajar as it enjoyed Cali's ministrations. "Myna, the youngest of us, was murdered for being defiant. She refused to be a slave. Our captors killed her in front of us and simultaneously killed the fight in me."

"It wasn't your fault."

A slow shake of her head and a woeful chuckle prefaced Cali's next words, "I am the oldest of my sisters and their alpha. I could have used my power to alter my sister's temperament. Myna would have submitted to our captors, but I said nothing." Cali's shoulders slumped. "I thought our rarity was a shield." She shook her head, eyes stretched slightly, as she replayed the horror she witnessed. "I heard rumors of the Host of the Trades. They waste nothing. In the Trades, they sell every part of a product." Cali pressed her hand to her chest. "Slaves are merchandise. I learned later, to my new mistress's delight, my sister was dismembered. Every part of her was sold, even her blood."

Onyx swallowed. She'd heard of organ harvesting back in her world but harvesting body parts and blood was crazy.

"My remaining sister and I were sold to a white Orcess. She was a regular in the Trades. She knew what

Aria and I were. Upon our delivery to her home, she tortured and questioned us about our powers. Our mistress sought to harness them. Aria took her life rather than endure a lifetime of abuse." Cali sighed. "I could have stopped that too."

"You were both being tortured! How is this on you, Cali?"

"I suffered, yes, but I could have born my sister's pain to give her peace. As alpha, my power lies in my capacity to take on the pain of others, both mental and physical. My sisters' abilities were limited to physical healing. Mine are far more. Only an alpha can be the king's healer."

She tapped her knee. The little bird turned in time with the tapping. "After my sister's death, my mistress worried that I would flee or do the same, so she had me warded." Cali pulled the collar of her tunic. A series of faint sigils lined her collarbone. "I could not run or end my life without her permission."

"Is that why she took your arm?"

Cali shook her head. "No." She stared at her empty sleeve. "My arm was the price of the magic she used to bind me to her."

Onyx covered her mouth to hold back her outraged cry. It took a few moments for her to recover before she asked Cali a question. "If you were bound to her, how did you end up with the Wandering?"

A sad smile crossed her face. "Captive slaves have few they can trust, but I met someone special. She's still in chains," Cali took a deep breath before continuing, "and she's a human."

"Human!"

Cali nodded. "Yes, but they're not here by choice." She shrugged. "At least, none that I know of." Her gaze settled on the bird on her knee. She repeated what she did with the other, looping the collar around its neck. "My friend is a human with magic." Cali looked over at Onyx. "I believe you call her a witch."

"So, humans can use magic here."

"Magic is magic. All of it works in Penumbra. The difference with humans is their connection to the magic of their world is severed once they cross over into Penumbra. What my friend and I learned by watching our mistress, is human witches reconnect with their magic. It takes a little time.

"Since humans are not recognized citizens, their magic flows undetected. What my mistress and most in Penumbra cannot acknowledge is that humans evolve. They're curious. My friend discovered how to read the spells cast to bind me. She also discovered a way to mute them."

"How did you get away?"

"My friend built her own ties within the Trades and inside Oracaii. She used them to help me get away."

"What happened to your friend?"

"She lives." Cali smiled as she looked up into the dim cotton-candy sky with its dark gray border. The Wandering traveled through the territory between the Odious and the Alluring. Cali enjoyed the stark contrast between the two. It was also a constant reminder to be always alert. "She stays behind to protect the other humans, especially Mouse."

"Mouse?"

"Mouse is a human girl brought here as a child. Our mistress enjoys terrorizing her. Mouse is tiny and always scared. My mistress craves power. She even seeks the throne, but as a female with no royal blood she cannot. She has no power which makes her cruel to those who are subject to her. She is queen of her slaves."

"She sounds like a bitch to me."

Cali chuckled. Her face was suddenly serious. "Would you save my friend and Mouse if you had the power to?"

"Whoa, look, I can't help them." Onyx stood and reclaimed her seat on the rock.

"So, you'll let them die."

"No! This isn't on me." Onyx shook her head and waved her arms in denial.

"You are the Chosen. What happens in the next two days is on your shoulders." Cali looked pointedly at the hand with the Challenge Mark. "I failed to use the power I had to save my sisters."

"That was beyond your control."

Cali arched a brow. "Was it? I was their alpha. It was my job to protect them, even if it meant forcing them to submit to our captor to buy us time. Together we could have gained our freedom."

The third bird hopped on Cali's knee. She looped its collar around its neck. "As the Orc Elite and queen, you can bring my former mistress to justice. You can save the Wandering by making us your people through blooding. It would be you who could deliver punishment to those who abduct humans from their world. It is you who are the hope for many of us, even if you deny it."

"I didn't ask for this!"

"Fate isn't about permission. It just is."

"Look, I can't." Onyx rose and walked away from the stone. The tightness in her chest had returned. Her breathing came in quick bursts, barely filling her lungs before the next inhale. Tremors coursed throughout her body. Her legs were failing as her stomach rebelled.

"You are the only one capable of defeating those who challenge you." Cali insisted.

Indignation chased away her tremors. "I'm not an Orc! Hell, I'm barely a quarter of their body weight if Joseph and Gryk are the standard." Onyx pivoted, aiming an accusatory finger at Cali. "I'm going to get you all killed!" The fire in her words died abruptly. Her arm fell docilely to her side. "Willow, Nancy Mays, my mom..." Onyx scanned the space in front of her, seeing nothing but the pained faces of those she cared about. "All of them hurt or dead because of me." She turned her back on Cali, wrapping her arms around herself to keep herself from falling apart.

"I'm nobody's savior."

"Yes, you are," Cali whispered fiercely. "The High Spirit chose you for a reason." Cali came up behind Onyx, the three birds perched on her shoulders. "Your father provided you with everything you need for victory."

Onyx pulled out of Cali's grip, spinning to face her. "Where is this miraculous equipment?" She threw up her hands, then covered her face as she shook her head.

"All kings have a tie to their ancestors." Cali pointed at the Knowledge Stone under Onyx's turtleneck.

"So, do I bribe my way into the winner's circle?" Onyx

pulled her hands away from her face. "It's just a damned piece of jewelry." She pressed her hands against it, dragging them down her neck and stopped at the stone. "It's a beautiful piece of jewelry."

"It's not just jewelry," Cali insisted. "The Knowledge Stone holds the collective wisdom of the former Orc kings."

"How do you know that? More importantly, how does it work?"

"I know many things because of my service to kings. I know many of their secrets. It comes with the job." Cali shook her head. "I do not know specifically how the Knowledge Stone works. I know that it only works for the Chosen."

"Of course." Onyx stomped her foot. It was childish, but she was *done*. Everyone had all these expectations of her. Demanding she save their world. She glared at Cali's back as she headed back to the stone Onyx had abandoned.

Cali hopped on top of it with the ease and grace of the birds she carried. The birds flapped their wings but did not fly away. Cali settled in a lotus position, legs crossed, back straight, with two birds on her right knee and one on the left.

She held out her arm without losing her balance. The bird on her left knee hopped into her open palm. She brought the little bird close to her lips. It tilted its head as she told it a secret. It straightened, hopped backwards, then spread its wings. In a single flap, it soared into the sky, gone by the next beat of its wings. This repeated with the others. Once all the birds were gone, Cali hopped off the stone, collected the gilded cage and walked over to Onyx.

"Onyx Jones, daughter of Ryza the Black." Cali sighed loudly before her next words. "I am sorry you are stuck here. I am sorry that our world and our problems are weights around your neck, but I am not sorry that you are here." She picked up the gilded cage, raised it, tapped the edge against the collar, then brought it back to rest at her side. "Let go of what you know. Listen to the whispers of warning and calling." Cali's smile was wistful. "Whether you are willing, or not, fate is pulling you along toward your destiny." She tipped the gilded cage toward the mark on Onyx's left hand. "It's your choice to embrace it or not."

Cali headed for the mouth of the trail which led to the clearing where they stood. Onyx moved to follow, but Cali stopped her.

"You should stay here and consider what Cassius and I have said. Decide for yourself if the lives of the Wandering are worth saving. But know this, the lives of those on the other side of Penumbra are equally at risk."

"How am I supposed to get back to the tent?"

"Joseph will come for you," Cali said as she began down the path. "I will go help Gryk and Cassius prepare for our journey."

The trail swallowed Cali and her gilded cage, leaving Onyx alone with her questions and doubts.

CHAPTER 17

Penumbra
The Wandering

FRUSTRATED TEARS DISTORTED ONYX'S VISION, FORCING her to stop at the water's edge. She crouched down, arms crossed over thighs and stared into the shimmering waves. What was she supposed to do? How was she going to make everything better for everyone? It was her life that would be forfeit in the end. She was here to make things right for Mama Mays. She owed Mama Mays a leg.

After Cedarville, Mama Mays stood in front of television cameras and told the world she would testify against Rico's crew. So, they came after her. Cecil Davies, who went by Big Cec, took a hammer to Mama Mays's knee. He only got one blow in. No one knows who or what stopped him, but no one saw Cecil Davies after that. Onyx worried that his psychotic mom would come for

Mama Mays, but she didn't. Angela Davies moved out of Chicago.

Onyx couldn't restore the missing limb or the pain she endured over the years, but she could save the Community Center and Youth Home for her. They were everything to Mama Mays. They meant everything to Onyx, too. It was a safe place to sleep where there was no yelling, no pulling at her to do and carry everything. There was quiet and acceptance.

The clearing had gone silent. No leaves stirred. The wind had stilled. Even the errant splash of the rampant stream had slowed. She glanced up at the sky as a thick patch of clouds spread across it, a sheer hand covering the setting sun, breathing life into shadows which spread into the clearing. The shimmering stream sparkled under the glow of moon lilies along the stream's edge. Their sudden bloom filled the surrounding air with a delectable scent, then it changed, taking on a rich musky aroma both masculine and familiar. The shadows bled across the ground, darkening the grass, roots and flowers. They stopped at the water's edge. Then she felt it.

It shifted behind her, barely within her peripheral vision. The weight of it caused a minor tremor when it moved. Her back stiffened and the need to look nearly turned her head, but weeks of its presence kept her gaze straight. Her eyes fastened on the glittering purple water.

She waited.

"Why do you fight them?" His voice rumbled, low and deep, but there was something else in it. Sadness?

"They want me to be what I'm not."

"The throne is yours. Take it."

Onyx flicked the collar. The soft tinkle of metal against her fingernail was pleasing to the ear. The shadow moved closer. "I'm not what you think I am." Onyx hugged herself.

The shadow growled. It didn't frighten her; it reinforced what she'd been trying to tell all of them. She was a disappointment. She wasn't worthy of the throne they were trying to set her on.

"Stop fighting who you are and embrace it." His words slid through his teeth. He moved closer, so close the heat of his body chased away the growing chill of dread. The heaviness of his hands hovering close to her shoulders tingled. He withdrew them. Onyx imagined him curling them in regret, then pressing them to his sides as he backed away.

"Listen to Gryk. Listen to Cassius. Trust them. They will not lead you astray." Leaves crunched behind her. Several small twigs cracked beneath his feet.

"They're strangers." Onyx pressed her knuckles against her temples. "This place is alien to me." She ground her foot into the ground. "It's not my home."

"Is that apartment in Chicago home?"

Onyx stiffened, her hands falling away as the lump in her throat cut off her words.

"Your place is here. The Wandering will embrace you." She felt a shift in the space to her left. "Joseph adores you. Gryk worries over you like he worries over Joseph and Cassius is never far."

"Cassius is a perv."

The shadow laughed, low and genuinely amused. "He is a feline Shifter."

"Not funny."

"Trust them." He moved closer, step by step, with each word spoken. "Let them guide you."

"I just want to go home and forget all about this place."

"Where is home, dearest child?"

Hubbard Community Center filled her mind. It was the only safe place she'd ever known.

"What made you cross over? What drew you to follow strangers into a portal?"

Mama Mays's face floated to the forefront, but Onyx remained silent.

"Remember why you crossed. Consider what will happen if you don't carry this to the end."

Onyx wrapped her arms around herself. It took everything in her to remain standing. For her to fail would mean failing Mama Mays again, only this time, she wouldn't lose part of a limb, she would lose everything.

"Trust your company." His breath was warm against the crown of her head. A soft metallic hum drew her gaze to a wash of red light at the base of her throat. The Knowledge Stone glowed. "Cali knows the royal court, its rules and the politics."

Speckles of sunlight broke through the clouds, piercing the dark spots in the clearing.

"Your reluctance will cost those you love most." She felt him recede with the shadows as the muted sunlight burned through the cloud cover, breathing life into the clearing.

"Why me?"

"Cassius told you who you are. It's up to you to believe."

Onyx turned full circle, just as the last of the shadow vanished.

CHAPTER 18

Penumbra
The Wandering

DAMPENING STONES. THEIR VIBRATION FELT GOOD ON Joseph's skin, unlike some noises that scratched and picked at him like the tips of claws. He didn't like those. Warm colors pulsed from the center of each stone, spreading down to the very bottom then surging into the neighboring one. It was like watching ring around the rosy. The lights danced and swayed without missing a beat. Joseph's eyes followed the dancing lights for a while, then wandered over to the tree-lined edge of their camp. Onyx was in there, close enough to see them through the trees, but he couldn't see her. She had asked him to give her a minute. When she asked, she laid her soft hand on his cheek, graced him with a smile and he made a promise. Promises were meant to be kept and he always kept his promises. Joseph was an adult in age, size and strength, but his mind was young. It stopped growing when he was hurt. The day Gryk saved him and made him his son.

A smile lingered on his face as thoughts of her filled his mind and heart. He liked her. It wasn't because she was pretty. She was like him, trapped in her feelings. Feelings tangled him up, stole his words and siphoned his courage. Joseph squinted at the collection of trees, wondering if it was a good idea to leave her in there. He promised and he would keep his promise, but he still worried.

A large arm circled Joseph's shoulder. It was the only arm big enough to wrap around him, his papa, Gryk. He tugged Joseph toward the others. Cassius and Cali sat on opposite sides of a small fire. There would be two more members of the Wandering who would join them once Onyx took her place at the circle of meeting. Joseph cast one last look at the forest before turning away and following his father.

Joseph took his place to the right of his father. Cassius sat to his left and Cali sat directly across from Gryk. Another Orc sat outside the circle, to the right of Cali, reflecting her status.

"I should wait for her." Joseph twisted in his spot, again scanning the forest for Onyx.

Gryk patted Joseph's shoulder. "She'll come when she's ready."

"The Chosen has much on her mind." Cali placed her hand over Joseph's, reclaiming his attention. "She has to figure things out for herself before she joins the circle of meeting."

"She's scared," Joseph said, again, turning to the forest, which hid Onyx away.

"We all are," Gryk chimed in.

Cassius agreed.

"It's a scary time for us all." Cassius reached across Gryk and squeezed Joseph's wrist. "We're being called to do things we've never done before."

Joseph shook his head vigorously. "But she's not from here. She doesn't know all the rules."

Cassius withdrew his hand and stared into the flames.

"It's not fair!" Joseph smashed his fists on the ground, kicking up a cloud of dust.

Gryk pressed his hands over them, locking them in place and waited for Joseph to meet his eyes.

"Nothing is fair in this world or hers," Gryk said as he squeezed Joseph's fists.

Joseph pouted, dragging his hands from his father's. He wanted to wrap them around himself and turn away from them all, but his father taught him that the field was no place for tantrums. He had to put his feelings in a box and let them go once they returned home. If they were too big for him, his father always helped him work through them enough so they could make it home safely.

Joseph pressed his fists into his thighs, rubbed them back and forth, reddening the skin. Gryk tapped the backs of his fists and he stopped.

"It's still not fair."

"It's not, but it can't be helped." Cassius thrust his arm north. "We've got a long way to go with barely any time to properly plan for battle or the court."

"But all this talk of battle makes her sad."

"Yes, it does." Onyx stood at the edge of the forest. Joseph jumped up from his spot and ran over to her. She smiled widely as she braced herself for affection. Joseph stopped just shy of touching her, then folded her in his embrace like a flower. Onyx let herself remain in his embrace for a minute, then signaled for him to release her. Joseph stepped away, grabbed her hand and pulled her toward the others. She let him. His sweetness made her happy.

Onyx sat beside Cali, though Joseph tried to coax her into sitting next to him. She appreciated the enthusiasm, but she needed to put on her big girl panties and get the lowdown on the road ahead.

She emptied her mind, lifted her head and looked to the old Orc, Gryk. "So, what happens now?"

Gryk bared his teeth in a smile, before motioning for her to join them in the circle of meeting.

"You need to meet the rest of your company." Gryk pointed to a spot behind Cali. A short, squat Orc—it looked like a child—stepped into the firelight. It was dressed in a simple long tunic slit at the sides where her hips began. The front and back of the tunic ended at the knees. There were no brands or piercings on the Orc's skin. The tusks were small and blunt. Its head, unlike Gryk's and Joseph's, was shaved. At the top was a patch of crimson braids held together by a black band with silver studs. Additional bands held the middle and the ends together, creating a singular mass. It wore breeches the same color as the band. The breeches were tucked in moccasin-style boots.

The little Orc stopped beside Cali, who pressed her hand on her shoulders.

"This is Makhaira, known to us as Mak. She will tend our capals, equipment and maybe do a little spying." Cali spoke as if she were planning a shopping trip.

Leaves rattled overhead, followed by a buzzing sound. Small starbursts of soft yellow light surrounded the thing descending from the canopy. It drifted like the leaves it dislodged toward the center of their fire. The little orb of flickering lights dimmed, revealing what looked like a walking stick. Its sheer leaf green hands lifted in a wave. Onyx waved back. Its eyes shifted between luminous green and black. Lack of clothing or any sort revealed its sexless nature. A body like a twig and dewy leaf-green limbs.

The lights it produced had to be from magic. Onyx stared in fascination as membranous wings like a firefly's propelled it toward her. It landed on the back of Onyx's outstretched hand.

"What is this little guy?" Onyx raised her hand to get a closer look at the little creature.

"This is Bella. She's a wood sprite and our alarm."

Onyx stared, examining the sprite. "She's too little. Her voice must be as small as she is."

Cali grinned. "Don't be fooled by her size. Bella is rare. She can sense the approach of predators." She looked off into the surrounding forest. "Right now, we travel along the edge of the Darkest Forest and the Alluring. We have the Alluring's light to ward off predators."

Onyx looked away from the sprite and at Cassius,

Gryk and Joseph. "Well, what would be bloodthirsty enough to attack a pair of Orcs and a Shifter?"

"A lot," Cassius said.

"Just because we're large doesn't mean there aren't beasts in the wilds that are bold enough to test an Orc." Gryk said. "We are close to the Vampire kingdom of Taldor."

"Vampires?"

Gryk nodded grimly. "There are also nurls, night hares and the Darken."

"What are those?"

"You don't want to know," Cassius said as he leaned over to rub Joseph's knee.

Onyx eyed Joseph. He paled when Gryk mentioned nurls. His eyes darted around their little camp, inspecting every shadow.

"Joseph doesn't like nurls." Gryk planted a firm hand on his son's shoulder.

"What are they?"

"Hairless felines with five rows of teeth. They are as tall as your shoulder." He pointed at Onyx. "It's hard to see them because they can blend in with their surroundings."

"Pretty scary," Onyx said, eyes fixed on a smoldering pile of ash.

Gryk hugged Joseph to him. "I slaughtered one to save Joseph when he was a youngling."

"It's how Joseph came to be with the Wandering." Cali shifted so she could touch Joseph. She squeezed his other knee.

"He was beaten nearly to death because of his differ-ence." Cali rubbed his knee. "He was barely a teen."

Onyx scowled. "He was a kid. Who would hurt a child?"

"He's half human," Gryk said.

"So?" Onyx growled.

"It matters to Orcs." Gryk pulled Joseph so their fore-heads touched. The stiffness in Joseph eased. "Predators by nature make prey of the weak. Joseph being half human made him an outcast, making him prey among Orcs." Gryk turned his head, still touching Joseph. "Joseph was carried into the Darkest Forest, beaten and left for the predators. It just so happens, a nurl was nearby." Gryk rubbed the back of Joseph's head. "It sank a row of teeth into Joseph's skull, which was already damaged from the beating. I killed it."

"He brought Joseph to me." Cali's affection for Joseph shone in her eyes. "I was able to help him heal." Cali's hand slid from his knee.

"I'm broken but safe," Joseph whispered.

"Yes, you are safe but not broken," Gryk corrected.

Joseph buried his face in the crook of his father's neck."

You are safe," Gryk repeated.

"Safe," Joseph whispered.

"What is my promise, Joseph?"

"You'll be with me always, even when you take your final sleep. You'll watch me from the stars and whisper in my ears when I am in trouble."

Gryk smiled, wrapping is arm around his son. He leaned his head so it touched Joseph, who visibly relaxed.

"Ghosts exist in Penumbra?" Onyx's brows formed a deep V.

"Why wouldn't they? We have Shifters, Magic, Fairies of all varieties, Vampires..."

Onyx gestured for Cali to stop. "Alright. Alright. I get it. Strange things happen here."

Bella drifted away from the group and spun toward the trees. Her fluttering wings created starbursts of light, which ceased. She grabbed her stomach as she twisted toward them and screamed.

Bella's shrill cry hurt Onyx's ears; it was severed by a nurl which leapt into their camp. It swallowed Bella whole mid leap. It roared at the others the moment it touched the ground. The hairless feline fixed its amber eyes on them. Gryk shoved Joseph behind him as he took up a nearby battle-axe. Cassius half shifted into a werecat, unleashing a roar of his own. A second nurl burst from the trees a few feet away from Joseph.

Onyx watched in terror as the nurl fixated on him. It crouched and drew back its snout, displaying rows of teeth as its tail whipped behind its lean body.

Onyx resisted the hands pulling her away from the deadly standoff. She searched the array of weapons propped up beside trees or on the ground near sleeping mats. All useless.

She measured the distance between herself and Joseph, who sat frozen with his hands over his eyes. The nurl's muscles bunched up to prepare for a jump. Onyx broke free of the hands that bound her. She dashed over to the closest tree, took up one of Gryk's battle-axes and launched it at the leaping Nurl.

The battle-axe cleaved it in half. Its halves landed on either side of Joseph.

Gryk and Cassius made quick work of their nurl. Gryk dropped his battle-axe and rushed over to Joseph. Onyx moved past them, plucking the battle-axe from the earth and swinging it so the handle rested on her shoulder.

She felt everyone's eyes on her, so she turned to face them.

"You saved me," Joseph whispered.

Cassius shifted back into his human form, eyes blazing red as he moved over to the fallen nurl. Onyx noticed a flaming heap behind him that was not part of their campfire.

Cassius glanced at her, then knelt beside the nurl. He ran the tip of his claw along the nurl's breastbone. "Look at this." He motioned to Gryk, Cali and Onyx.

They all stared as marks on the nurl's chest filled with molten light. The light blackened the surrounding skin. It washed across the corpse in the blink of an eye, turning the remains to an ashen heap.

The group moved away and shared a look among them. Gryk was the first to break the silence.

"Magic."

"It was an assassin's mark." Cali's hollow voice turned their heads toward her. "The nurls were sent here."

"No one knows about this camp." Gryk waved his hand around their little clearing. "The dampening stones hide us from magic and keep all sound among us trapped within it."

"Yes, it does, but the nurls had a homing beacon."

"A what?" Onyx was all kinds of confused.

"Someone must have taken out a kill contract on us," Cali looked to Onyx, "or you." Her gaze returned to the pile of ash. "The nurl was the method of execution. But there had to be a homing beacon planted among us which led the nurls to our camp."

"Like Bella," Gryk and Cassius said in unison.

"Sadly, yes," Cali confirmed. "She must have wandered far enough away to be captured, marked, then sent home before anyone noticed."

"So, the nurls followed her scent?" Onyx asked.

Cali shook her head. "They followed the magic planted within her."

"What happens now?"

"We must speed up our plans." Cassius met Onyx's gaze.

"I'm not ready," Onyx said.

Cassius's gaze ticked up to the battle-axe before meeting her eyes. "You're ready." He pushed past her, stopping at the tree line. "I'll give you a few minutes to collect yourselves, then we talk."

Cassius shifted into his cat form and dashed into the forest.

CHAPTER 19

Penumbra
Ivy's Cottage

IVY'S ANGER HAD COOLED AFTER A BRIEF WALK THROUGH the forest. She burned off her aggression by killing night hares. Her pride was satisfied when she made them cower. One of her charms vibrated during her stroll, alerting her to the Chosen's presence. It would serve her well to know the Chosen's every move. There was too much at stake. She hurried back to her cottage.

"What do we have here?"

Ivy's thick fingers shifted, then slid deeper into the ports near the Seer's eyes, trapped in a disturbing scene. Ivy's left eye was milky-white like the Seer's. The edge of her sight was clouded by the Seer's unique magic.

Nurls tore into the girl's camp, devouring her little spy before turning on the others. She glimpsed the shimmering magic on their chests.

Both Ivy and the Seer watched as the Chosen moved, pulled away from her friends, grabbed a weapon and split one of the nurls in half. The girl moved like a seasoned warrior, swift, precise and without fear. The girl's speed troubled Ivy, but more so, the red tint of her eyes the moment she took up her weapon.

Magic revealed itself in the eyes of its vessel. Ivy had thought the girl was ordinary. She showed no signs of magic in the human world. There was something else, beyond the shimmering haze of her aura. It didn't form, at least not as she shared sight. Sharing sight allowed her access to the Seer's vision, but some details were lost in the ether of the Seer's magic.

The Seer's old master had warned her of it. Ivy didn't believe her, though her story didn't change, even when she took her life. The Seer's existence was a myth to those in the Host of the Trades. Should anyone discover the depths of her sight, it would be the end for Ivy.

She had the Seer bound to her through an Oath. The Oath granted Ivy the ability to share sight. The only way to break the bond was through Ivy's death. Ivy had no plans of dying.

Ivy shifted the Seer's sight to ascend above the place where the battle was at its end.

Where were they?

The Seer's magic banked, then glided around the clearing like a bird. It sounded like the beating of wings as it narrowed, focusing on the girl who had piqued Ivy's interest. She would be a worthy wife to Jahll. Any child she produced would be strong. A boon to their line. The only deficit was her humanity. It would taint their blood just as her royal blood would strengthen it.

"Mother!"

Ivy jerked her hands from the Seer's ports. The little human hissed, collapsed, clutching her head as she curled into a ball.

Ivy was in the basement of her cottage. The basement was where she worked magic. Correction. Borrowed magic. She conducted many experiments and had murdered quite a few humans for the sheer pleasure of it.

The floor overhead groaned under Jahll's weight. The groaning halted. He had probably noticed Mouse, who was already several shades of purple, blue and red. Ivy had bruised her, but she would heal. She always did.

Jahll knew about Mouse, at least what Ivy had told him of her. She was an orphaned human who stumbled into Penumbra through a Juncture. Trapped. Since she had no place to go, Ivy housed her. What her son didn't know was that she had an Indenture Contract. The contract bound slave to master. Like her bond to the Seer, it could only be severed in death.

Ivy wiped away the clear potion which activated the link on her shawl. Her head tilted toward the ceiling as she watched small dents form under her son's weight. Clouds of dust fell with each step, messing up her basement.

"Mother!" Jahll bellowed.

Ivy rearranged her shawl. She sprayed a spelled fragrance to hide the scent of rot which permeated her workspace. She'd grown accustomed to it, but her son would ask questions.

On Jahll's third bellow, she unlocked the spell, sealing her away from prying ears, then nullified the hex on the curtain separating the basement from upstairs. She pushed back the curtain.

Jahll stood in front of her podium, blocking it from sight.

"What!" She stormed into her living quarters, baring her teeth at him.

He curled his lip, lowering his head slightly, aiming his tusks at her and growled.

"Did you stop it?" He closed the space between them, grabbing her upper arms and dragged her until she was flush with his body. He glared down at her, waiting.

"Yes."

Jahll let her go. She stumbled backwards, regaining her feet quickly.

"Have you considered that others may want to harm her?"

Jahll's growl deepened.

Ivy moved around her son, heading for her podium. The book lay open, which meant Jahll was flipping through it as he called her. She always closed her book when she finished with it. Her slaves were too afraid of it to touch it.

She ran her hands across the pages. "What were you looking for, son?" The pages were black like the magic it detailed. She looked over her shoulder at her son.

"I need her to survive and bear me a child."

Ivy spun and faced Jahll. "Granted, a pairing between you would be ideal if the situation were different. Your younglings would fortify your legacy, but what you desire is impossible."

"It is possible."

"She must die if you are to become the new Elite."

"I know that."

"You cannot sire younglings with a corpse."

"I will be added to Ryza's line."

"But you will be the Elite. It cannot be done."

"It is what I wish, Mother."

Ivy gawked at him.

Jahll moved her out of his way, poised over the book. He tapped a claw on one spot. Ivy moved to stand beside him. Her mouth fell open as she read what he wanted.

"*Mortalis Paradox*," the words tasted bitter on her tongue. She looked askance at Jahll.

He nodded, pressing the tip of his claw into the page. "You will make this happen."

"But..."

Jahll arched a brow. "Don't tell me you have reservations in using dark magic."

Ivy narrowed her eyes at him. "Of course not."

"Make it so."

"She must die for you to gain immortality and total rule of all the Orcs."

"I know this, Mother." He looked down his nose at her. "The Mortalis Paradox will allow for her to die at my pleasure, but her body will carry my seed and produce my offspring."

"The High Spirit..."

"When do you worry about the High Spirit mother, or

the Prophet?" He gestured around his mother's home. A scroll made of human skin hung over her bed and a dead female lay in it, one of his mother's playthings. There were artifacts and books in every corner.

Jahll was aware of his mother's twisted needs and bloody habits. His mother thought she was all-knowing, but he kept his own secrets. He could read magic as well as he could read his mother. She saw him as a path to the throne. She would be a queen without the crown, or so she believed.

He watched the wheels of her devious mind turn. Her annoyance lifted the moment decision took root. She would carry out his wish because it did not obstruct her path to the throne.

Jahll graced his mother with a warm smile and a grateful embrace when she said yes. His hooded gaze hid his anger. She thought he was stupid. A proxy to be manipulated. He turned his back and headed for the door.

"Thank you, Mother," Jahll said before leaving his mother to her work. He paused outside looking into the dimming sky. The throne was close. Soon, everyone would learn his true nature.

Ivy snatched up a satchel then threw on her cloak. She yanked open the door, stepped across the threshold, then stopped.

"When I return, have my Mouse ready to travel."

"Yes, mistress," the Seer said.

"You will join me." Ivy slammed the door and was gone.

Carol, The Seer, stared at the door, wondering what mischief her mistress was up to. Whatever Ivy's plans, she would watch and listen for a way to up-end them.

CHAPTER 20

Penumbra
The Wandering

CASSIUS MOVED THEIR CAMP A LITTLE DEEPER INTO THE Darkest Forest. They managed the move in less than twenty minutes. Cali created a flameless pit which was a circle of orange glowing stones. The stones heightened or lowered the heat needed with a word. The rippling air around it was evidence of heat.

The magic surrounding their camp was on steroids. The spell work on the stones was fortified, then redistributed around the border. Cali mentioned the addition of some nasty shielding to prevent future intrusions like the nurl attack.

Onyx squinted at the darkness. She had become the sentinel of their company, patrolling its edge. Cali and Mak tried to convince her to sit. She couldn't. Not after what happened. She watched the once vibrant grass lose its color as the sun sank.

They're not going to stop. Onyx thought as she glared into the shadowed sea of trunks. Under the dim light of sunset, they resembled teeth, thick at the root, narrowing to points at the tops. Every shifting shadow was a potential assassin. Onyx ran her hand up and down the staff of the spear she'd taken up. The grooves of Orcish script beneath her fingers reminded her of the benefits of battle madness. It sharpened her sight and stripped her of doubt, making her aim true.

A mountain formed a wall at the end of the sea of trees. The darkness thickened, becoming absolute by the eighth row. Swirling mists, clicks and chittering insects taunted her. Should any of her company wander into their depths, there would be no return.

"Come eat, Chosen." Cali's presence reminded Onyx of her fragile courage. She lifted the spear and tipped it forward, loosening her grip on the shaft. She looked over her shoulder at Cali.

"I'm not hungry."

Cali made a face. "You must eat. We all have to rest so we are ready for the last leg of our journey."

"The capital. We're supposed to be there in two days."

Cali shook her head then gestured toward Cassius and Gryk who stood under a tree near the capals. Joseph was busy feeding them as Mak went around checking the packs still strapped to the animals.

"We have to get there sooner."

Onyx pointed into the darkness to the mountain. "I

don't think we can get through that riding capals. They would need wings for us to manage that."

Cali grinned. "Don't worry about the how. We will reach our goal before sunrise. We will ride toward the capital with the mountain at our backs and the sun in our faces."

"But won't the Orcs in the capital attack a group of approaching strangers?"

Cali grabbed Onyx's free hand and led her away from her post, back to the fire. Gryk and Cassius knew how to get them to the top of the mountain. "No."

"How can you be sure?" Onyx studied the woman beside her.

"The birds I sent away earlier are our messengers. They bring word of our arrival to the proper members of the Oracaii court and our allies."

Cali squeezed Onyx's hand. "Don't fret over the details of our trip. Trust us, your company, to get it done. It's our honor." Cali dragged Onyx back to the camp's fire.

Cassius rubbed the back of his neck. It didn't hurt. It was a habit when his mind was too full. Onyx patrolled their camp, searching for enemies that were not there. She carried a heavy burden. One he wished he could help her with, but the High Spirit and the Prophet would frown on his intervention. He could, as the former king's left hand, escort the Chosen to the capital, but their plan required his absence at her side.

He beat his head lightly with the edge of his fist. They

were entering a tricky leg of their journey. If any part of their plan failed, it would end them all.

Gryk squeezed his shoulder, forcing him to abandon his worries, to meet the old Orc's gaze.

"You worry for nothing." Gryk glanced at Onyx, then returned his gaze to his friend. "She is ready." He'd drawn the map in the dirt between them, a mockup of the capital. Several bold X's marked crucial parts of the capital building.

"She is not battle-trained." Though Cassius had encouraged her earlier, his confidence wilted.

"She bears the knowledge of the old kings around her neck." Gryk aimed a clawed finger at Cali and Onyx. "You saw how she handled the Nurl. The battle-axe!" Gryk waved his arms around his head. "She is stronger than we think. A normal human can't lift an Orc axe, not even the bloated ones they call body builders."

"He promised she would be safe," Cassius mumbled to himself.

"She is safe," Gryk said with conviction.

"But he never showed me how the Knowledge Stone works. If he did, I could show her. Offer her an advantage."

"I know little about the stone except it shares its knowledge with its Chosen." Gryk swung his stick toward the mountaintop in the distance.

"What if she doesn't figure out how to use it?" Cassius laced his hands together on top of his head and paced, mindful of the map.

"We must trust the will of the High Spirit."

"I know." He stopped abruptly, unlacing his hands to

wrap them around himself. "I wonder about the magic of the stone." He looked off into the darkness. "I don't smell magic." He blew out a frustrated breath and shrugged. "I never smelled magic when Ryza was wearing it." He looked at his friend. "It makes me anxious."

"Your problem is you are Orcish in your thinking. The Knowledge Stone isn't about magic. It's about blood. It's about birthright."

"We have weapons and a plan." Cassius scanned the array of packs strapped to the capals. "Will it be enough?"

"We'll make sure of it." A sly look bloomed. Gryk bared his teeth. "The flowers in your blood is our way across the mountain and will lead us to victory."

"What does an insult have to do with this?"

Gryk pointed at Cassius's ears and repeated the phrase, flowers in the blood. Understanding dawned. He was not only the king's left hand, but the bastard son of the Elf kingdom of Myleiu and Shifter Kingdom of Oakheart. His father, an elven general and his mother a cat-Shifter. Cassius possessed fae magic, though he hated using it. Like Onyx, it was his birthright. He preferred living as a Shifter in honor of his mother, but he knew magic and could wield it, though untrained. It was instinctual and shifted to meet his needs. Cassius didn't know if it was the mix of Shifter and Elven blood that caused his magic to work how it did. He gazed at the mountaintop and the vivid moon lingering inches away from its peak.

As left hand to the king, he was a spy, a guard and he had the honor of being a friend. None of the Orcs knew him outside of his cat form. A deeper appreciation for

Gryk settled in his heart. He would use his magic and spy for her. Find the Orcs behind the assassination attempts. If opportunity presented itself, he would eliminate them, as he had done her childhood assassins. It was his pleasure to murder all of them, feeding terror into them as he stalked each one. He took them in sets of two or three. He ended them all and made himself a nightmare to the others. It kept Nancy and those she cared for in the Center safe, which included Onyx.

A queen's hands were always dipped in blood. It was his pleasure to spill it on her behalf. Onyx would have the crown if he had to slaughter every official in the high court to make it so.

CHAPTER 21

THE BOOM OF JAHLL'S FIST CRASHING DOWN ON THE balcony railing startled those passing underneath. They froze; several dropped whatever they were holding to cover their heads. The cries of children blossomed, followed by cooing mothers and the slow restoration of movement, as neighbors gathered what had fallen, at least the salvageable bits.

Jahll stepped back, removing himself from their sight. His hands slid from the railing as he righted himself then descended into his sleeping chambers. Taqual would bring news soon of his bride's arrival. She was due by next sunset. After that, he would wed her and lock himself in Ryza's line. He would be of royal blood, one way or another. His mother would make sure of it.

"Sire."

Jahll's head jerked in the direction of the voice. It came from the other side of the thick door bearing the crest of Ryza. He moved to the king's chair, which sat in an angle to the door. Ryza himself designed it. The armrests had levers underneath. With the flick of a finger, daggers were readily available. Other such devices were built into the bed, the closet, the chest and places he had yet to discover. What he did know, he learned from an inebriated advisor. The placement of the king's chair was also Ryza's design. Its angle gave him a warning of intruders, allowing him to gather weapons and cover. The chair itself was forged of the same steel as Orc shields.

Jahll looked around the room at all the seemingly plain furniture and wondered what was beneath. He'd only gained entrance to the royal quarters in the last seven days, since the presence of an heir seemed impossible.

"Sire, are you in your quarters?" Taqual's gruff call redirected Jahll's curiosity.

Jahll adjusted his posture before speaking. "You may enter."

Taqual entered the room executing a military pivot which ended in a bow befitting a king. Jahll was pleased but troubled by Taqual's scowl. Jahll watched the other Orc, fingers sliding to the levers on the underside of the king's chair and waited for him to speak.

"Sire, I bring news of the Chosen."

Jahll straightened, his fingers still near the switches. "Speak."

"The Chosen was attacked."

Jahll felt anger rise like venom. It pooled on the tip of his tongue, which he held. His grip on the armrests distressed the wood. He eased his grip but kept his fingers near the switches.

"Explain."

Taqual kept his eyes on the floor, raising his voice enough so Jahll could hear. "A pair of Nurls attacked her camp."

Jahll rose with a blade in each hand. If the next words were not to his liking, Taqual's head would connect with the floor.

"Her mother watches over the Chosen. She sent word that the Chosen and her company made short work of them." Taqual held his hands up in submission, lowering his head.

Jahll slammed a dagger into the floor. It sank nearly to the hilt. "When?" Jahll closed the space between them, setting the tip of the blade at the crown of Taqual's head. Blood bloomed and began a slow cascade down his scalp to his forehead. It lingered along his brow then dripped off the tip of his nose.

Jahll replaced the blade buried in the floor with his own short blade. It was poised to take off Taqual's head should he wish it.

"Today. I don't know when, but near sunset."

Jahll snatched the blade from Taqual's scalp. He stalked to the other side of the room, sheathing his short sword but still gripped the curved handle. He banged his fists against the wall, it cracked from the blows, as he roared.

The rapid cadence of the guards filled the hall. Jahll

roared louder, turning away from the wall, to face the door which was still open. The guards lingered at the threshold, weapons half raised, as the captain leaned in for a look.

"Away!"

The guards lowered their weapons, acknowledged Jahll in salute, then vanished from sight.

Jahll stalked over to a still kneeling Taqual. He towered over him, fists curled, hot breath streaming from his nose. His lips peeled back from his teeth. "Did she survive?"

"Yes, sire."

The muscles in his neck and arms relaxed, drawing his shoulders down and his fists uncurled. He took a few steps back then grunted. Taqual was slow in lifting his eyes to him, but Jahll reassured him when he offered his hand.

Taqual took it and was pulled to his feet. Jahll released the other Orc. His chest was filled to near bursting with heat of rage, making it hard for him to breathe, so he moved to the balcony. He leaned on the railing, his forearms sliding over them, hands limp. He rested his chin on his left bicep and watched the Commons go about their lives in the streets below. He lifted his eyes toward the sky, the sun was setting. The birds were beginning their migration back to their roosts, except for one. A white bird. It flew leisurely across the market, settling on a canopy below.

Jahll turned as Taqual approached. "How did you know about the attack?"

"Spies." Taqual stopped at the top step, there were only five that led to the balcony.

"Why didn't your spies intervene?"

"Sire, I didn't know they were supposed to."

Jahll growled, head angled down, as his neck stiffened. His tusks aimed at Taqual. "She is to survive her journey." He beat his chest. "She will come to me."

Taqual's confusion showed. "It is not my place to ask why."

"No, it isn't," his words were guttural.

Taqual ducked his head so Jahll couldn't see his frustration. He drew his hand across his chest, a salute to his future king, but a reminder of his deed. Underneath the arm plate burned a secret. One he could not hide for long. One that would get him killed if Jahll were to discover it, or that witch mother of his. Taqual backed away from Jahll just as a white bird landed on the balcony railing.

A little white bird with purple and gray plumes looked up at Jahll. Around its neck was a messenger tube. He held out his hand. The bird hopped on it without fear. It blinked several times before tilting its head to allow him access to the twine. Jahll removed the odd necklace from the bird, which took to the air the moment it was relieved of its burden.

Jahll popped the top of the tube with a gentle squeeze then shook it until a scroll slid into his waiting palm. He used the tip of his claw to nudge it open.

Jahll,

As second to Ryza the Black, it is your honor to receive the queen's company. We will arrive at the capital by tomorrow's sunset. Please have the proper envoy to escort us from the gates to our rooms in the palace.

The Queen's Lady

Jahll crushed the message in his fist, his eyes shifted to the main gate. The guards' silhouettes moved about. His gaze drifted to the bruised horizon and the tiny white dot in the distance. His heart was heavy, but hope kept it from going to a dark place. Tomorrow he would get the answers he sought. If they weren't to his liking, he had a plan for that.

Mortalis Paradox. Carol had heard it whispered in the darkest corners of the Host of the Trades. It was a spell those in the Trade were reluctant to use. To verbally ask about it could easily earn the caster and the purchaser a visit from the Shades.

The Mortalis Paradox was a type of necromancy, dark fae magic. The spell bound the victim to their host, which allowed the host to use the victim however he or she pleased. The Mortalis Paradox could resurrect the victim to near full life. Its magic hid the victim from the eyes of the Prophet and the High Spirit, yet alive enough to reproduce. For the spell to work, the caster would need to get their target to drink the potion or turn it to powder, in which a single puff of air would do the job.

Ivy left the cottage in a hurry, which meant Jahll left no room for her to disobey. Both mother and son were mad, twisted things, Carol thought. Ivy despised the males of her kind. She barely tolerated the females. She ranted about it from time to time. Carol deduced Ivy was rejected by both sexes, so she chose creatures that were not of her kind to harass.

There was no such thing as love in Ivy's chest. Carol didn't believe Ivy possessed a heart, so she imagined a barren, black spot with ghostly echoes of a heartbeat. She cared for her son, but that was because of how he could elevate her in Orc society. She tolerated him.

Mouse groaned in her sleep. Carol ran tender fingers along her swollen jaw. Ivy loved to torture Willow. She did terrible things to her for the sounds of terror and eventual catatonia they provoked in Willow. It was strange, the moment Willow succumbed to catatonia; it frightened Ivy. She feared breaking Willow completely. Carol didn't understand why.

Ivy was a sadist to her core. Carol was her Mouse before Willow arrived. Only Carol shut herself down when the torture started. She left her body. Her mind closed itself to pain. There were several times she nearly died, but when Ivy discovered Carol's talents, the torture stopped. She was treated better. Ivy left her alone, gave her freedoms. After the upgrades, Ivy gave her even more freedom. Freedom allowed Carol time to think. It gave her magic time to connect with her. Though she was no longer on her native soil, magic still found her.

Carol used to believe magic came with the moon. Since her time in Penumbra, she now understood that magic was about the blood. She held up her free arm, turning it around in the shadows, as small delicate glyphs shimmered beside a pair of tiny white wings. The light was coming from her blood, not the skin. She discovered that too when she witnessed Ivy's many attempts at harnessing magic for herself. She bled human witches, stored it in jars and vials in her downstairs workshop and would drink it. Once the blood settled inside her she would recite incantations. Sometimes they worked. Sometimes they didn't.

When Ivy allowed Carol the freedom of not only movement but mind, she discovered a lot of things about herself and what she could do.

She looked down on the battered younger woman and vowed she would set her free. Only in freedom would Willow find herself, find her power. Right now, the girl squirmed in the throes of a nightmare. The writhing ceased when Carol dragged her index finger across her face. She did this three times; on the fourth, she drew glyphs. Each one set to quell the nightmares so Willow could sleep.

A peal of tiny bells drew her from her dark place, setting her eyes searching for the source. A fluffy white bird with purple and gray plumes was perched on the middle finger of the dead girl. It cocked its head, blinked, then flew over to Carol. It landed on the curve of her knee.

It bore a little twine necklace with a messenger tube. The little bird tilted its head, making it easy for her to remove its little collar. It lingered on her knee, as she removed the scroll and read it. She closed her hand around it and pressed it to her chest. The little bird flew away.

Carol looked down at Mouse, blinking away her tears. "Your friend is on her way," she whispered as she stared at a small tattoo at the center of her wrist: a pair of stylized wings with an eye in the center. A secret shared between the only friend she had among Ivy's slaves. The only slave to escape Ivy's hold. The tattoo was a promise that help would come to free not only Carol, but the others.

She stroked Willow's matted hair absently as her gaze returned to the window. Help was coming.

Three white birds with purple and gray plumes soared along the diving line of the horizon, where Penumbra's mountains and the sky met. The first banked right, gliding upward as the others followed. The triad formed a single line and one by one they burst into glittering white dust.

CHAPTER 22

Penumbra
The Wandering

A STRANGE TRILLING PULLED ONYX FROM HER FITFUL slumber. Despite her earlier denial, she was exhausted. As soon as her head touched her pillow, she was asleep. She blinked her way into consciousness as she focused on the strange sound. The trilling shifted into a mournful, howling wind. She rolled onto her stomach, coming face to face with moccasin-clad feet. She looked up to Joseph's smiling face. He wiggled his fingers in a wave, then offered her a hand. She grinned, raised her arms and was lifted up.

Joseph set her gently on her feet, releasing her immediately, which was new for him. He liked to touch her, not in a pervy way, but in his Joseph way. A hand on her shoulder or a touch on the knee. He would encourage her to touch him. She'd learned through observation that certain people's touch brought him comfort.

A sphere of light rotated behind him. Familiar silhouettes stood in front of it.

"What's that?"

"Cassius."

Onyx gazed into his soft blue eyes, noticing his braid had been redone. The ribbons were one color, royal blue, which was more masculine. Maybe it was their way of keeping him safe while maintaining his beauty.

Her mouth ticked up as Joseph swung his arms and looked around. He caught her staring and he blushed.

She rested a hand on his bicep. His gaze met hers.

"What's wrong, Joseph?"

"Nothing." He pulled away, but Onyx gripped his arm. He stopped but didn't look at her.

"What's wrong, Joseph?" She squeezed his arm gently. "Truth."

"I'm scared." It was barely a whisper.

Onyx laid her head on his chest, then pat his arm. "We're all scared, Joseph."

"I don't want to be by myself again."

"You're not by yourself." Onyx leaned back so she could look into his face. "You have your Papa, Cassius, Cali and the girls who do your beautiful braids."

He dropped his head, chin pressing on his chest as he rocked. He shook his head slowly. "No Papa. No Cassius. No friends. No pretty braids."

"Joseph, you have all those things. None of that is going to change."

"If you leave, it will."

Onyx opened her mouth, but her voice failed her.

"I'm scared." His eyes desperate as he searched her face. "If you leave, the Wandering become no one's people." He averted his gaze, fixating on the trees behind Onyx. "We become nothing." His last word had a morbid finality.

Onyx squeezed his arms. "But you're strong, Joseph. You, your father and Cassius can keep everyone safe."

Joseph shook his head vigorously. "No." The word popped like a gunshot in the quiet clearing. His gentle gaze hardened when he it settled on her again. "Your papa kept us safe. He made us his people." Spittle flew from his mouth, from the force of his words. "He made us his people, like Papa made me his son." He beat his chest, eyes watering, as the fire of his frustration waned.

"Please stay. I want to be your people." His hands broke apart, falling limply to his sides. "I love the Wandering." He tapped his chest. "They're my family." He looked lost. "I don't want them hurt."

"Joseph, look, I..."

"Hey!" Cassius bellowed. "You two comin'?"

Joseph flushed; eyes cast to the ground. "Sorry. Sorry. Can't be late."

"Joseph," Onyx began, but Joseph pulled away.

He did an about-face before throwing over his shoulder, "We have to leave now." He trotted over to the camp, leaving her behind.

Onyx stared at Joseph as he trotted over to the others. She wanted to tell him she wasn't going anywhere. She lifted the hand with the Challenge Mark, noticing it claimed more of her arm. She let it fall before jogging over to the huge swirling light. The trilling seemed to resonate around its edges. She peeked inside. It differed from the psychedelic portal from before. It was total darkness, dulled by a sickly green light. The floor of the portal was a glistening black, similar to glass. Cassius stood with his hand raised, palm open, near the edge of the sphere. The sigils on his chest glowed brightly.

She looked around at the others, each mounted on their capals.

"Where's my ride?" Onyx asked Cassius.

He hit her with his perviest grin, then shifted into a Maine Coon cat.

Onyx arched a brow, her hands defaulting to her hips. "Really? You're too small to carry all of this."

Cassius roared. Spindles of green light danced around his body, which grew until it was the same size as the surrounding capals. He bowed, pressing his forelegs forward, his claws peeking from their sheaths. He arched his hindquarters in the air. Onyx got the message and hopped on. Cassius righted himself, careful not to dislodge her. His tail swished behind him as Gryk entered the portal first, drawing his battle-axe as he did so. Cali was next, followed by Mak, then Joseph. Cassius entered last, roaring once they were in. The trilling intensified along with the light. Onyx clutched Cassius's fur as a wave of vertigo swept through her as the light behind them died. A small dot appeared a few feet ahead of Gryk, who swung his capal toward it. The others did the same.

The light joined the trilling. Trilling shaped the dot into a sphere which grew big. As soon as it was big enough, Gryk rode his capal through the trilling sphere and the others followed. Cassius and Onyx were the last to exit. Like before, Cassius roared upon exit. The vertigo Onyx felt before vanished with the portal. She inhaled the fresh air, catching hints of spices. Another deep inhale introduced the scent of seasoned pork. She turned her head, following the smells.

In the distance stood an ivory castle; within its walls was a black palace. Onyx looked behind them. The tips of trees poked through gray mists. Flickering lights moved underneath. She swung her gaze back to the castle.

"That is Oracaii," Cali said as she dismounted. The others did the same. She noticed Joseph stuck by his father's side, which was far away from her.

She slid from Cassius's back and he shifted back to his human form.

Onyx wandered over to the edge of the mountain. There was a simple trail leading from their spot safely to the mountain's base. She looked around at the trees. They were tall enough to keep their presence hidden but gave them a clear visual of the open plain between the mountain and the capital.

"How are we going to make it to the capital without being seen?"

Cali came up beside her. "Our objective is to be seen."

The trilling started up again. Both women faced the growing portal. A small, child-like being stepped out of it with handheld high, sigils blazing bright in her palm. A long white braid danced in the air of her magic. Behind her, a black capal emerged beside a colossal figure covered in a black hooded cloak. The portal trilled but did not close as the girl moved to stand beside it, as the capal and the cloaked figure approached the group.

Gryk and Cassius inclined their heads when the cloaked figure stopped. The capal looked around at the collection of people, its dark eyes settling on Onyx. It made a strange braying sound as it pulled at its reins. The cloaked figure released them. The capal trotted past the others and came to a stop in front of Onyx. It offered its head, which she scratched.

The cloaked figure pulled back his hood. A senior Orc, with hair as white as a cloud, stared in awe.

"It knows her," the senior Orc's awed whisper resonated among them.

"Of course, she is Ryza's offspring." Cassius watched the black capal bray excitedly as Onyx continued to scratch a spot between its horns and ears.

"Akyr." Gryk joined Cassius and the historian.

Akyr stared at Onyx and the Capal. She turned toward them when she felt their gaze. The capal rested its chin on her head as she erupted in giggles.

"Mosnat!" She managed between giggles. "Mosnat, cut it out."

Akyr, Cassius and Gryk gaped.

"How does she know..." Akyr moved toward the pair. He joined them, capturing Mosnat's reins and scratched his chin. Mosnat stretched his neck so Akyr could reach more of his sweet spot. He grunted his pleasure, basking in the attention.

Onyx glanced at the elder Orc without missing a beat as she continued to lavish affection on the black capal.

"How did you know his name?"

Onyx's hands froze. She stared at the capal then shrugged. "He looks like a Midnight, so Mosnat seemed appropriate."

Mosnat butted Onyx with his nose. She resumed rubbing his snout before slipping her hands under his chin.

Akyr watched the pair, noting that red gleam beneath her odd tunic.

"My Chosen," Akyr inclined his head. "It is an honor to meet you."

Onyx stopped loving up on the capal and acknowledged the elder Orc in kind.

Akyr laid his hand over his heart. "I am Akyr, royal historian. If you need anything, summon me and I will come." He bowed his head, his joy apparent as he passed the reins to her. "Mosnat is now your capal."

Mosnat raised his head at the sound of his name. Akyr lay a hand on Mosnat's snout. "Serve your new master well."

Mosnat grunted, then bobbed his head, which pleased the elder Orc.

Akyr gave one final bow before returning to the portal. He paused beside Gryk.

"All is ready. I will wait on the steps among the greeters." He and Gryk clasped each other's forearm. "May the High Spirit bless your purpose."

"May it be so with you," Gryk replied.

Akyr pulled up his hood and stepped into the portal, followed by the little white-haired female. The portal vanished behind the pair, leaving Onyx and her company staring after it.

Cali went over to Onyx and her new capal. She stroked Mosnat's snout. "We need to prepare for sunrise." Both women stared at the pitch-black sky. "I will join Cassius and Gryk to discuss our plans." Cali took up the reins and aimed them at Onyx. "You will retire to your tent." She jerked her chin at a dark gray tent several feet away. Two sleeping pads lay on either side of the flap. "There you will find your clothes for the morning and your weapons."

"I don't..."

Cali shook her head sharply. "No time for disputes. Your gear is inside, along with fresh water and some fruit. Sleep if you can." Cali returned the reins, squeezing her hand. "I will share all you need to know at the appropriate time."

"Shouldn't I be in on the plans?"

"No. A queen doesn't need to know what her right and left hand are doing. All she needs to know is that they move in her favor."

Cali did an about-face, leaving Onyx with her new mount and a thousand questions.

CHAPTER 23

Penumbra
Oracaii

THE RHYTHMIC CADENCE OF JAHLL'S GUARD WAS A SONG IN the barren palace halls. There were twelve in his company. All dressed in their royal blacks. Weapons slapped against muscle as they jogged down the main steps into the small courtyard. The second line of rear guards fanned out to form a half circle around him. Should someone strike, his guard would close the opening with their bodies while the others attacked.

Jahll and his company flowed through the narrow streets of the market toward the main gates. All the Commons were restricted to the windows and rooftops of their abodes. Only royals were allowed in the streets today, a proper welcome for his future mate. Jahll lingered behind his guard, preferring anonymity as he previewed the Chosen. He wondered if she was more Orc than human. Was she scrawny like the humans his mother kept? He would get the answers to his questions before facing her. It would spare him the shameful display of emotion in front of the others. A king is stone. A king is law.

A horn sounded. Three long blasts followed by two short ones. Clanking chains and the grunts of the Orcs pulling them disturbed the silence. The sluggish gates opened, revealing the glare of the morning sun. Its light blotted out everything except a trio of silhouettes.

Ryza's bull capal, Mosnat, brayed as it stepped out of the glare. The light receded as he pressed forward at his rider's prompting. The Chosen sat, back rigid, head high in Mosnat's saddle. She was a small Orc and dressed in armor unlike any he'd ever seen. She donned a midnight-black form-fitting tunic that covered her neck and arms, a black metal breast plate with her father's mark over her heart. Around her neck lay the Knowledge Stone. Sunlight amplified its brilliance.

As her company drew closer, Jahll noticed her tusks were lacquered in black. Silver chains hung from each tusk, ending at the ear. Black braids flared like outstretched wings in the squall of wind; silver beads clapped together like chimes. Her claws were the same smooth lacquered black as her tusks. Her feet were covered in thick-soled black boots made from animal hide. As she rode past, a flash of red caught his eye as she adjusted her grip on Mosnat's reins. The intricate lines of a Challenge Mark were etched on the back of her left hand. It disappeared into her sleeve. How far along was it and who issued the challenge?

He growled as he considered the Chosen's companions through narrowed eyes. To her right was Gryk the hammer astride his capal, Dagalush, or Imp, in Orc tongue, dressed in blood red armor. He also bore the mark of Ryza over his heart. Twin battle-axes arched like grim wings at his back. His sword, *Kafsog*, rested in a scabbard strapped to Dagalush's saddle. A little wooden flower danced on a cord tied to *Kafsog's* pommel. The third member of the Chosen's party rode to her left. A pale, willowy female dressed in white linen breeches with a blood-red synched outer corset over a beige blouse. It was her right arm which fascinated Jahll. A black witch-marked metal arm flowed from the sleeve of her blouse, a stark contrast to her natural pale limb. He wondered if it functioned like a normal limb.

His lips curled at the prospect of testing it. He raised his fist and gestured for his company to double back. Jahll spotted a hooded Orc slinking along the inner walls near the gate as he was about to fall in step with his guards. The Orc had blunted tusks. He wore a hooded cloak with its hood down. A brilliant flaxen braid swung like a rope at the Orc's back. Jahll would address the trespasser later. He shrank into the shadows to join his company, missing a second intruder's entry.

Inside the capital were vacant streets covered in black sand lined with stark white skulls. A foot or so behind those skulls stood soldiers, a wall of muscular chests and nipple piercings complementing their partial armor.

Onyx glanced at the buildings behind the wall of soldiers. Apartments, painted slate gray, bone white and deep blue rose six stories above the tallest Orc. The Orcs inside them were not as fearsome as the soldiers as they leaned from the windows of their apartments. They wore plain clothes: tunics, basic dresses, with little to no piercings. No one said a word, but their looks spoke volumes. She was an aberration and a miracle.

Gryk cleared his throat, which meant her head had turned away from the path. She corrected her mistake as she adjusted her grip on Masnat's horns and arched her chin. Her helm gave her the look of an Orc, with its gleaming tusks and faux piercings. Jingling chains and tinkling braids were her banner as Mosnat's stature set her above the tallest Orcs. Yet her heart beat faster than a rabbit's. Anxiety obstructed her airways when she swallowed.

Remember, slaves don't make war. Queens do. Chin up, my Queen. Cassius flicked his tail. He lay across Mosnat's saddle making him invisible to onlookers. He rose and made his way to the top of Mosnat's head where he sat, chest out, looking down his feline nose at every Orc they passed. Awed whispers erupted among the Commons and the officials. Cassius stiffened his spine, striking a regal pose as they rounded the corner and entered the courtyard.

Mosnat slowed as they neared the palace steps. An assembly of Orcs dressed in finery lined them. They parted as a group of soldiers pushed through. A formation of four sets of three soldiers filed down the stairs and fanned out as an Orc in a hooded black robe separated from the mass. He stopped several feet in front of the assembly. Mosnat halted and snorted at the Orc, who pulled back his hood.

Onyx pushed back her helm and looked down her nose at the Orc with the pink left eye. A streak of white hair in a braid fell across his shoulder. The rest of his hair was loose and dull black.

"Welcome to Oracaii." He did not bow but bared his teeth.

Onyx learned by observing Gryk that the bearing of teeth without dropping his head and aiming his tusks at her was a smile. She did not return it. A flicker of something ugly rose in those eyes. In a blink, it was gone.

A hollow buzz sounded to her left. Cali caught an arrow mid-flight in her metal hand and threw a blade with her right. All within seconds of raising her shield and drawing her blade. Gryk's battle-axes were in his hands and Cassius hissed in the odd-colored Orc's face.

Onyx didn't move a muscle. *Trust my company.* It's what she promised. It's what her father told her to do.

The oddly colored Orc seemed satisfied. He bowed, offering his name upon rising. "I am Jahll, Lord of Oracaii and Ryza's second. Welcome."

"Oracaii has no Lord," Onyx stated. "An elfson like you brings shame to my father." Onyx slid from Mosnat, lingering at her saddle.

Jahll snarled, but it was cut short. Onyx made a show of casually turning to investigate the sudden silence. Cali balanced on the snout of her capal with her sword at Jahll's neck. Gryk had one of Jahll's guards underfoot and the edge of both his blades at the necks of two others.

"She is right," an aged voice cracked the silence like thunder. A rumbling of agreement joined Akyr, who stepped forward. Several senior guards followed. Akyr stopped a few feet away from them. "Only a no-sack would dare an assassination of the Chosen instead of facing her in the arena!" Akyr spit his words at Jahll's back before turning his ire on the crowd.

"Do you fear a woman?" Akyr snorted, pushing hot air from his nostrils. He bared his teeth, angling his head, tusks positioned for a fight. He jerked his arm at the surrounding soldiers, then aimed a claw at Jahll. Neither Gryk nor Cali withdrew their weapons. "Are you such pussies that you would attempt a kill in secret? Assassination by the limp hand. None of you are Orc enough to stand in the arena with the daughter of Ryza the Black."

Onyx noticed the light of interest rise in the eyes of onlookers. She kept her eye on Jahll, his eyes fixed on the ground. He hadn't moved a muscle, but it didn't mean it cowed him. There was a tremor, barely noticeable, in his arms. She didn't miss the flexing of his hands, or the droplets of blood splashing on the ground.

Akyr waved the red flag in front of the bulls. So far, no one took the bait and attacked. Maybe there was honor among beasts. Onyx flexed the hand bearing the Challenge Mark, then thrust it up for Jahll to see.

"I'm assuming you did this."

Cali and Gryk lowered their weapons but did not sheath them.

Jahll scanned the Orcs within his line of sight before leveling his gaze with Onyx's. The sleeves of his robes covered his hands. "Yes," he lied.

"You aim to kill me." Onyx folded her arms across her chest, fixing Jahll with an unimpressed look. "I don't plan on dying." She scanned the assembly behind Jahll.

"Can someone take care of Mosnat and take me to my quarters?" She gave her capal a scratch along his jaw before brushing pass Jahll. Cassius hopped off Mosnat and trotted behind her with both his tail and head held high. Onyx paused when her foot settled on the palace steps. She looked back at Jahll. "I'm done here." She faced forward and jogged up the last of the steps.

A white Orcess met her before she reached the palace entrance. She wore a thin shawl which did not hide the ornate assortment of necklaces. The Orcess donned a pure white cloak. Thin bangles beat against each other, setting off a fragile chime. She wore no rings, but there was a fine line of tattoos along her wrists blurred in the clutter of bangles.

A pair of petite children dressed in rags shadowed the Orcess. Onyx couldn't tell if the children were male or female. Both were painfully thin. Their matted hair hung in matted ropes. The frayed ends of their tunics were black from dirt. Their feet were bare and caked in dried mud.

The Orcess did a half curtsy. The children mimicked the move. "If it pleases you." The Orcess pressed her hand to cover her heart. "I will escort you to your rooms." She waved her arms toward the children. The smallest of them flinched when the Orcess swung her arms toward them. For a second, the Orcess's magnanimous mask cracked. In the blink of an eye, it was back in place.

Cali stepped forward. "And you are?"

"I am Ivy." She did another half curtsy.

"It pleases the Chosen and her company." Cali sheathed her sword. Ivy couldn't hide her fascination with Cali's metal arm, specifically the witch marks. She used her normal hand to gesture for Ivy to lead the way.

Ivy did an about face and began their journey to the sleeping quarters. She stopped in the foyer when she noticed Gryk joined them.

"He cannot share quarters with you," Ivy huffed.

"Do not act as if you don't know me, Ivy. I lived in this palace." He gestured at the grand halls and its high ceilings. "I know these halls." There were three corridors on either side of them. "I will deliver them to their quarters." Gryk adjusted the packs he pulled from their capals. He slung a pack across his left and right shoulder. The third pack hung awkwardly from the crook of his arm. He adjusted them before heading for the right corridor. Cali and Onyx followed. "I know the way."

Ivy watched the trio through narrowed eyes as the trio disappeared down the corridor. She tapped her girls, who raced to catch up with them. They knew what to do.

The crowd felt like needles being shoved into his skin as Joseph pushed through the crowd. A hiss buzzed in his ear like a fly. He swatted his ear hoping it would stop when something tugged at his cloak. He stopped.

"Lift your hood!" Mak whisper shouted.

Joseph did so instantly, ashamed of the oversight. He was so intent on getting inside, following the plan to help the others, he forgot the simplest of the instructions. *Let no one see you.*

His job was to memorize the layout of the capital, every street, alley and any hidden passageway he stumbled across. Joseph could do that easily. He might be broken but his memory was the best part of him. He never forgot a trail. He never got lost. He couldn't do his job if he got caught.

Joseph muttered an apology, falling back so Mak could take the lead.

He didn't like Oracaii. The last time he was here, Jahll and his friends had nearly killed him.

CHAPTER 24

CASSIUS PADDED THROUGH THE HALLS OF THE PALACE TO the king's room. The interior was unchanged. Statues of the old kings lined the halls; beside each king's statue was his favorite weapon, encased in unbreakable glass. The floors were plain. The only color to them were rectangular carpets gifted by the fae to Ryza after the peace treaty. Sandalwood incense burned, Ryza's favorite scent. It would burn until morning, to be replaced by the new ruler's scent or removed.

Muffled voices rumbled behind the black door. He rubbed his feline body against the thick wood, leaving a little of his fur behind.

He walked away from the it, spun three times, then sat on his haunches. The tip of his tail swished left, right, then stopped. It curled up when he meowed. The hairs he left on the door shimmered as his magic flowed through them, amplifying the voices inside. Ivy and her son were in a heated discussion over Onyx's arrival.

Not surprising.

He and Gryk briefed Onyx on Orc etiquette, which translated to her tapping into her inner bitch. She treated Jahll like the dick he was. She gave him her back, ignored his posturing, flexed her muscles and showed her authority. Jahll could have struck but Gryk would have killed him. Law and pride locked Jahll in place. He accepted the shame, but vengeance was a serpent that hid in the grass. Jahll would strike. It would be sudden and vicious. Cassius's role was to expect the strike, glean knowledge, read the careless conversations and deliver what he learned to the others.

"She made a fool of you!" Ivy hissed.

Cassius twitched his ears.

"Let her believe I am simple." Jahll was unphased by his mother's barb. "She's Ryza's daughter. I would expect nothing less."

"The others…"

"The others will know soon enough what I am capable of." Jahll paced. "As for the girl, her fight means sturdy sons. It adds pleasure in breaking her."

Ivy mumbled something profane. Jahll snarled and the floor rumbled.

"I know you think me a fool."

The chill of Jahll's words penetrated the thick wood and crawled down Cassius's spine. He'd lived an exceptionally long life among Orcs. He understood what they were capable of. Add in madness and a slaughter was inevitable.

"Did you bring what I asked for?" Jahll moved around inside, the floor a thunderous reverberation with each step. The smack of flesh and the clink of glass against claw told Cassius Jahll's request was fulfilled.

"That's the first half."

"Mother!" Jahll growled.

"Patience! The spell is in two parts. The first you will deliver by coating your weapons with what's in the vial," Ivy said.

"What of the second?" Jahll pressed.

"I still need to finish it."

A loud boom shook the door on its hinges.

"The Rising challenge is tonight."

"And won't it look suspicious if you pour a potion down her dead throat in the middle of the arena?"

"I would do no such thing."

"The deed must be done away from the eyes of the council and the battle called in your favor before you make a move to complete the spell." The rough soles of Ivy's feet scraped against the floor as she moved about.

"I'm not a fool, Mother."

Ivy grunted her disbelief as endless bangles clinked together. "I have planned for the girl's corpse to be delivered to my cottage, where I will wait for you with the last portion of the spell."

"Good."

"Remember."

"I know. I know. Every spell has its cracks."

"Magic doesn't always yield to its caster."

A bestial chuckle devoured the quiet. "She is half human, mother. Humans are weak." Silence lingered for a few seconds. "All that belonged to Ryza will be mine. She will be mine." The chuckle returned. "My pet."

"You cannot toy with her or entertain second thoughts. She must die," Ivy said, a flurry of chimes and the swish of fabric punctuated her words. "The spell must be completed before sunrise."

"Don't worry, Mother. I know what to do."

Footsteps in a military cadence sent Cassius scurrying under a nearby statue of an old king off to the right of the room. The marching ceased inches from the door. The bickering inside quieted as a brave soul requested entry.

Jahll pulled the massive doors open. His body filled the entry, barring their entry.

Cassius pressed his body to the floor and crawled forward. He stopped at within the reach of shadow, eyes hooded as he watched the Orcs. There were four. All bowed as if Jahll were already king.

"I need you to retrieve a few things for me." Jahll plucked a folded piece of paper from the waistband of his breeches. The lead soldier stepped forward and took it. He unfolded it, scanned the contents, then passed it to the others.

"We will find this blond Orc," the lead solider said as the others saluted Jahll.

"I need him delivered to my quarters before sunset."

The soldiers bowed, then did an about-face and headed down the hall. Cassius turned away from Jahll, who disappeared into the room again. Slinking within the shadow of the statue, Cassius watched the soldiers until they turned the corner. A sensation, like a hand not quite touching the skin, tightened his muscles and he prepared to run. Before he could move, everything went dark, then he was hoisted into the air.

He hissed and mewled as he unleashed his claws on the interior of the bag. Fine slivers of light flared after each passing of his claws. The cuts disappeared, mended by the receding light.

"Jahll will be pleased with this," Cassius heard his captor say, as Orcish laughter accompanied a sudden rise. "You will help him ascend to the throne." The Orc thumped the bag. Cassius hissed and swatted at the spot the Orc thumped. The Orc laughed even harder, swinging the bag as he carried Cassius to his fate.

Jahll and Ivy were whispering furiously when Taqual returned. He waited in the doorway with a writhing bag. The furious whispering stopped once Ivy caught sight of him.

"What is that?" She approached him slowly. Jahll flanked her.

Taqual hoisted the writhing bag higher.

"Ryza's pet." Taqual bared his teeth, pleased with his offering. He thumped the bag again, chuckled as the fresh round of hissing and twisting resumed. He passed the bag to Jahll.

Jahll took the bag from Taqual, whose smile faltered. Taqual expected joy or even relief to be clear in Jahll. Instead, there was something else. Something cold. Jahll handed the bag to his mother before turning his attention back to Taqual. The iciness had vanished. In its place, determination.

All things considered, Jahll had endured much since Ryza's fading. The girl had shamed him before the assembly. She possessed the totems of kinship, authenticating her role. She was Chosen, heir to Ryza's throne. Ryza's pet, his capal and even the Knowledge stone had found their way to her when they should have come to Jahll.

Jahll laid his hands on Taqual's shoulders. Taqual was large for an Orc, but Jahll was bigger. Jahll squeezed Taqual's shoulders, touched his head to his, their tusks just shy of touching.

"Thank you, Taqual, for this gift." Jahll stepped away from Taqual to let his mother pass. She rushed from the room with the irate cat in tow.

Taqual bowed his head and pressed his hands together, before lifting his head. "It is an honor to serve my king."

Jahll patted Taqual on the shoulder again. "I will send word for you to join me."

Taqual lay a fist over his heart. "I will await your word."

Taqual spun and headed down the hall, not seeing rage rise in Jahll, who bared his teeth and aimed his tusks at Taqual's back.

Ivy took her usual route to her cottage, ducking into the alley leading to the old tunnel which opened and spilled into the Darkest Forest. Her anger made her reckless. She failed to check to see if anyone followed. She missed the short, stout figure trailing her. The little shadow clung to the darkness. Ivy touched one of her magicked necklaces to the old lock. It popped open. Entering the tunnel, Ivy recited the words then resealed the lock without missing a step. Her shadow held the door ajar as the lock sealed. The shadow waited until Ivy was several yards ahead before slipping in behind her.

CHAPTER 25

Prenumbra
Oracaii Guest Suite

AFTER DAYS OF SLEEPING ON THE GROUND, A PROPER BED was like winning the lottery. Onyx stretched like a cat, pressing her hands into the soft mattress then flopped onto her back, sat up and looked around the room. It was masculine in its color and furnishings. There was a stag with wings the same fawn brown color as its coat, stuffed and mounted high on the wall. Cali said it was a fae mount called a Peyton. Its glassy-eyed stare was fixed on the ceiling. Beside it was a hideous black, scaly horse-like creature, its wings leathery. It was a Riolin which was mounted on the high wall, posed to display the spines where the mane should be and its serpentine tail. A real Beauty and the Beast vibe. She wondered if the person who set them in place had that in mind when positioning the creatures.

Cali moved into view. She was still wearing her metal arm, which painted an odd picture as she flitted around the room, humming while lighting incense. Stress seeped from Onyx's body as fragrant moon lilies permeated the space. Cali went over to a plain beige satchel and pulled three luminous orbs from it: lavender, olive green and dark blue. She approached a large tapestry bearing the symbol of Oracaii. Under the symbol was an Orc soldier dressed for battle. She shoved it aside, then vanished into an adjoining room.

Curiosity pulled Onyx off the bed. She padded across the floor, stopping at the tapestry. Someone knocked on the door just as she reached for it. Onyx moved to answer the door when Cali stopped her.

Pressing her fingers to her lips, Cali asked, "Who calls?"

"The mistress's servants," a soft, feminine voice replied.

Cali and Onyx shared a quick look before Cali went over to answer the door. She cracked it open. Onyx came up behind her.

The two dirty children who accompanied the white Orcess waited. The smaller of the two refused to look up at them, while the older one looked Cali in the eyes.

Cali stood aside, allowing the girls entry. She closed the door behind them. The children did not venture beyond the point of entry. They waited, heads down with their hands clasped in front of them.

The smaller of the pair wrapped her hand around her left wrist. Anytime Cali got too close, a distressed whine would start and the girl would twist something on her wrist. Cali stepped back. The whining and nervous twisting ceased.

"What is your purpose?" Cali inquired.

The older of the two girls responded. "We are here to help as needed and to spy."

The younger girl gaped at her older friend, who made a face.

"It is truth."

"But the mistress will be angry." The words "will be angry" were so soft, only the older girl could hear them because she stood next to her.

"Our mistress is always angry," the older girl said.

The younger of the pair turned her gaze to the floor. It was probably safer than witnessing her friend's brazen rebellion.

Cali's radiant smile cut through the tension between the pair. She walked up to the bold one and embraced her. The sigils on the metal arm glowed.

"What are you?" Onyx had moved to stand beside them, eyes fixed on the sigils. She and Mak helped Cali put on the arm. At first sight, she thought it was a mechanized prosthetic, but it wasn't. It was hollow, but the metal was heavy. It took the combined effort of her and Mak to get the damned thing aligned with Cali's missing limb. Once lined up, the sigils lit up. Cali's flesh became pliant. It reached for the magicked metal like globs of Play-Doh. The metal did the same. When flesh and metal touched, a seam formed which bound them together. The entire process looked painful but once the arm connected, Cali stretched it out, moving the fingers, turning the wrist as if it had been part of her all along.

Onyx glanced over to Cali. "Why is your arm doing that?"

To Onyx's surprise, the talkative girl answered. "It will always extend the protections of its magic to the rest of her body when in the presence of another magical being."

Onyx cocked her head, brows furrowed. "What are you, a dirt sprite?"

"Ha! Ha!" the talkative girl threaded her laugh with sarcasm. "I am a witch."

"What species or creature are you?"

"I am a fully grown human adult and my name is Carol."

Onyx straightened, taking a step away from the trio. Carol wore a veil she had yet to remove. There was a protrusion between the temples and ears that gave the impression that she was something other than human.

Carol jerked a thumb between herself and the smaller girl. "We're both adults and very human."

It surprised Onyx how the smaller girl stood upright. She was so thin. She looked malnourished, yet there was something familiar about her. What was with her obsessive grip on her wrist? What was she protecting? Onyx's attention shifted to Carol. "But you're a witch."

"Yes, I am. Believe it or not, there are witches in the human world." Carol's mouth twitched then spread into a smile. "Human witches tend not to advertise, those who do are usually wannabes." Carol shrugged; her posture relaxed. "I only believed in witchcraft before I was dragged over here."

"You were kidnapped?"

Both girls nodded.

"Couldn't you have used your magic to fight your abductors?" Onyx wiggled her fingers.

"No. Magic was ritual for me in the human world. I attended pagan festivals, tried love spells and mixed healing potions which were herbal teas. My greatest desire was to be connected to the earth. I wanted to feel her breathe, help her heal, if that was possible."

"So, you're a healer?" Onyx encouraged the women to take a seat, but they didn't. They remained close to the door, as if they were going to make a run for it.

Carol shook her head. "No. I'm a Seer."

"You're some kind of psychic?"

Carol shook her head again, then flipped up the veil and turned slowly in a full circle.

Onyx and Cali gasped. Carol's skull had holes drilled in between the temple and the ears. There were three ports; inside were shimmering sigils unlike the ones on Cali's arm and the dampening stones. Harsh, jagged script formed an ugly green spiral. "I catch visions here and there, but my vision has reach. I can see great distances through the eyes of others. It's not as clear, but with the focus of the magic inside my ports," Carol tapped the space above the left ports, "I can see things unfold as clear as you're standing here."

Carol glanced at Cali's metal arm.

"She can read magic," Cali said then extended her arm, turned it over, curled the fingers, then flexed it, before letting it fall to her side.

"I can read magic, mute it and I've learned how to break bindings," Carol announced.

"Wow." Onyx ran her hand across the intricate patterns along the sides of her head.

"Wow, indeed." Carol's chest swelled with pride.

"How long have you been here?" Onyx asked.

"I've been in Penumbra for twenty years," Carol said.

"What!" Cali's disbelief evident. "It is forbidden for us to trespass on human lands."

Carol shook her head. "It is law, yes, but those with twisted appetites have created a trade."

"Such crimes would bring down the Shades!" Cali said.

"They would, if the magic behind it was detectable."

"What do you mean?" Onyx asked.

Carol glanced over at Cali before speaking. "There's something about human magic that is undetectable." She dragged her fingers through matted hair. "Maybe it's because we're not native to Penumbra." Her hands dropped abruptly to her sides. "Whatever it is, word spread. If I were to be honest, our mistress pioneered this new demand."

"But she collects rare species among the Penumbran clans. Those who are near extinction are her favorites." Cali pressed her hands on her chest. "Like me."

"Well, interest has expanded to the human world." Carol's eyes darted to Onyx then back to Cali. "Human trafficking is a thing now in the Host of the Trades. Non-magical humans make the best slaves, especially to the weakest of Penumbra's creatures. And you know the way of the Trades, if it has value, they will acquire it and sell it."

"How long has this been going on?" Onyx asked.

"I was taken twenty years ago." Carol looked over to her little friend. "She was stolen eleven years ago."

"Where are you from?" Onyx sat on the edge of the bed. It was that or collapse on the floor.

"I'm from Montana."

Onyx looked over to the smaller girl. "Where are you from?"

The smaller girl's eyes widened as her shoulders drew up. Her mouth opened and closed like a fish.

"I...I... I'm not sure." The girl's eyes filled with tears.

"Do you know your name?" Onyx coaxed.

The girl shook her head vigorously, her tears creating clear streaks on skin that had little exposure to sunlight. "I'm Mouse," she whispered. "I've always been Mouse."

Carol hugged Mouse to her, stroking her hair. "Don't worry, Mouse, I know your name and more."

"But..." Mouse wiped her face with the sleeves of her tunic, creating a dirt smear across her cheeks.

"What's going on?" Onyx stood.

Cali gestured for her to wait.

Carol and Cali shared a look then Cali went over to the large window. She carried a small, synched pouch. Opening the pouch, she began chanting as she placed the lip of the pouch to the windowsill. She dragged it along the border, creating a fine silver line. Once complete, Cali stood back and examined her handiwork.

While Cali was lining the windowsill, Carol did the same along the bottom of the door. Carol grabbed Mouse by the crook of her arm when she finished and pulled her toward the tapestry. She jerked her head for Onyx and Cali to follow.

The musty odor wafting from the other side of the tapestry gave Onyx pause.

"Trust me, Chosen. All is well. The room is safe." Cali took Onyx's hand and led her inside.

It looked like a roman bath. Turquoise water formed an oblong pool in the center of the room. Large white stones surrounded it. They instantly made her think of quartz. The stones weren't jagged, but smooth. A groove was carved in each, like a seat. Eight gray stone pillars lined the path between the pool and the walls. Each pillar had an ornate sconce stretching toward the pool. The torches were lit, but the light was dim.

The orbs Cali carried into the room earlier lay on a yellow blanket next to the pool. Carol led them over to it. Cali bent and collected the orbs, handing the olive-green one to Onyx. She passed the lavender one to Mouse and kept the dark blue orb.

Carol directed Onyx and Mouse on where to stand. She positioned them parallel to each other along the side of the pool. She and Cali positioned themselves on the shorter ends.

Carol looked at each of them before speaking. "Cali will enter the water with me. Once inside, she will tell you when to pour the contents of your orb into the pool. When the contents coalesce around myself and Cali, you must keep your position." She pointed to their feet. "Don't move, no matter what you see."

Onyx fumbled with her orb as she backed away. The

orb didn't fall. She curled it securely in her fist. "What do you mean?"

"My Chosen, time is short. Death is coming. Who it takes depends on how we move?"

Onyx swallowed loudly.

"You have done well with the guidance we have given you but know that your enemies are already working against you." Cali gestured to Carol and Mouse. "Lucky for us, Cassius has been hard at work pushing your father's plan." She held up her wrist, revealing a tattoo of stylized wings with an eye at its center. "We have friends among enemies."

Carol held up her wrist, revealing an identical tattoo.

"You have no reason to be afraid of Carol, or what she shares with us." Cali met Onyx's eyes. "She set me free and remained in chains for this purpose."

"We're going to make that bitch Ivy pay," Carol growled.

Onyx relaxed her grip on the orb, switching it to her palm. She carried it like an offering to the edge of the pool, stopping where she was told and gave a nod to the pair in the pool.

Cali poured the contents of her orb into the water before sliding her fingers into Carol's ports. A dark blue ring formed around them.

"Daughter of earth. Seer of Penumbra. Share your vision with me. Your eyes are my eyes, as mine are yours. With one eye we see past and present."

Onyx and Mouse twisted their orbs, tipping them so their contents flowed into the waters. Trails of olive green and lavender slithered toward the pair. Their progression stopped the moment they touched the blue ring. The slithering colors formed a tight line from the pool's edge and the women at the pool's core.

The turquoise waters morphed into a gray, reflective mass like a mirror as Carol's left eye formed a cataract and Cali's right eye did the same. Voices echoed through the bathing room as images drifted to the surface of the gray water.

Onyx's heart grew taut as the image of Cedarville came into focus. It was the shadowed underbelly of the abandoned complex where she and Willow would hang out. The vision moved through the halls like a camera. The complex was full of cops. Onyx's twelve-year-old self stood in the middle of two cops, a social worker and Mama Mays. She remembered that day. All the questions gave her a headache. At some point she stopped answering them because they wouldn't let her see Willow. Rico had hurt her and Onyx needed to know she was okay.

Onyx watched as her younger self began shouting her wish to see her friend. While Onyx yelled, three men, the same ones who delivered legal papers to Mama Mays, snuck behind the EMTs tending Willow. Two snapped their necks while the third took Willow from the gurney. They moved freely in the chaos, unnoticed by the others. It would be another hour before anyone discovered Willow was missing. The bodies of the EMTs hid Willow's abduction. Willow's trauma was documented as too much for her to process, leading Willow to run away. Her file was closed, leaving Onyx with questions no one wanted to answer.

The image faded, replaced with another. Again, Onyx was covered in blood, clutched in her mother's arms. She shielded Onyx from the ugly blade protruding from her back. Onyx recalled the pinch of the blade tip above her belly button. A monster, unlike the Orcs, stood over her mother. Its body was not muscular like an Orc, but doughy. It had a single eye and a stomach which hung over its fur-lined loin cloth. Its breasts were heavy but not round like a woman's. The only muscular parts of the beast were its arms and legs. It put its foot on her mother's back and pulled the blade free. Lifting the blade with both hands, the monster swung downward.

It never completed the swing. An enormous black Orc snatched the monster by its neck, snapping it, as it flung the monster away from Onyx and her mother. Onyx couldn't remember how her mother died. It was a memory she didn't want, so her mind hid it away. The gray waters in the pool shoved the memory in her face and with it, the image of her father. The one everyone told her about.

Ryza the Black sank the monster's blade into its skull, roaring at its fallen form, before turning to them. His hair was a black velvet curtain mixed with silver bands twined with battle braids. He pushed it over his shoulders as he knelt before them. His eyes were full of regret, rage and hope as he turned her mother over. He untangled Onyx from her mother's grasp, setting her between his knees. He lifted her mother and laid his hand over her heart. A desperate moan slipped from him as he lowered his head, exchanging his hand with his ear. He was careful of Onyx, shifting an arm between them, allowing room between his bulk and her mother's body.

She saw him mourn Olivia Jones as a second person joined them. No, it wasn't a person but a cat. The same kind that hung around the Center. The cat shifted into a familiar form. Cassius knelt beside the enormous black Orc and lay a hand on Ryza's knee.

"We must not linger." Cassius moved away from them. "I'll gather a bag for her."

Ryza laid her mother down, then gathered Onyx to his chest as he rose. He lay his chin on Onyx's head as they both watched as Cassius ducked into Onyx's room. He emerged with one of her mom's vacation bags. An aqua-blue bag with the word "Bahamas" in white letters scrawled across it. He slung the straps over his shoulders and headed for what remained of the door.

"We have to go." Cassius stared into the hall, then looked back at them. "The Shades will be here soon. They will do what they do." Cassius jerked his chin at Onyx. "We must do what's best for her."

Ryza followed Cassius out of the apartment she shared with her mother. A wave of color washed across the surface of the pool, wiping away the vision, replacing it with the back door of Hubbard Community Center. Cassius sat with Onyx and her bag on the step as Ryza entered into a portal in the middle of the playground. The portal sealed as the door opened. Nancy Mays collected the child, the bag and the cat.

Another wave washed away the vision. A flash of faces surfaced: a light-skinned black man with a closely cropped gray afro, a heavily made-up white woman with platinum hair and her aunt Helen. Those faces sank into the gray depths of the pool with the last image being Jahll. His face faded, replaced with a glowing vial.

"Mortalis Paradox," Cali and Carol said in unison.

Ivy's face shattered the vial as her body rose, forming an imprint on the surface of the water. The sleeping form of a newly abducted Willow lay in the corner of Ivy's cottage, dressed in a brittle tunic which fell past knees tucked close to her chest. Ivy squatted low, leaning in to pat the soles of her feet.

"You, my dear, are the chink in the Chosen's armor." A nasty smile flashed across her face and was gone. "My little Mouse." She rubbed her hands together, her avatar sinking into the gray waters.

Cali's and Carol's heads turned to Onyx. In one voice they spoke, "Light of Oracaii, shield between two worlds, embrace your calling. Haven to the un-clanned, voice of truth, speak. Fate of Oracaii, lead the way."

The gray receded, restoring the pool to its turquoise tint. Lavender, olive green and dark blue from the orbs became vapor. Carol blew at the dark blue mists surrounding her and Cali. All the mists crystalized and fell into the water, the magic and color fading as it sank to the bottom.

Cali removed her hands from Carol's ports. Their eyes regained their color.

Onyx dropped onto one of the white stones, face buried in her palms. Cali swam over to her. She climbed out of the pool, then knelt at her feet. Gently, she pulled Onyx's hands away from her face.

"Chosen."

Onyx looked away, focusing on a torch on the far side of the room.

"Onyx."

She looked sharply at the woman, who had never called her by her name.

"Hold on to what you saw." Cali tapped the face of the Knowledge Stone. "Countering the moves already in play requires the knowledge of kings."

Cali wrapped her hands around Onyx's, raising them to her forehead.

"By the forge of my soul, my life for yours. This day I bind myself to you as shield, counsel, healer and friend."

Onyx pulled her hands from Cali's as the other woman raised her head, a look of resolve in her eyes.

"I am honored to serve the first and future queen of Oracaii."

"I'm not anyone's queen."

"You will be," Cali spoke resolutely.

Onyx placed her hands on the collar, the tips of her fingers resting against the Knowledge Stone. "I don't know what to do."

Cali looked across the pool to Carol, who sat next to Willow.

"Carol will show you how."

"How does she know?"

"A seer's powers are connected to the soul. Visions are attached to the fates of individuals. To see one's path, I must touch their souls," Carol said without looking away from Willow. "The Knowledge Stone is not only a collection of the old king's knowledge, but also a home for their souls."

"But the High Spirit claims the souls of the fallen," Cali said.

"She collects the spirits which belong to her. The souls are the essence of our being. A collection of knowledge, of life. The spirit of the Orc kings is with their maker, but their knowledge lies in the stone." Carol lay her hand on her neck.

Onyx pulled her hands away.

"All that forges the future of Oracaii and all connected to it will happen by sunset."

Cali squeezed Onyx's knee. "You can do this." Onyx lay a hand over Cali's, who covered it with her metal one.

"Light of Oracaii," Cali whispered reverently. Carol and Willow echoed Cali's words. Willow raised the wrist she kept concealed. A worn bracelet with Onyx's name on it hung loosely. Onyx raised her own. The bright beads and its worn nameplate with Willow's name were displayed for all to see.

Hope crept into Onyx's heart. She could do this, make things right for all of them.

CHAPTER 26

Penumbra
Ivy's Cottage

RYZA'S STUPID PET BEGAN WRITHING THE MOMENT SHE opened the door to her cottage. It sneezed, hissed and swatted at the top of the bag. Ivy ground her teeth, then gave the bag a single violent shake. The cat stopped its writhing as she slammed the door and stalked across the main floor of her cottage. She stopped at the black curtain, pausing long enough to retrieve her key. Opening the door, she descended the spiral steps. There was something satisfying the moment her bare feet touched the dark soil. The soil wasn't black. It was the color of dried blood. She spilled a lot over the years. It seemed a natural transition from its original soft brown tint.

The room was an enormous square, which was wider than the top floor. To a stranger, Ivy's cottage was a simple one-story structure with a single window. The roof was warded to repel the predators lurking in the Darkest Forest. Even the grounds were warded for twelve feet, forming a barrier which added protections against scrying and other such magic. Dark magic flowed freely in the Odious. Ivy's activities triggered no alarms since the Odious was a place where bad things were free to indulge their appetites. As long as they did not spill into the Alluring, all was well.

Each of the four walls in Ivy's workshop held crucial instruments to her craft. Cages lined the far-left wall, stretching to the ceiling. In them were her human witches, four of them, a few lesser fae and a Nurl. She kept the Nurl in stasis. Nurls were hard to keep. Their ability to blend into the environment led to deadly mistakes.

There were two open cages reserved for future purchases. Once Willow served her purpose, she would dispatch her and purchase a bound fae and perhaps another human. She would watch over Jahll's kingdom. Keep an ear to the gossip and decide her next move. First, she would break the Chosen's ties to the Knowledge Stone. Jahll expected her to survive the Mortalis Paradox. Ivy rolled her eyes. She loved her son and the power he would bring her, but to let her live would be foolish. For Ivy to break the girl's bond to the Knowledge Stone required blood. Ivy altered the spell she gave her son, which would allow her to kill the girl but keep the blood alive. She would have to cut him to transfer Onyx's blood to him. The enchantment she taught Jahll would activate the blood stone she bonded to a bone in his wrist when he was a child. The Knowledge Stone would respond to him.

Ivy moved deeper into her workshop. The rear wall held instruments of torture. Humans made the most interesting noises when in pain. The right wall held several tables, all of them empty. She used them to dissect the humans who died in her care. She did the same with the minor fae and creatures foolish enough to wander into her territory. Beside each table was a cabinet and a sink. Underneath each table were surgical instruments, vials and boxes.

The center of her workshop held two rectangular tables. The table on the right held an array of jars, vials and small to medium-sized cages. Beakers, scales, Bunsen burners and hot plates, all trinkets from her trips into the human world. They made her work easier. She gained the services of a protected human to wire her workshop for electricity. He supplied a small generator and had it spelled to hide the noise of its engine. Ivy enjoyed electricity. Using her human in Chicago, she purchased a small refrigerator in which she kept some of her specimens.

The table on the left was less cluttered, so Ivy tossed the bag unceremoniously on the table next to a medium-sized cage.

Ivy unlocked the top of the cage, opened it, then dumped the cat inside. She slammed the cage shut, locking it before the cat could react. The beast narrowed its eyes at her, then hissed. Ivy lowered herself to eye level with the animal.

"Let's see how long you keep that attitude once I get to work on you."

The cat slammed its body against the front of the cage. Ivy scurried back. Animals of all kinds cowered before her. She was unaccustomed to such aggression in beasts other than nurls. Any being with sense knew better than to test a nurl.

She glanced at the sleeping nurl's cage. Her malice returned as she glared at the cat.

"You'll be purring for me soon," she promised as she turned away from the cat and began sifting through vials. Laying several on the table, she bent down to pull a box full of stone bowls from underneath when something crashed overhead.

Someone cursed.

Ivy lay her box on the table beside the cat's cage.

The ceiling dimpled overhead under the weight of the intruder. Her girls had not returned. They were too light to make impressions like the ones she witnessed. Besides, her girls were trained to announce themselves when they entered.

Ivy stalked over to the stairs and ascended them without fear of being heard. Her workshop was warded to conceal its presence and her work from others. Jahll suspected she had such a place but said nothing.

Ivy reached the top of the stairs, growled at the door, then snatched it open.

Mak's skin tingled from the magic both inside and outside of the cottage. She followed the white Orcess through the hidden tunnel, all the while wishing Joseph was with her. She had never gone into the Darkest Forest on her own. It was always with a company of three. Everyone preferred exploring new territories with Joseph. He was annoying, but he never got lost.

She and Joseph were separated in the crowd. Some colorful item probably distracted him. There were in an unmanned bazaar. The booths displayed their goods, which meant the Commons could move freely once Onyx and the others made it into the castle.

The show Jahll and the others put on was just that, a show. Several attempts had been made on Onyx's life from the moment she crossed the Juncture into Penumbra. Mak bared her teeth at the spineless acts of a bunch of no-sacks. Only a coward would hide his or her face during a kill. Orcs murdered in plain sight and always with a purpose: either war or revenge.

Mak held a finger under her nose. Her own scent dulled the odor of magic, which had already started her stomach to churning.

Mak looked across the room, her gaze settling on the frozen graying form on the bed. The faint scent of decay worked its way through the magic. Mak was no sorceress, but her talent lay in scenting magic. Magic bothered her skin and nose. She learned the various levels of magic by smell. The scent of blood and lemons belonged to blood magic. The sole purpose of blood magic was murder. Death by blood magic guaranteed pain and suffering.

Dark hex magic was milder but just as bad. They

smelled like old dirt and brine. Hexes made the victim sick. There were some hexes that could cripple, but that was rare. Milder hexes took on the scent of its avatar, but underneath was always the scent of the wildflower or vine powering it. Hex avatars were typically food, flowers, or some animal. They carried dangerous magic to the victim, driving him or her to consume, inhale, or touch the spell. Once unleashed, there would be discomfort, but it was momentary. Like a tummy ache. It went away on its own.

Mak covered her nose with her hand, hoping it would cancel out the smells coming from every inch of the cottage. If she waded in it much longer, she would start sneezing and give herself away. The white Orc was here, but not in plain sight.

"Damn it!" she hissed, being mindful of her volume. The Orcess was carrying a black bag. It had to be in here somewhere.

Mak stopped wandering around and looked. Cali taught her the most insignificant things held the greatest secrets. The space was open, sectioned off by furniture. There was a nest positioned against the wall across from the bed, which was the room's center. On the opposite side of that bed was a vanity with an array of bottles, with colorful liquids inside. Beside the vanity was a closet with its curtain drawn back, exposing a messy array of gossamer and silks.

A squall of scents clogged Mak's airway. She spun in the direction from which the odor flowed. A black curtain trembled, setting off a shimmering cluster of sigils and unfamiliar marks. The curtain stilled and the smells faded. What was behind it?

Mak crept closer, allowing several feet between her and the curtain. The curtain pushed out, then retracted like a breath. This time there were no shimmering sigils, but the stench resurrected. It wasn't as strong as before. Mak moved forward six steps, then stopped.

A loud trilling erupted. Mak covered her ears and gagged from the pungent odor of death and lemons. She backed away from the curtain as it trembled furiously, then parted. The white Orc stood in a doorway behind the curtain. The smells coming from the other side filled her with a desire to peel the skin from her body and tear off her own nose.

She fumbled with the sheath strapped to her outer thigh, but she drew her blade. Though her eyes had narrowed to slits from the trilling and the smells, she could still track the white Orc's movements. The Orcess bared her teeth, aimed her decorative tusks at Mak and bellowed.

Mak mimicked the action as she tracked the vulnerable spots on the other Orc's body. Mak might be easy prey to the other Orc because of her age and size, but Mak knew how to fight through discomfort. It was the life of an outsider. A Wanderer.

Mak balanced herself to prepare for the fight to come.

The Orcess charged. Mak let loose her own roar and surged forward to meet her.

CHAPTER 27

Penumbra
Guest Chambers

CAROL HUGGED HER FRIEND CALI AS SHE GRINNED AT THE sight of Willow and Onyx huddled together in excited conversation. She and Willow were expected back at the cottage. Carol dreaded the trip and wasn't sure of Willow's reaction upon their return. Would she respond to Ivy's pet name? Would she do something reckless and get herself killed?

Carol released Cali and summoned Willow to join her. The trip back to the cottage would give Carol time to convince Willow to pretend a little while longer.

A boom echoed through the room, turning all heads to the door. It jostled on its hinges. Each woman looked to the other.

Another boom followed by a crack ate up the momentary silence.

"You cannot enter the Chosen's room."

A growl answered Gryk's warning.

Cali rushed over to the door and pulled it open as Jahll rose to his feet. Pieces of the floor tile fell from Jahll's back. Jahll dressed in common clothes. Gryk placed himself between the open door and Jahll, dual axes drawn. Cali stretched out her arm. The sigils along the enchanted metal flared, a sword filled the palm of her metal hand. She closed her fingers around the pommel and drew into a battle stance.

Jahll's gaze mocked her. He curled his lip, baring his canines at her before returning his attention to the armed Orc between them.

Onyx pressed forward. Cali stopped her, keeping her out of Jahll's line of sight. Gryk was in the middle of the doorway. He positioned himself in a way that should he fall in battle, his body would not trap them inside.

"Why are you here?" Cali barked.

Jahll stopped his pacing. "So the Chosen's servants speak for her now?"

Onyx surged forward, but Carol and Willow stopped her. Willow pressed a finger to her lips followed by a sharp shake of her head. "Don't."

Onyx stepped back and held her tongue.

"Are you cowering inside?" Jahll taunted.

"I see your mother's madness has taken root," Gryk countered. Jahll's eyes cut to Gryk, who swung his left axe over his shoulder while letting the right hand lie docilely at his side.

Jahll bared his teeth but did not drop his head or tusks in challenge. Instead, he flashed them, though there was no humor in his discolored eyes. "I am here with an offer for the Chosen."

"You have nothing she desires." Cali put herself back in Jahll's line of sight.

He laughed, a disturbing sound. "I'm certain she does not wish to battle." He walked a slow circle in the space he occupied. He inspected his claws as he made his rotation. "I have no desire to engage in battle with a human female."

Onyx ground her teeth as a snarl built. Again, she surged forward. Again, Willow and Carol blocked her.

"There is no sport in slaughtering something so weak."

"Or is this another one of your shows?" Gryk prodded. "Do you fear a mere female that you would barter for your life?"

A rapid succession of steps ended the taunt as they all watched Taqual round the corner. He jogged over to them, slowing to a brisk walk. His pace slowed further as he noticed Gryk's weapons and Cali's drawn sword. He laid his hand on the hilt of his own blade should he need to intervene.

Jahll motioned for him to stop as he turned back to the group before him.

"I know about your problem." Jahll dropped his voice and raised his unblemished left hand. He tapped the back of it.

Onyx looked down at the mark on her hand. It progressed up her arm, ending at the elbow. Carol and Willow stared open-mouthed at the Challenge Mark.

No one spoke.

"I can make it go away." Jahll laced his hands behind

his back and rocked on his heels. A flick of his fingers and he called Taqual forward.

"Why would you do that?" Onyx stayed where she was. Curiosity pulled the question from her.

"Simple." Jahll was swift as he removed a small axe from its hiding place, a strap to his back. The loose tunic kept it from pressing against the fabric. In one swing, he removed Taqual's head. He caught the left wrist of the dead Orc. A second swing and Jahll removed Taqual's arm at the elbow. A slow pivot and he raised the severed limb dramatically, displaying the Challenge Mark.

Jahll flung it into the room. Onyx gazed down at her arm. The mark faded. Onyx opened her mouth to thank Jahll. What he did next made her grateful that she didn't.

"As my right, before the thirtieth day. I challenge the Elite for the right of ascension. That I may stand as the true Elite to the Orcs."

Onyx dropped to her knees as a new mark seared into her hand. It sliced through her flesh, crawling up her arm, ending on her shoulder. Her arm throbbed. It felt like the mark cut into her bones.

Jahll retrieved Taqual's head, then called to Carol and Willow.

"My mother waits for you," he barked, moving in front of Carol as she attempted to pass him. He bent low, meeting Carol's eyes. Lowering his voice, Jahll leaned close to her ear. "I know what you are and what she uses you for." He rose slowly, his gaze never leaving Carol's as he lifted Taqual's head. "Show her what you've seen. Remind her I am not a toy but her king and she will treat me as such. If she chooses not to, then I am no longer responsible for her fate."

Jahll moved out of Carol and Willow's way. Both women hurried down the hall and did not look back.

Jahll bowed dramatically. "I will see you in the arena." He did an about face and marched down the hall, leaving a trail of blood in his wake.

No one spoke until he was out of sight.

"Why didn't you kill him?" Onyx asked, cradling her arm to her chest.

"He was within his rights. He did not break protocol and he did not attack you," Gryk said.

Onyx gestured toward the bloody trail.

"He used intimidation, which is no crime." Gryk aimed the tip of his axe at the bloody corridor.

"He killed another Orc."

"Again, it is not a crime. He relieved you of a challenger none of us could identify, so he did you a favor."

"But..." Onyx waved her free hand along the marked arm.

"Any Orc can extend a Rising Challenge within the thirty days. Today is the last day." Gryk gestured at the mark with his chin. "The mark will race toward your heart."

"I have to kill him."

Gryk and Cali nodded their heads.

"There is no other way," Cali said, unable to look away from the headless corpse yards from where they stood.

"Killing him is a service to Oracaii." Gryk returned his battle axes to their sheaths as the three of them stared down the barren halls. "He will draw Oracaii back into the Odious and kill us all."

"He's one Orc," Onyx said.

"Who has eager followers. Orcs will again descend into the Dark Times, though Jahll believes his cause is righteous. Orcs will again invade territories not their own. We will become rabid dogs that will force the High Spirit to put us down for good." Gryk's voice took on a haunted tone.

"Once the Orcs are no more, the Wandering will be next," Cali said.

"Why would anyone hunt the Wandering? You've harmed no one." Onyx looked between Cali and Gryk.

"For the moment, the Wandering are Orcs. We were blooded and the High Spirit is honoring that bond. The moment the Orcs fall, we return to what we were, a traveling band of rejects. We are the sin of Penumbra. Mixed races living as a community." Cali shifted her gaze from the empty corridor to her bare feet.

"That's not a crime," Onyx reasoned.

"Our existence breaks a crucial rule." Cali dragged the tip of her sword across the floor.

"Which is?"

"The law of territories is clear; clan members must stay within their territories. Only when invited by another can a differing species enter. But when invited, the guest of the host clan is not allowed to use their abilities. To do so, brings down the Shades," Cali said.

Onyx moved between Cali and Gryk. She turned to Cali. "I thought the Wandering traveled the line between the Odious and the Alluring."

"We do, but as a clan, we flaunt the sin of many. Our mixed species breaks the law of territories by default. Our lack of land is another. We easily encroach on the territories of others even when we access Junctions to pass through them."

"Why hasn't anything happened to you before now?" Onyx asked.

"Ryza blooded the Wandering. He was favored by the High Spirit and well respected among the other Elites. His standing allowed the others to look the other way. Those who were hostile honored us to stave off Ryza's anger." Gryk leaned against the door frame, arms folded across his wide chest.

The reality of their situation finally registered. Onyx used ignorance as a shield. It authenticated the artifice of her defiance. Not acknowledging the plight of others made indifference easy. Indifference had no price. The headless corpse outside of her temporary room showed Onyx the true price of ignorance. If she continued rejecting the full weight of her calling, all of them would end up just like the corpse. She had until sunset to get her shit together for all their sakes.

CHAPTER 28

Penumbra
Ivy's Cottage

CASSIUS'S EYES GLOWED RED AS HE STOOD UP IN THE CAGE, arched his back then turned in a circle within the confines of the cage. The moment his fur connected with the wire it ignited, flaring molten orange then collapsed in a pile of ash. Cassius stretched his feline body then plopped down onto the floor. Little ashen clouds formed around him. He sneezed, shook his snout, then inspected the room. He was on a mission and time was of the essence. The battle would happen tonight. Onyx had until sunrise.

Chaos rose the moment the six Elites faded. It exposed long hidden factions. Madness was taking root within the other clans. There was infighting and it wasn't for the honor of the calling, but a desire to resurrect archaic practices. Becoming the next Elite was a chance to break unifying bonds of being a clan, returning to internal factions devoted to caste systems. It would destroy Penumbra. It would destroy the clans. Penumbra would become a place of war. In war, the innocent suffered for the sake of another's glory.

He meowed, hopped over to the other table, then rose on his hind legs to examine the captives in cages. He counted four witches. The corpse on the bed upstairs had to be the fifth. All of them were in poor health. Each wore a brass collar, which bound their powers, rendering them helpless.

The Shades were on their way and so were the familiars belonging to the captive witches. The Prophet entrusted him with their rescue the day of Ryza's fading.

Cassius dropped back onto all fours, hopped off the table and trotted around Ivy's shrine of perversion. Crawling under tables, behind cabinets and pausing to inspect random boxes, a fine sliver of light caught his eye, stopping him in his tracks. Arching his head up, he scanned the expanse of the back wall where the light emanated. A white sarcophagus leaned against the wall. It was open. Short spikes covered the interior on both sides. Light streamed through the hinges along the middle of the sarcophagus. Cassius padded around it, searching for a safe point of entry. He found a small gap between the sarcophagus and the wall. He squeezed into it.

He stretched up, again rising on his hind legs. Using his paws, he pressed the wall, the pads of his paws connected with sigils. The room's hazy lighting hid their presence well, but his magically enhanced night vision revealed Ivy's Plan B, should she ever get caught: a literal back door. He examined the warding on it. Like the curtain upstairs, it was spelled to compel ignorance of its presence. The spell work didn't affect animals on this side of the door. Cassius spotted a few trigger spells, alarms to warn Ivy should someone other than her attempt to use it. As he continued his inspection of the spell work, he discovered a nasty one meant to mutilate. Once his inspection was completed, he trotted between the central tables and shifted into his human form.

Focusing on the array of vials scattered on the right table, he sorted through them, withdrawing what he needed. Cassius combined the contents he gathered into a nearby stone bowl. He inspected his handiwork before taking up the bowl. Holding it in his right hand, Cassius positioned his left over it. He spoke the words which activated the spell. The sigils over his heart filled with green light with each word spoken. It faded at the spell's end.

He walked over to the cages, stopping in front of the first with a witch inside. He knelt before it, dipped his fingers into the bowl. Reaching through the bars, he drew a sigil on the witch's forehead. The sigil shattered the binding spell, which fell from her like a torn spider's web. Vibrant brown eyes blinked slowly, as if emerging from a deep sleep. The witch grabbed the bars of her cage. Cassius set the bowl on the floor and pressed his clean hand to his lips then pointed up. The woman in the cage nodded her understanding.

"I'm here to set you free but we have to move quickly."

The woman opened her mouth. Cassius again pressed his clean finger to his lips. "We have no time for questions. Those will be answered once we are safely away from this place." He pointed to the bowl then to her and whispered, "If we are to get out of here before chaos ensues, I need your help to free the others."

The woman nodded again. Cassius grabbed the lock and crushed it. Moving the bowl aside, he helped the woman out of the cage. She needed his aid to stand but once she gained her balance, she grabbed a bowl from the table. He explained what she needed to do as he poured a portion of the potion from his bowl into hers. They went to work freeing the other witches.

Once free, Cassius shared his plan. They would move the sarcophagus. He would unlock the door. A white bird with a purple and gray crest waited for them outside. They were to follow it. Members of the Wandering would meet them and lead them to safety. Hell was coming to the Dark Forest. It was their decision whether to wander blindly or follow the bird.

Cassius pressed his index finger to the center of each witch's collar which broke away then he went over to the sarcophagus, nicking his palm on one of the spikes before closing it. After pushing it out of the way, he pressed his bloodied palm to the door's center. His mixed Shifter and unseelie fae blood protected him from bad magic. It also broke it. The crackling of wards filled the room. A series of clicks followed as the door's locks disengaged. Ivy's workshop lit up like a Christmas tree as a myriad of spells fell away.

Disengaging the spells removed the soundproofing. Roars erupted upstairs. Witches screamed as the scrape of claws and the crash of bodies broke out overhead. Cassius ushered them outside. One of Cali's white birds hovered a short distance away from the open door.

The witches darted out. Cassius left them to their fate as he dashed across the room and up the stairs. Something crashed against the main door, knocking him against the railing. He moved out of the way, waiting on the second step, listening intently to the fight on the other side. The intensity of the battle shifted away from the door. Cassius took that moment to enter the room.

Dark blood smeared across the floor in the path of the Orcs locked in battle. Mak was small but she used it to her advantage. It allowed for quick, darting attacks. She moved in close, struck and slipped out of reach. The Orcs broke apart the moment he entered the room.

Ivy had a deep cut over her right eye and any more across her cheeks, arms, along her ribcage and legs. The hilt of a blade protruded from her left leg. She turned her rabid gaze on him and roared. Ivy was caught up in blood lust. She would not cease fighting until she was the last one standing. Cassius shifted into his werecat form. His body bulked up in muscle and his limbs lengthened. The bones in his face shifted, his canines dropped past his jawline. He returned her challenge with his feline roar as he moved in.

Mak could use a break. The small Orcess held her ground but not without injury. Her right arm hung limp at her side and her right eye was swollen shut. She had her share of ugly bruises yet was poised with her blade ready for Ivy's next charge.

Ivy looked between them then charged Mak out of convenience. She was closer but Cassius was faster. He slammed into Ivy, knocking her off her feet. She slid across the floor. The cottage shook from the impact of her body connecting with the wall. Cassius stood in front of Mak, who dropped to a knee. He didn't like the sound of her breathing.

Ivy rolled onto her feet. She roared but it turned into a howl. Her wild eyes fixed on him as she dropped her head and tusks.

The door to her cottage swung open drawing all their attention. Ivy spun, immediately charging the small human as she crossed the threshold. The little human sank her hand into the pocket of the cloak she wore. She drew the contents to her lips as she dropped into a crouch and blew. A black cloud with silver particles engulfed the charging Orcess, who dropped like a stone. The momentum of her charge propelled her body forward. It stopped inches away from the open doorway.

The Orcess's human servants stepped into the cottage. The smallest of the pair went over to Ivy's body and kicked it.

"Is she dead?" The girl glared at Ivy.

"No, Willow," the taller of the pair said. "She's unconscious."

Willow shrugged but seemed displeased with Ivy's status among the living.

A wave of warm air and magic flowed through the open door. Cassius shifted into his human form. He went over to Mak and picked her up then hurried over to the door.

"We have to leave, now!" He pushed past the humans. "If you like living, I suggest you do the same."

The girls followed him out of the cottage. They had just moved onto the trail that would lead them to the others when the human called Willow said she had to go back. Her companion lingered in indecision. Cassius ground his teeth and stopped.

"We can't be here! Death is on its way and it will take us all."

Willow was already gone. The remaining human waved Cassius off before turning to follow her friend. Cassius wished them a quick and painless death. He clutched Mak tight as he shifted into his werecat form and ran.

CHAPTER 29

Penumbra
Oracaii Guest Suite

THE INCANTATION MUST NOT BE SPOKEN ALOUD. IT IS A CALL *from one soul to another.* Those were Carol's words to her as she placed her hands on the sides of Onyx's head. There was a jolt, not quite like electricity. Words filled her mind along with the ritual that made them work.

Onyx dragged her arm across the turquoise waters of the pool, relishing the ripples spreading across the surface. She looked down at the deep purple orb cradled in the palm of her hands. Carol left her with the incantation she needed to call forth her ancestors while Cali gave her the orb. She said it was to help her body to accept the knowledge the elders passed along. The transfer of wisdom would be rigorous.

Onyx clutched the orb, drawing it to her lips. The bruised sky outside filled her with worry. All her life she'd existed between self-doubt and anger. After Carol's visions, she learned Jahll's mother had orchestrated everything. There was nothing wrong with her. She carried no curse, yet a tendril of doubt remained.

Her father had done his best to keep her alive. He sacrificed a lot for her survival, even extended his protections to a clan that was not of his people. She could do the same.

Onyx inhaled deep as she lowered the orb. She blew out the breath she held and twisted it. Her eyes closing as she did. Its contents flowed down her body into the pool as instructed. Releasing the emptied pieces of the orb, she laid her right hand over the Knowledge Stone. Her left hand lay over her heart and opened her mind.

> *Fathers, Kings, Brothers, Advisors*
> *Come forth.*
> *Your Chosen seeks knowledge.*
> *I call for Oracaii's sake.*
> *Our survival hangs on your word.*
> *Enter this vessel, willing and empty.*
> *Grant me this honor, my kings.*

The surrounding water bubbled. Her eyes popped open as several, the same size as the purple orb, floated into the air. One bounced off her cheek but did not pop. She stood in the middle of water that seemed to boil, but it did not burn. Geysers of steam rose all around as the bubbles drifted lazily. A familiar scent mingled in the rising steam.

Vaporous tendrils crawled along the surface of the

pool and spread across the floor and walls. Soon the entire room faded into the ether along with all sound, except Onyx's breathing. She sat in silence for what seemed like an eternity before she felt movement. It was like her dreams. Shadows lingered just beyond her line of sight.

She lowered her head, fixing her eyes on the only spot of color, the Knowledge Stone. Red pulsed between her fingers. Gryk gave her a brief history of the Orc kings. There were twelve. Eleven were brutal until her father. He chipped away the stone from the heart of the Orcs.

A touch fed Carol things Onyx had yet to discover. She read the souls within the Knowledge Stone. All twelve kings were inside, but she warned her that not all would come. Some held tight to the old ways and would not be quick to acknowledge a female as leader of the Orcs. Time had changed some. She encouraged Onyx to trust the kings who approached her. They were the ones who would help.

Onyx felt silly sitting in silence, so she tried something.

"I seek the counsel of the kings."

Someone grunted in the distance. It came from the left.

"Your chosen has come in search of knowledge," Onyx tried again.

A chuckle erupted north of where she sat. Another followed. It danced around her from all directions.

Fine, Onyx thought. They were being dicks about it. Mak taught her a few Orcish insults. She considered the risk. The kings were already dead, so what could they do to her?

"So, I guess this place is full of a bunch of fat whores."

Several growls caused the surrounding vapors to tremble.

"I come seeking knowledge of war."

Someone spit, sucked their teeth then replied. "Slaves don't make war."

"I am no slave. I have been Chosen by both the High Spirit and the Knowledge Stone."

"A woman is not worthy of the Knowledge Stone, much less the Orc throne." The speaker sounded like he was gargling rocks.

"None of you no-sacks ever wore the Knowledge Stone!" Ryza barked.

Several grunts echoed from all directions.

"Why are you part of the Knowledge Stone if you have no knowledge to share?" Onyx prodded.

"It is a king's choice of disciples. You are a woman," a gruff voice said.

"Unteachable," another king said. His voice a booming baritone.

"You're wrong!" Onyx challenged.

She felt the air stiffen.

"You are ignorant even in death," Onyx continued. "If you do nothing, there will be no more kings."

One of the kings huffed. "We'll have a king soon enough."

Chuckles drifted from all directions. "As soon as one of the males kills you."

"You wish to give Ivy's son the throne?" Ryza said.

Three Orcs in full battle armor stepped out of the mists. Their bodies were sheer. Each wore silver armor which sparkled as if it were under constant sunlight. The light within their armor distorted their faces, but Onyx could make out a few of their tusks. One of the three Orc kings was missing one.

A fourth king stepped into Onyx's line of sight. His skin was no longer midnight black but dark gray. Ryza wore the same silver armor as the others. He knelt before her, removed his helmet and smiled.

Fathomless eyes scanned her from head to toe.

"What do you need from us, daughter?"

One of the three Orcs behind them cleared his throat.

"Apologies, brothers." Ryza waved his arm at the first king on the left who inclined his head.

"I am Nkin the Reaper."

"Reaper?"

"I am good at killing." He dimmed the shimmering armor and flashed his teeth. "I am good at figuring out how to kill my opponent while fighting. I find the weak points and it's not always about the armor." Nkin stepped back.

The Orc in the middle stepped forward. "I am Vzaah the Bold."

"I take it you are fearless," Onyx offered with a smile.

The grin he returned confirmed her assessment. Vzaah stepped back and the third Orc, the one with the broken tusk, took Vzaah's place.

"I am Braken the Berserker."

"What does a Berserker do?"

"Put his people in the path of the Shades."

Onyx sobered.

"I led my people down a very dark path." The radiance of Braken's armor faded completely. Braken's body reflected years of war. Both ears were torn. A deep scar ran down the left side of his face. He had no left eye and was missing a few teeth. His body was covered with claw marks, keloid scars and sunken places that were missing flesh. Nkin and Vzaah had their share of scars, but none as gruesome as Braken's.

"Blood is life. Blood is victory. Blood is everything." Braken's words were solemn. The others echoed them, including her father.

He placed his fist over his heart. "I learned the ways I chased were about my pride. It was a madness, an addiction to conquest and suffering." He pulled his fist away, dropping it to his side. "It wasn't until the Prophet warned me of the Shades that I came to my senses."

Braken began walking in a small circle in the space between Onyx and the others. "The Shades were coming."

"Why are there still Orcs?" Nkin asked.

"Like her father, I offered my spirit as payment for what I led my people to do."

"She took it," Onyx said.

"Yes. My soul bought the Orcs another chance." Braken looked to Ryza.

"You saved us. Three centuries of peace."

Ryza grunted. "Not peace. I fertilized the roots of bitterness. Despite being able to hand the most battle-hardened Orc his ass, they still thought I was soft because I showed compassion."

"Kindness is weakness in the eyes of our kind, yes, but

its fruit is undeniable," Nkin said. "Orcs see it as soft, but it gained us a place in the light. They associate Orcs with honor and wisdom. Others sought your counsel on how to wage and win at bloodless wars."

"To what ends? Before my fading, I discovered Ivy and others were slipping into the human world."

"You didn't stop her because of me." Onyx cut in. Ryza didn't look at her.

"I crossed over into your world hunting down the Orcs I'd heard were stealing humans."

"That would be Ivy," Onyx said.

"She wasn't the only one," Ryza corrected.

"I can't stop them," Onyx said.

Nkin laughed. "You're human."

"She's also my daughter." Ryza bared his teeth and aimed his tusks at Nkin.

"How are you going to stop Ivy?" Nkin challenged, which drew a growl from Ryza.

"By killing her son and becoming the Elite."

"How are you going to do that?" Nkin folded his arms over his chest and arched a brow.

"That's why I'm here. I'm from Chicago. I've lived there all my life. I know nothing about Orc culture except the little I learned from Gryk and Cassius. I have no idea how to use most of the weapons besides a knife or maybe a small battle-axe."

"You've already accepted a battle with Jahll," Nkin said.

"Not sure if it shows but look at my left hand."

The trio of kings cursed in unison.

"He slaughtered another Orc. I believe it was one of

his personal guard. This guard had issued the challenge first. Jahll killed him, then issued his own."

"It is within his right to kill another for the honor of challenging you to be the next Elite."

"Is it okay for him to get his mother to brew up a spell that will resurrect me as a slave?"

"Orcs don't tamper with magic," Vzaah declared. "Even I know not to do that."

"Why don't Orcs use magic?"

"We are dark by nature. Add magic and it can twist us," Vzaah said.

"Well, Ivy uses it liberally."

"That's impossible," Nkin said.

"Ivy's harnessed human magic. She uses it liberally in Penumbra." The three kings, Nkin, Vzaah and Braken stared at her, mouths agape.

"Why hasn't she been killed or visited by Shades?" Vzaah asked.

"Human magic is invisible to the powers that be in Penumbra." Onyx tilted her head as she sifted through her thoughts. "It's like human magic flows on a different wavelength."

"Our people are doomed," Braken said.

"Not if you help me," Onyx interjected. "Share your knowledge. Teach me how to win and I will deal with Jahll, his mother and hunt down the Orcs that have trespassed in the human world."

Onyx measured the Orcs before her. All were not kind or her idea of good in life, but they had the skills she needed to deal with Jahll.

"A human that has crossed into Penumbra may not return to their world," Nkin stated.

"But I'm only half human." Onyx said.

Three kings considered Onyx's words. Ryza sat next to his daughter, waiting for the others to make up their minds.

"Tonight, is the Rising," Ryza said. "The challenge has been issued and a decision must be made." His gaze shifted between the three kings. "Do you want Ivy's madness to infect the clan, or do you want the Orcs to thrive?"

The three kings walked over, forming a circle around Onyx. Ryza stood in front of her.

"Blood of our blood. We honor your request. Knowledge you seek. Knowledge we share." The four kings spoke as one. Nkin, Braken and Vzaah laid their hands on Onyx's head. Knowledge flooded her mind, creating an ache around the crown of her skull. Her father laid his hand over the one clutching the knowledge stone.

"Daughter of mine, what I have is yours." A slow burn built on the back of Onyx's hand. "All I know, I give to you."

"As blood calls to blood, we honor you as queen." The four kings removed their hands. "May iron flow through your veins and lead you to victory."

The heat in her hand grew and like fire to dry leaves, it spread through her body. The four kings vanished into the mist, leaving her to burn. In her agony, she screamed.

CHAPTER 30

Penumbra
The King's Room

JAHLL STROLLED ACROSS THE ROOM, GRABBED A CHAIR AND spun it around. He straddled it. Folding his arms across the top, then laid his chin on them. He considered the bruised, pale orange Orc blubbering at the feet of his men. He tilted his head. The Orc before him should be dead.

Jahll thought he killed him back when he was new to the guard. He and his company stumbled upon him as a youngling. He was playing with toys meant for small children, which should have been the first sign of his unworthiness. Physically, the pale orange Orc was not quite a teen. He seemed fit. A future soldier. Jahll discovered he was broken when they questioned him. His mind was stuck. It was maybe five years old.

The more questions they asked, the more agitated the

pale orange Orc became. His whining irritated them. Jahll wasn't the first to strike him, but it was his idea to kill him. There were senior soldiers around and no Commons to tattle on them, so he and his company dragged him into the Darkest Forest. Screams were common there, so no one would interrupt their game. They tortured him for hours until one of his company reminded them it was their turn to inventory the weapons and polish the senior guards' armor. It was menial work, but it gave them an audience with battle-seasoned Orcs, which they hoped to be.

They left the pale orange Orc in the forest. His blood would draw carnivores. He was too simple of mind to fight them off. How did he survive?

Jahll tilted his head to the opposite side. The Orc was clean, well fed and from the bows in his hair, he was cared for. He arrived at the same time as the Chosen's company. He did not approach the castle, but he entered the gates. Despite the beatings his men delivered, the pale orange Orc gave no names.

Jahll rose from his chair, mourning the loss of potential. Had the Orc's mind been whole, he would have made an excellent guard.

Jahll moved to his bed, where an array of weapons lay. He had two hours to kill before he needed to meet the Chosen in the arena. He would not kill the Orc, he thought, as he ran his fingers along the collection of blades. Plucking up a small blade, Jahll closed his hand around the hilt. The blade was long and sharp, like a needle. He did a slow pivot and waved the blade slowly.

The pale orange Orc cowered, covering his head and

closing his eyes. His sweat kept the blood on his skin from drying. His pretty golden hair was torn from the neat little braid. Maybe he would cut the braid off, Jahll thought as he noted the way the peach Orc kept it in his sight. It hung over his shoulder and draped across his stomach.

Jahll crouched low, making himself level with the Orc. He snatched up the braid and sliced off the tip.

The Orc wailed, yanking his braid free. He curled his body around his damaged braid and screamed.

Jahll rose, satisfied. He backed away from the distraught Orc, wiped the blade on his tunic and returned the blade to its place.

He ordered his men to hold up the weeping Orc but to do him no harm. Someone loved him enough to give him shelter and cater to his disability. The Orc's screams would bring his caretaker. If it was the Chosen, Jahll would bleed him in front of her. Being female, she would suffer with the pale orange abomination. It would weaken her resolve, making her easier to kill in the arena.

Jahll summoned his armor bearer, instructing him to prepare his armor for the Rising. He'd already sent word to the kitchens to prepare his favorite meal. Tonight, he would feast and tomorrow he would break in his new slave.

Cali helped Onyx back into the principal room. The summoning of the old kings was exhausting and Onyx needed to regain her strength quickly. Onyx wore a simple shift which clung to her curves, but the rising heat dried both her skin and the shift. Cali helped her into the bed then busied herself with laying out Onyx's battle clothes.

The Rising was tonight. Cali was grateful others had not challenged Onyx to become the next Elite, but she wondered what Jahll and his mother did to make that happen. There were very few people outside of those belonging to the court when they arrived. The Commons were confined to their quarters, their sight stunted by distance. None of them bore witness to the marks on Onyx's hands, or the capal she rode. The tallest Orcs lined the streets. Their height was another obstacle to onlookers.

Onyx groaned, curling her body into a ball as she digested the information imparted from the old kings. Knowledge sharing was not only mental, but physical. The kings shared their centuries-old experience as kings and generals, but also muscle memory. Both Gryk and Cassius worried over her lack of battle training. What she needed to survive only the old kings could provide.

Cali went over and sat on the edge of the bed. She leaned over, placed her hand on her forehead to check for fever. Finding none, she slid her hand along Onyx's bare arms. Her skin had cooled down but hadn't returned to normal. The purple elixir used in the pool would speed her recovery. Cali decided she would make her a drink before they departed for the arena. She had some herbs that would help her shed her lethargy. She patted Onyx's arm when a wail filled the halls and bled into their room.

Onyx bolted upright. "Joseph!" She scrambled from

the bed and raced for the door. It swung open before she and Cali reached it.

"Stay here." Gryk jabbed his finger toward the ground. "You cannot let yourself get distracted."

A scream echoed through the palace.

"Joseph's hurt!" Onyx was on the verge of tears herself as her mind filled with every scenario that could lead to him screaming like he did.

Her legs buckled, but Cali caught her before she fell. Gryk picked them both up and sat them on the bed.

"Joseph's my son. I'll see to him." Gryk jogged toward the door, pausing in the entryway, glancing back at Cali.

"See that she makes it to the arena."

"I can help you," Cali offered.

"No! Stay with the Chosen. I'll fetch Joseph and you can heal him later."

Cali nodded just as another scream tore through the halls.

Gryk turned on his heels and sped off.

Cali and Onyx watched him until he disappeared around the corner, leaving Onyx and Cali with a sense of foreboding.

CHAPTER 31

Penumbra
King's Room

DEATH CRIES FOLLOWED BY THE SQUELCH OF STEEL SINKING
into flesh alerted Jahll to the arrival of the pale orange
Orc's caretaker. He signaled for his guard to get into position. They dragged the Orc over to the balcony and laid
him at the foot of the steps. Jahll's guard spread out. Two
were positioned on either side of the door. They were far
enough away that should it break, they would still be fit
for battle.

Bodies crashed against the door. It shuddered, wood
splintered, but it did not break. More bodies collided
with the door. It took the hits and did not break. Jahll
slipped several blades on to his person before walking
over to the pitiful Orc. He kept the most intimidating of
his personal blades out.

Another body struck the door. This time it cracked.

Splinters sailed into the room like arrows, striking some of those closest to the door. None flinched.

Quiet settled in the outer hall. The guard raised their weapons. A shifting of feet moved them all in a ready position when the steady bang of a boot against the door started.

Roars echoed throughout the wing during the brief pause in the assault. The banging resumed. Each kick cracked the door even more.

"Joseph!" the Orc roared, and the pale orange Orc answered.

"Papa!"

Jahll grinned as he placed his boot on Joseph's chest. He sneered as the pitiful Orc cowered and resumed his whining.

The kicking intensified until the door finally fell. Chunks of it flew across the room. His guard ducked but did not leave their positions.

Gryk stood in a sea of corpses. His battle-axes soaked in blood, Gryk promised murder to every guard he lay eyes on.

Jahll's guard moved as one. Their numbers staving off Gryk's advance but did not stop him. For an old Orc, Gryk possessed the speed and precision of an Orc in his prime. He used both his axe and fists to break through Jahll's guard, whittling down the numbers as he fought his way to Joseph.

Jahll stood before Joseph, lifting his blade and resting it against his neck. The act sent his guards to their death quickly, as Gryk moved with murderous intent toward Jahll.

Metal sang as Gryk continued to carve his way to Joseph. Jahll gave a nod to his guard positioned near the door.

"Stop!" Jahll added pressure to the blade pressed against Joseph's throat. A trickle of blood flowed around the blade's tip down Joseph's neck.

Gryk stopped advancing, keeping an eye on Jahll yet remained aware of the guards before him.

"Release him and I will let what remains of your guard live."

Jahll bared his teeth but did not drop his head or tusks. Thoroughly amused, he removed the blade from Joseph's throat, aiming it at Gryk. His guards formed a tight line in front of him, weapons ready.

"You think you hold sway here?" Jahll tapped the blade against his cheek as if he were contemplating the offer.

"I will kill you all!" Gryk growled, his gaze darted to Joseph and back to Jahll.

"What will you give me in exchange for his life?" Jahll shifted the blade from his cheek to his chin.

"Anything." Gryk looked Jahll up and down and sneered. "No matter my offer, you will kill him."

"No," Jahll lied for the fun of it. "I need something from you."

"I have nothing of value."

"Oh, you do possess something of great value," Jahll mocked. "You will help me break the Chosen when she enters the arena." He tucked the blade he beat against his chin in his hair, leaving his hands free.

"Never." Gryk lifted his axes, his gaze drifting to

Joseph who lay curled in a ball against the balcony steps. He covered his ears as he whimpered.

"You don't have a choice," Jahll said as he pulled his axe from the sheath strapped to his back. It hung low, above the waist of his breeches for easy access.

Gryk looked up as the axe swung home. Jahll's guards hit him simultaneously, taking his head which rolled toward the balcony. Jahll stopped it with his foot. He reached down and grabbed the hair, wrapping it around his fist then hoisted it up.

Everything he needed to secure a swift battle was in hand, he thought as he walked over to the body. Jahll doubted the girl knew anything about battle. If she did, it was probably taught in haste. He stared down at Gryk's body. If he had time to train her, Jahll would have something to worry about.

He lifted the head and stared into its lifeless eyes. So many underestimated him. The advisors whispered things about him. His mother believed he was her puppet. Jahll set the head spinning with the prodding of a finger. All of Oracaii would understand the kind of king he would be. An immortal king. He would lead them to glory. Restore the old ways with tact. He grinned and lowered the head; it bounced against his hip as he walked.

Jahll called his soldiers to him. One of them tossed him a bag. He dropped the head in and cinched it. He moved toward the ruined door.

"Sir," one of his guards called.

Jahll spun and acknowledged him. "What is it?"

The guard pointed to a still cowering Joseph. "Do you want us to kill him?"

"No. I have a better use for him." Jahll picked his way through the debris, stopping once he reached the doorway. "Bring him to the arena."

The guards saluted Jahll who jogged down the hall. A low chuckle echoed in the emptiness.

Jahll's guards converged on Joseph, oblivious to Gryk's spectral form standing next to his corpse.

There were so many bad sounds. Noises that pinched his skin and filled him with fear. Joseph's papa screamed and roared at the Monster and the Monster laughed. He had not changed, the Monster. Still mean. The pain of others made the Monster happy.

The noises stopped but Joseph was still scared. It wasn't safe to open his eyes, so he kept them shut. He jumped each time the floor trembled when an Orc fell. The moment the falling stopped, either the Monster would get him, or his papa would save him.

The quiet was broken by the slow rhythmic taps of boots. The Monster's guard!

Joseph started rocking back and forth, hands still pressed tight against his ears, eyes closed. The Monsters were coming!

Something cool and familiar touched his forehead. His papa's scent wrapped around him drawing his eyes open.

"Papa?" Joseph noticed his papa looked different. His body was as sheer as an old piece of parchment paper held up to the sun. Tiny particles of light flickered beneath his skin, but the weight of his arms pulling him into an embrace were the same.

"Papa." Joseph sighed as he relaxed in his papa's arms.

"Why is the prettiest warrior in the clan weeping?"

Joseph used his forearm to wipe his tears. "I'm scared," he whispered.

"You're strong, Joseph." Gryk cupped his chin, coaxing Joseph to look up. "I taught you how to protect yourself and others."

"Yes."

"I need you to be strong, Joseph." Gryk held Joseph's face between his palms. "Onyx needs you to be strong."

Joseph was filled with both worry and a need to protect.

"She needs you now."

"But you and Cassius keep her safe."

Gryk shook his head. "No, son. My time is done."

Joseph wept.

"No, no, son. There's no time for crying."

"But..."

"I'm here still." Gryk put his see-through hand over the space where his heart should be. "What did I promise from the time you were a youngling to this very morning?"

"You'll be with me always, even when you take your final sleep. You'll watch me from the stars and whisper in my ears when I am in trouble."

"Good." Gryk nodded then pressed his phantom hand over his heart. "Remember that when you're scared." He looked up at the approaching guards. "Now, get up and show them you are my son. Show them what you do to protect your friends."

"I'm scared, Papa."

"I know, but the Monster will hurt Onyx like he hurt me." Gryk lowered his head so he was eye to eye with his boy. "She needs you to be her right hand. It will be your duty to keep her safe. Can you promise me you'll keep her safe?"

"I promise." Joseph's shoulders relaxed. His limbs loosened as he felt the prickle of the guards getting closer.

Gryk released Joseph's face and squeezed his shoulders. "Now. Let's show the Monster's guards just how scary you can be."

"Okay," Joseph said. The promise he made stripped away his fear and dulled the pinching noise. Promises were oaths, sacred and held power.

"That's my boy," Gryk said then faded.

Joseph waited until the laughing guards reached for him. He made a fist and punched up, under the guard's arm. A bone cracked and the guard screamed. His Papa always said to make the most of a distraction and Joseph did. Three rapid punches and he cracked the knees of a guard who seemed frozen in place.

Joseph felt the swing before the blade reached him. He rolled out of its path and scooped up the nearest weapon. A battle-axe. He tossed it from hand to hand, spinning it a few times and grinned. It was his papa's axe. He had scratched a flower on the handle. His papa helped him fill it with color. When he made it, Joseph was into the color purple. The petals were several shades of purple with a thin green stem. Joseph liked flowers.

The Monster's guards were cautious when they approached him. There were only two standing. They charged at the same time from different directions. Joseph liked dancing too and spun out of striking range. He reversed his spin, bringing the axe down. It sank into the guard's shoulder. The last guard struck the moment Joseph's blade struck his companion. Joseph let go of the handle, rolled out of the way and snatched up a sword from one of the fallen guards.

Joseph memorized the room and everything in it. He could walk through it with his eyes closed and not bump into anything. It was a game he and his papa played when they discovered his gift. Joseph held on to his promise and his need to get to Onyx as he sized up the guards in front of him. They needed to go away so he could get to the arena. It was the place Cassius said they would all meet up to bear witness.

He felt the bite of metal before the guard completed his blow. Weapons made noises and like noise, it pinched his skin without touching. His sensitivity worked in his favor when he danced with the guard. The guard's strike missed but Joseph's didn't. His missed swing tilted him forward, allowing Joseph to plunge his sword through the back of his neck. It was the only way to make sure the guard didn't get back up.

The guard whose shoulder still bore his papa's axe was still struggling to get it out. Joseph put his foot on the back of the guard he dispatched and pulled. With his sword free, Joseph sank it into the heart of the other and left it there. Joseph grabbed the handle of his papa's battle-axe, looked around the room for more guards.

Seeing none, he yanked the battle-axe from the dead guard's shoulder and headed for the door. He picked up the blade's twin without missing a step and jogged into the hallway.

He hadn't been in the palace since he was a boy, but he knew the way to the arena.

"I'm coming," Joseph said then took off, running at full speed toward the arena.

CHAPTER 32

Penumbra
Oracaii Arena

CALI'S WHITE CLOAK WAS STARK AGAINST THE ABSOLUTE dark hanging over Oracaii. Torches lit the path they followed to the arena. Onyx was a bundle of nerves as she held her head high, eyes forward as the high stone walls of the arena came into sight. Akyr and another advisor flanked her. They would be witnesses. Another of the elders, Heran, held the torch which lit their path. He whispered the rules of the Rising Challenge to her before plucking the torch from the wall and led them into the night.

The scent of moon lilies drifted across their path, conjuring an image of Joseph who was as sweet as the flowers. Gryk and Cassius kept much of their plan from her, including Joseph's mission. She found herself worried over him. It wasn't because he was weak. In such a short time he'd taken root in her heart, made her care, which fed her need to make sure he was safe.

Chains rattled as unseen guards turned levers which started the lethargic swing of gates. Her company stilled as they waited for the gates to open completely before resuming their procession. Onyx ran the tip of her finger along the cords holding her hooded cloak together. It was black and hung low, concealing her face. She imagined herself a reaper without a scythe. Her purpose was survival, which meant death for her opponent.

Her procession reached the bottom of the fighting stage. There were thirty Orc-sized steps carved from white stone with intricate design work etched in each. The etchings were filled with black coloring. Onyx was grateful for her long legs as they began to climb them. Light flared above the trees a short distance away. Swirls of flame burst above them showering the sky with embers. She wondered if it was Phoenix fire.

Cali came to an abrupt stop. The torch Heran carried came into view when he tilted it to the left and touched it to what looked like a string. Once the flames touched it, Onyx realized it was a wick. The wick spanned the length of the platform which the chain of candles revealed was a long rectangle. A silver glint from below caught her eye. Spikes grinned at her from a pit which ended at the base of the stair and according to the light wrapped around the platform. Heran tipped the torch lighting another wick on the right side. The same hiss of candle wicks catching fire echoed until the last candle burned.

Heran jogged up the last of the steps, leading them onto the platform. He led Onyx to a small dais on the right side. On both sides of the dais were an assortment of weapons: spears, a whip, swords and knives. There was a pedestal to the right of the dais. On it was an ornate knife called a Troth and a stone bowl. She looked across the platform to the left side. It was set up the same as hers, but there was no pedestal.

Apparently, there were stairs on the opposite of the arena because Jahll stepped onto the platform a few minutes after she did. Jahll was dressed in a fur-lined loin cloth. It was made of rough leather with a large silver skull covering his crotch. A belt with two empty sheaths dangling from it held the loincloth in place. Both hands were bearing partial gauntlets with spiked knuckles. On his shoulder was a spiked pauldron. His legs were bare and he wore dark leather boots which stopped at the knee.

A guard walked onto the platform carrying two bags and handed them to Jahll, then moved to sit behind the dais. Whatever was inside the bags leaked. Thick drops of liquid rained on the platform's surface. The lead in his procession touched his torch to a wick along the ledge. Wicks hissed and popped as they caught fire and spread light onto the face of the platform. Onyx noticed the symbol of the capital at its center.

Cali prodded her gently, directing her to step onto the dais. She took her place, not liking the view. Jahll sneered at her. She tucked her feelings away. Gryk had constantly reminded her, every chance he could, to not let her feelings rule her while in a fight. His words were, "Orcs are prone to bloodlust. It drives an Orc into a berserker state. In that state, an Orc is both deadly and vulnerable. We're bloodthirsty and the desire to mangle our prey is strong, making us lethal to our opponent. It also makes us blind. In a bloodlust we are shortsighted and we lose the discipline of battle. Every swing must have a purpose. In bloodlust that is lost. It's easier to cut us down."

Jahll was crazy and freaked her out, but he was full Orc. Onyx knew how to control her crazy. She didn't want another Cedarville.

A cluster of sparkles formed in the platform's center as an orb of light grew. The orb stretched vertically, forming a slender silhouette which filled with color. Soon a cloaked figure stood between Onyx and Jahll. It raised its hand, revealing a fragile wrist. The cloaked figure was female.

"As the Prophet to the High Spirit, I call this Rising Challenge to begin. The High Spirit's price is due at its end." The Prophet looked to both ends of the platform. Onyx and Jahll acknowledged her words with a nod. She then pointed to the pedestal and gestured to the blade next to the bowl.

"Once the Troth has been drawn, the time for challenge is done." The Prophet looked out into the darkness. "Who challenges the Chosen for the right to become the next Elite?"

"Here," Jahll called out. The Prophet did not acknowledge him but waited.

"There will be no others," Jahll said with a conviction that turned the Prophet's head. He lifted the bags, then dropped them beside the dais upon which he stood. He made a show of opening each one and inspecting the contents. Taking up one of the bags, he reached in and removed the contents, lifting it high for those outside of the arena to witness. Taqual's head spun as Jahll roared as he turned in a circle on the dais. After completing a full rotation, he slung the head toward the center of the platform, then jerked his chin toward it.

Baring his teeth, he said, "He planned to take my place as Elite." Jahll spit on the empty bag.

The Prophet's gaze moved to the second bag. "Is that another challenger?"

Jahll chuckled. "No. It is the first of two gifts I have for the Chosen."

Again, Jahll made a show of rummaging through the second bag, using both hands to remove its contents. He held Gryk's head between his palms. Both Cali and Onyx gasped.

"Gryk," Onyx whispered. Grateful she had not pulled back the hood of her cloak, her surprise remained in the shadows. She locked her knees, willing them not to fail.

Jahll laughed heartily from his end of the platform, then motioned for someone below to approach. The humor on his face faded when no one came forward.

A voice from Onyx's side of the platform rose with each step. "Since we're doing show and tell," said Cassius as he stepped onto the platform. Carol and Willow followed. Willow was covered in blood and sported a feral grin as she moved in front of Cassius. Her arms were wrapped around Ivy's pale white head, frozen in shock. "We have a little something for you."

Willow adjusted her grip on the head and thrust it forward with pride. She beamed as if presenting a prize.

Jahll bellowed. It morphed into a long, anguished wail. He stretched out his hands to Willow. "Give her to me!"

Willow shook her head, folding the head into her tight grasp.

Jahll snarled as his arms fell to his sides, hands curling into fists.

Willow dashed behind Cassius.

Cassius turned his head toward the steps again. Joseph trotted onto the platform carrying Gryk's bloodied battle-axes. "Were you looking for him?" Cassius taunted.

Joseph faced Jahll and beat the blades of the battle-axes together and let loose a roar that shocked Onyx. He flashed his teeth and aimed his tusks at Jahll. Onyx reached for him, placing her hand on the small of his back.

It was like a switch flipped. Joseph calmed and looked at her with those sweet blue eyes. She pulled back her hood so he could see her happiness.

Cassius spoke. "I come as witness and left hand to the Queen." He bowed to the Prophet, who returned the gesture. Cassius took his place in a set of seats that reminded her of orchestra seats at a concert.

Joseph winked at Onyx before facing the Prophet. "I come as witness and as right hand to the queen." He mimicked Cassius's bow. The Prophet did the same and Joseph took his place beside Cassius.

Cali stepped forward. "I come as witness and as the queen's silent blade." She paid tribute to the Prophet, then took her place beside Joseph. Heran and Akyr did the same. The last four of Jahll's witnesses stepped forward. All high-ranking guards. They settled in their seats. Only ten witnesses could be present during the Rising Challenge.

Onyx undid the ties to her cloak and let it fall. She faced Jahll sporting black body armor. Form fitting breeches covered her legs. She kept her combat boots with a blade strapped to each. Several blades were tucked out of eyesight but were available for easy access. Wrapped around the fist bearing the challenge mark was a spiked gauntlet and her right hand was bare. On her left shoulder was a spiked pauldron with fur lining underneath. Cali had upgraded her turtleneck with black chainmail. She wore a hard leather corset over it. The knowledge stone shone like a crown around her neck. The stone itself glowed like a red sun.

Onyx took the Troth. She extended her left hand over the bowl and slashed her palm with the Troth. Her blood poured into the bowl.

"One has been called to take the claim, but to the High Spirit, I offer my name. Onyx Jones, daughter of Ryza the Black. Rightful queen of the Orcs."

Once the words were spoken, she lay down the Troth, closed her bleeding hand and faced the Prophet.

The altar vanished in a sparkling black cloud. It materialized beside Jahll. He repeated both the actions and words of Onyx, glaring at her throughout the process.

"May the will of the High Spirit speak through the victor." The Prophet moved off to the right side of the platform.

Jahll snatched up a spear and threw it at Onyx.

Onyx leapt from her dais, caught it, spun and propelled it back at him. Jahll ducked, but not before the spear sliced through his shoulder. He pulled out a battle-axe from the arsenal behind him and shoved a short sword into a sheath.

A weaponless Onyx snarled at him. Jahll was taken aback by the faint red shimmer of a familiar form. It was there for a moment, then gone. She twirled toward the weapons, drawing a whip. Jahll was halfway across the platform when she cracked it. It lashed his cheek. He reached for the end of the whip but missed. Onyx snatched it back. She danced, spinning just beyond Jahll's reach, snapping the whip several times, the end cutting into his bare legs. Her next swing, Jahll countered with his battle-axe.

He hacked at the whip's fall. The axe blade failed to sever it, allowing Onyx to snatch it away. She grabbed the fall, rotating her wrist, coiling the body of the whip around the length between her hand and elbow. Her eyes remained on Jahll, catching the moment he saw her as a real challenge.

She would make him pay for Gryk and Joseph. She didn't miss the bruises on Joseph. The cut over his eye, the one he winked at her with, set her blood on fire. His mother's sins were on his head. Ivy stirred up all the shit that was her life. Jahll had taken up her practice: torture Onyx.

Onyx shook the arm, baring the whip, forcing Jahll to keep an eye on it as they circled each other on the platform. She dropped a coil of the whip, drawing her arm back. Jahll took the bait and swung his axe as a countermove. Onyx snatched up the coil as she added speed to her sidestep. She jumped, spun low, missing

Jahll's doubling back with the axe. Slipping a long slender blade from the sheath under her corset, she plunged it in an angle, into his side toward his ribs. She leapt forward, sliding on her stomach as Jahll jerked away from her while kicking at the space where she should be.

Onyx wanted to bust out laughing at the stunned look on him as she rolled onto her feet. She ran along the edge of the platform to her weapons. Taking up a sword, she used the blade to knock down a battle-axe and spear. She kicked them closer to her dais.

Onyx waded into battle, circling Jahll, who withdrew the blade she deposited. Jahll's body was taut, ready to kill her the moment she let herself get distracted.

Jahll enjoyed taking heads. Onyx decided she would take his. She stayed out of reach, resolving to let him make the next move.

Jahll charged her. She held her ground. He dove, making a grab for her as he closed in. Onyx jumped, twisting midair. She shoved the sword into his shoulder as she descended. Jahll cursed but twisted as he slid across the platform and launched his short sword at her. This time it hit. She thanked God, the High Spirit and the Prophet for her leather corset. It took the hit but did not break. The force of the sword's impact knocked the wind out of her as she crashed to the platform. Landing on her back, the remaining air in her lungs fled. She wheezed from both pain and the need to restore breath to her lungs.

Her vision flickered as she rolled onto all fours. Jahll kicked her in the side, flipping her. She curled into a ball, the pain lacing her side, stealing away what little air she restored.

Move. She needed to hurry, but her limbs weren't responding to her brain.

The vibration of Jahll's approach filled her with panic. She closed her eyes, whispering to herself the goal: survival. The surrounding air warned her of an incoming blow. She rolled left. Instinct drew her arm back. The coil of the whip dropped. She swung it. The whip snapped. Jahll's head jerked in her direction. The whip's fall wrapped around his neck and Onyx laid all her weight into the handle, which tightened the coils.

Onyx grinned at Jahll's bulging eyes as she cut off his means to breathe. Jahll grabbed the whip's fall hitch, yanked, then rolled. Onyx let go of the whip the moment she felt herself rise. Jahll clawed at the whip. Onyx used his struggle to get to her dais. She took up the battle-axe and produced another small blade from her stash.

Jahll was slow to rise, but his gaze tracked her every move as he freed himself. He threw the whip on the platform and roared. He paced a slow line back and forth while tossing the battle-axe. The axe twirled, making a loud slapping noise when it connected with his palm. He was on his fifth rotation of pacing when a sudden spin locked Onyx in indecision.

He swung his battle axe but didn't release it. Instead, he set loose a secondary blade which hit home. It slipped through the space between the corset and her breeches, piercing the chainmail and sinking into her flesh. It was a shallow cut, but a cut all the same and it hurt like hell. Onyx wasn't used to pain. Being a half Orc in a human world, human strength wasn't a big deal. A full-blooded Orc was another story.

Damn, it hurt, but she pulled the blade out and drew him away from her side of the dais. They stared each other down as they circled each other again. Something flashed in his expression. She didn't like it. Like he'd won the fight.

Onyx bared her teeth at him. He smirked, an uptick of the lips. Her head swam for a second, then cleared after several slow blinks. The spot where the blade touched her skin burned.

Onyx spread her legs for balance, bending her knees slightly, as she moved her battle-axe in position. Jahll's neck was thick, but if she broke it, taking his head would be easy. She moved just outside of his swing radius. Jahll's arms were long and his weapons expanded his reach.

They watched each other. Jahll's chest rose and fell like he'd been in a workout. Onyx hoped the first blade she shoved in him hit its mark and punctured his lung. It wouldn't kill him but slow him down, if it worked the way she hoped.

Jahll came in fast. It wasn't a charge, but a grab. She let hope distract her, allowing him a subtle shift which put her within range. He flipped his battle-axe and swung the butt at her head. She ducked, but he was ready. He followed the battle-axe with an elbow.

She crashed onto the platform. Her battle-axe slid from her hand. She watched it slide over the platform's edge into the pit of spikes below.

Jahll was quick, straddling her, then pressed his knees

against her arms, locking them to her sides. His blade rested against her neck. He leaned in, baring his teeth.

"Don't worry, halfling," he whispered. "Your death will be temporary." He pressed the blade up, just enough to pierce the skin. Onyx hissed. The cut burned like the one he made earlier. "This will be only the first of many deaths," he crooned as he dragged the blade down her neck, sliding it under her silver collar.

Onyx teased a set of blades from their hiding place, bending her arms slightly as he resumed dragging the blade to rest between her breasts. The tip of his blade teased the ties of her corset. She sank the blades into the muscle just below his ass. She dragged them across. He bellowed, arched back to drive his blade into her chest, but she was free of his grip.

She rocked her body to the right, throwing him off balance. Using her forearms, she dragged herself over to Jahll's battle-axe. It was bigger than the one she lost, but it would do the job. Onyx rolled onto her back, reaching for the axe as she rolled. Wrapping her hands around the handle, she used her stomach muscles to pull herself upright.

Jahll was working his way up, using his forearms for balance.

"Jahll!" she shouted as she threw the axe.

A wave of nausea hit her as the blade sank into his skull.

Onyx rolled back onto her stomach and retched. What was wrong with her?

She heard her friend's cheer from her corner of the platform, but her head swam. Voices were garbled, like they were underwater. *Did he poison me?* Onyx wondered as frantic hands shook her and called her name.

Someone rolled her onto her side. She lay, unresponsive. She wanted to speak, but her mouth refused to work. So she watched. Joseph dropped to his knees beside her body and cried. The sheer size of his frame made it hard for her to see. He leaned over her prone body giving her a clear view of Jahll's corpse. A cloaked figure stood over Jahll's body. At first, Onyx thought it was the Prophet, but the robes were wrong. It had to be the High Spirit everyone told her about. According to Cali, she was the collector of the loser's spirit. Also, the cloaked figure was radiant, shimmering like a thousand stars, but for some reason the others didn't notice. She reached into Jahll's chest and pulled. A sheer version of Jahll stood over his corpse. He stared down at it as the beginning of fear rose on his face. He looked across the platform at Onyx. His eyes were vacant holes as black as a starless sky. Jahll opened his mouth to scream when the High Spirit vanished.

Cali was suddenly beside her. She turned Onyx to her, leaned in and pressed her lips to hers. Onyx felt the nausea seep from her body. The burn of her cuts faded. Cali leaned back, tilted her head to the sky. Lifting her arms heavenward, she shifted into an Orc-sized white bird. Only one of its wings was silver, like the prosthetic. In a single beat of its wings, it soared into the night. The second beat of its wings released a glowing dust like ash.

Onyx flopped onto her back, watching the bird until it faded from sight. Her eyelids grew heavy. Soon Onyx let them close. At least death didn't hurt.

CHAPTER 33

HELEN'S HAND TREMBLED AS SHE LIFTED THE PEN. HER LIFE was about to change forever. No more pretending to be rich. The papers she glanced through revealed several properties in the north, south, east and westside of Chicago. All in exclusive neighborhoods. There were other properties across the United States. She had her eye on the two in Florida: a condo on South Beach and a home in Orlando, close to Disney World.

Helen hadn't heard from Onyx in three days. There were no texts. She'd even staked out the Community Center, just in case. Nothing.

Gorman, the attorney, sat across from her. A plump woman who'd squeezed into a pretty plum-colored dress sat with her notary stamp. Gorman cleared his throat.

"Are you ready to begin?"

Helen was too excited to speak, so she didn't. She nodded her head instead.

"Perfect." Gorman leaned over and spread the four sets of documents in a horizontal line. "These four sets of documents represent the properties in your niece's name." He slid a fifth document forward and tapped it. "This gives you power of attorney over her accounts, properties and other items of value. Should your niece contest your actions, she will need to prove she is mentally sound." Gorman smirked. "I've set up enough paperwork to make that difficult for her to contest."

Helen and Gorman shared a genuine laugh. She flipped through the paperwork, stopping at the yellow sticker with the words "Sign Here." She pulled them closer, clicked the button on the pen, then signed and dated the documents, her mind instantly creating an itinerary of stores and restaurants she planned to visit in the next several days.

She returned the signed papers to Gorman who added his signature then passed it to the notary. Her stamp was about to come down and officiate the process when the doors to Gorman's conference room opened.

A tall, dark-skinned man in a suit entered. Helen figured he was Middle Eastern because of the long black braid. His hair had a sheen to it. She wondered what color his eyes were. They were covered with a pair of sunglasses. A familiar figure entered the room after him. Onyx, her niece, dressed in expensive, flowing, black silk pants, a white blouse and a cropped jacket that matched the design of the pants. She wore polished black flats. Helen couldn't make out the brand, but they were probably as expensive as the clothes. She was also aware that she wore the silver collar.

Helen opened her mouth to berate her when a blonde man built like a linebacker entered the room. He was also dressed in a black suit, like his slimmer counterpart. Like his companion, his blonde hair was long and done up in a braid. The only difference between them was that his braid had pastel-blue ribbons threaded in.

"What the hell are you doing here!" Helen demanded. She advanced on her niece; the slim Middle Eastern man blocked her path.

"I would return to my seat, if I were you." The man had the voice of a late-night DJ, smooth and sexy.

Helen backed up but did not sit down. Instead, she pointed at the silver collar with the rubies. "Are you the drug dealer who gave her the jewelry?"

The dark-skinned man snickered.

"You should be more concerned about what *you're* doing," Onyx said.

Helen drew up but did not move to strike Onyx. At least, not in front of her bodyguards. She'd separate her. Reestablish her dominance. Onyx owed her and Helen would remind her of that.

Gorman rose from his desk. "You have no place here." He fixed Onyx with a withering look. "And you have no authority over what's happening here."

Onyx smirked, snapped her fingers. Several men in suits filed into the crowded office. The first of them showed them his credentials.

"I'm Agent Phelps of the FBI." Phelps looked over his shoulder at a second man dressed in blue slacks and a polo shirt. "I think he's more interested in what's happening here than I am."

Helen put her hands on her hips and looked the man in blue slacks up and down. "And who the hell is he?"

"Oh, I'm just Norman Brooks of the Internal Revenue Service." He looked pointedly at the documents laying on the table then at the lawyer. "I don't have the authority to arrest you, but I'm sure Phelps and his friends can do that for me."

Two officers stepped forward, pulling out their handcuffs as they closed in on Helen and Gorman. The plump woman in the plum dress cried. Phelps assured her they weren't interested in her, but she might need to testify later. He instructed her to go out in the hall. One of the officers would take her statement and information before she could go. The woman thanked Phelps and hurried out of the room.

Helen yelled and cursed at the officer who cuffed her. "You can't do this! I'm her legal guardian! I have a right to the property and the money!" Helen twisted toward the desk, jerked her chin at the papers she signed.

"So, you think," Phelps said. "Everything in this place is fake, including the lawyer who set all this up."

Helen cut her eyes at Gorman, if that was his name.

"Look, I'm a victim," Helen beseeched. "Agent Phelps, he fooled me too."

Agent Phelps reached into his pocket and pulled out his cellphone. He tapped on the screen, launched an app before flipping the screen so she could see it.

It was a voice recording app. Agent Phelps hit play.

"Once you've acquired your niece's wealth, would it bother you if you never saw her again?"

"No. Once I've got the money, I have no use for her."

"What happens when people ask about her?"

"She's a grown-ass woman. She can come and go as she pleases. It just so happens, she left and I ain't seen or heard from her in however many days or months. Of course, dates and times will be adjusted based on who I'm speaking to."

Agent Phelps pressed stop, closed the app, and returned the phone to his pocket.

"What do you think, Brooks? Sound like this lady here is a victim?"

"More like an accomplice," Brooks said.

Phelps, Brooks, Onyx and her guys watched Helen and Gorman get escorted from the office. There were already agents and IRS inspectors collecting files.

Onyx learned after she woke up in her room in the palace that Cassius and her father had started a legal case against Gorman and Stein. Melissa Eldridge, Ivy's human avatar, employed the firm. At first, Onyx thought Melissa was a victim, but she wasn't. Melissa used the office as a front to launder money. It seems Eldridge ran a small investment firm which fleeced its clients. Her connections made her valuable to Ivy.

Ivy planned on erasing Onyx from the human world to keep her dealings secret. Cali's escape let the cat out of the bag. When she fled Ivy's place, she went to Onyx's father, Ryza. Ryza sent Cali to the Wandering. He also employed a few of the Wandering as sentinels to assist Cassius whenever he crossed over and to look out for Onyx.

The sentinels were Shifters and fae halflings which made it easier for them to blend in. Onyx finally understood why there were so many dangerous-looking stray animals who were kind to the kids at the center. They were protectors.

Agent Phelps ducked into the office and bid Onyx and her companions' farewell. Onyx followed him to the door. Joseph held it open. One of the female officers stopped and slid a piece of paper in his coat pocket, winked, then left.

Once the others were gone and the main door closed, Cassius laughed. Onyx smacked him on the shoulder.

"Cut it out, Cassius. You know Joseph is sensitive."

Cassius composed himself. "I'm sorry, but she was bold."

Onyx walked over to Joseph, who scratched along the arms of his shirt then yanked at the collar.

"Don't do that, Joseph."

"But it itches," he complained.

"I know, Joseph. Magic bothers your skin, but we need the glamour to hold for a little while longer." Onyx laid her hand on his forearm.

Joseph dropped his head. "Okay."

Onyx stroked his braid, pulling it over his shoulder. She ran a finger along the ribbons. "Thank you, my beautiful warrior."

Joseph blushed.

Onyx beamed. "You are the prettiest warrior in all of Penumbra, you know."

Joseph's blush deepened.

Cassius went over to the door and held it open. "Where to next, my queen?"

"Hubbard Community Center."

Cassius arched his brows and cocked his head. "Nancy's fine. She's the guardian of your property. Your foundation has set up the Community Center in such a way that no one can take it from her."

"I know, but I want to be there when the good Alderman shows up."

"Why?" Cassius wondered aloud.

"Two words: cops and cameras."

Cassius followed Onyx and Joseph into the hall. He didn't understand what she meant by cops and cameras, but whatever the meaning, it lit that spark in her. He would do anything to keep her inner light shining.

Her role as guardian between worlds established the Wandering as their own clan. They were under her protection as the Orc Queen. But their role as her sentinels allowed them to claim a territory. On it they could make a home for themselves. The gates to their kingdom would be open to those rejected by their kind. No one should ever be without a clan. Because of Onyx, there was no need for the rejected to wander.

EPILOGUE

South Side Chicago
Juncture, rear courtyard of Hubbard Community Center

ONYX LINGERED AT THE MOUTH OF THE JUNCTURE. SHE drank in the sights and smells of the small corner of Chicago that shaped her. For such a long time, Hubbard Community Center was the breath of life, its occupants her reason for being, but for the first time in her life, she felt whole.

Laughter trickled down from the open windows of the dorms. She giggled reflexively. Looking down the hazy corridor of the Juncture, she watched Joseph fidget on the other end. Cassius, Joseph and she were due back at the Wandering's camp. There, the first set of her new guard would be tested: The Arm of the Queen.

Unlike the old kings, it was necessary for Onyx's reach to extend to the Junctures her people had access to.

Considering the mischief Ivy and her son had caused, the Junctures needed guarding. The Wandering's mobility, diversity and unending talents gave her the edge she needed. Orcs were stubborn but most liked the path her father chose for them, but there were still those who didn't.

She had some vision correction to do. Orcs saw women as weak. Human women were useless. She smirked. In her mind, the old kings chuckled, causing the Knowledge Stone to flicker. Its light stained the ground red.

Orcs would soon learn that women are fierce creatures. They would learn. After all they survived, Carol and Willow decided to join the Wandering as clan. After their time with Ivy, Onyx couldn't blame them for staying as far away from the Orcs as they could. Besides, there were more humans trapped in Penumbra. If any sought refuge, Carol was committed to being their ambassador. For young human witches, she would teach them how to harness their power. Life in Penumbra wasn't the end of the world but a new beginning. Both Carol and Willow were a testament to that.

Willow found her voice and confidence wasn't far behind. She stayed close to Carol but was determined to overcome her fear. She wanted to enlist in the Wandering's Honor Guard, which were several small teams of highly trained clansmen. Each unit were skilled in combat, intelligence gathering, and field medicine in case of injury. Thanks to Ivy, the human witches that were freed from her little cottage of horrors would become a permanent part of the units. They would learn combat magic which includes cloaking, defensive magic, as well as unraveling spells.

Mak was now the healing teacher for the Wandering since Cali was one of her swords. It suited her. Though she was adept at fighting, healing was her calling. Her knowledge rivaled Cali's. The Wandering would be well cared for with Mak as their medic.

A soft meow drew her gaze to the black Maine Coon cat sitting outside the center's back door, which swung silently to a close. A soft click confirmed it was locked. Cassius trotted forward, head and tail held high.

Onyx watched him pass. She took one last look at her old home, released the edge of the Juncture and followed. Her steps were confident as she considered the many ways she would teach Orcs about a woman's power. The many layers of a woman, from the sharp tongue to the strength of her compassion, to the sharpness of her mind. Onyx was all those things and then some.

THE END

ABOUT THE AUTHOR

E.M. Lacey is an author who writes about diverse characters set in dark urban and dystopian landscapes. She writes what she loves to read which is, horror, YA, science fiction, and dark urban fantasy. Her characters gain power by embracing their authentic selves.

She's a coffee drinkin', meme postin', movie watchin' girl who loves to talk all things books and movies. You might bump into her at local comic cons and other such nerd fests. Whenever she's not getting her nerd on, she's writing, reading, binge watching Netflix, or communing with horror movie fans and other readers/authors online.

Join E.M. Lacey Online
www.emlacey.com

Sign up for E.M. Lacey's general newsletter here:
http://eepurl.com/hg1jrv

facebook.com/authoremlacey
twitter.com/author_emlacey
instagram.com/author_e.m.lacey
bookbub.com/authors/emlacey

ACKNOWLEDGMENTS

I'd like to thank Jessica Cage for inviting me to join such an amazing project. It's been a great experience. I got to meet and collaborate with some amazing authors: Kish Knight, Delizhia Jenkins, Jennifer Laslie, and Mikel Wilson.

Also, thank you to all of you who read Trials of the Black Throne. I hope you enjoyed it. As always, help an author out and leave a book review.

Thanks for reading!